I0662023

DIM
THE
LIGHTS

DIM THE LIGHTS

LINDSAY EVANS   VELVET CARTER
THEODORA TAYLOR

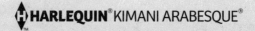

HARLEQUIN® KIMANI ARABESQUE®

DIM THE LIGHTS
ISBN-13: 978-0-373-09144-7

Copyright © 2014 by Harlequin Books S.A.

The publisher acknowledges the copyright
holders of the individual works as follows:

Recycling programs
for this product may
not exist in your area.

ISLANDS OF DESIRE
Copyright © 2014 by Lindsay Evans

LIQUID CHOCOLATE
Copyright © 2014 by Danita Carter

HER WILD AND SEXY NIGHTS
Copyright © 2014 by Theodora Taylor

Printed in U.S.A.

™ www.Harlequin.com

CONTENTS

Without these two wonderful women, my stories and the happiness I've found in writing wouldn't exist:

To Dorothy Lindsay and Cherie Evans Lyon.

And as always, I remain thankful for the women who have sup-
ported me through school and cancer,
sloth and indecision, ennui and everything else:

To Angela Gabriel, Carol Lindsay-Richards,
Khaulah Naima Nuruddin, Sheree L. Greer,
Kimberly Kaye Terry.

Thank you

ISLANDS OF DESIRE
Lindsay Evans

Dedication

Mario B.G., you are indeed the sweetest chocolate ever!

Acknowledgments

Although *Liquid Chocolate* bears my name, I work closely with my agent Sara Camilli, who is the best in the business!

A big thank you to my new publishing family Harlequin, and especially to Shannon Criss, thanks for adding the final touches to *Liquid Chocolate*.

As always, I'd like to thank my family and friends who understand when I have to go underground with my characters and live in their world!

And to you the readers, thanks for all of your support and I hope you enjoy *Liquid Chocolate* as much as I enjoyed writing it!

All the Best!

Velvet

Chapter One

Erica stood on the bow of the chartered yacht, the *Agape,* watching the undulating blue glory of the Aegean Sea. The sunlight glittered off the waves, catching the glints of turquoise buried in the dark and compelling blue of the water. She squinted, trying to see past the haze that obstructed her view of the island formation that the vessel sailed smoothly toward.

The high wind buffeted her body, clad in a pair of white high-waisted sailor shorts and a pale yellow tank top that complemented the deep brown of her skin. Erica felt the appreciative eyes of other passengers and some of the crew wander over her slim frame as she stared out to sea.

Around her, the voices of the nine other passengers on board the one-hundred-foot yacht, headed for a three-day island excursion, rose and fell in excitement. They'd just left the port of Thira in Santorini. Excited about the journey, Erica had quickly dropped off her bag in the cabin before coming back up on deck. She'd been lucky, one of the crew told her, that she'd scored a deluxe cabin, complete with queen-size bed and close to the communal bathrooms. She'd only shrugged and accepted the unexpected upgrade with a smile.

Too bad Colette wasn't there to enjoy it with her. It should have been her room, too. Erica's mouth turned down at the thought of her good friend and fellow law school graduate. Colette had promised she'd come along with her on the celebratory trip to Greece. Law school graduated. The bar passed in two states. Then, fewer than three weeks out, her friend had canceled, confessing that her boyfriend insisted two weeks away from him was too much. It helped Colette that the boyfriend had offered to pay her back the money she'd lost from canceling the trip so late. But that didn't help Erica.

She had been disappointed, even a little angry since she'd booked the hotels with consideration for her friend's preferences. But she'd shrugged those feelings off soon enough, determined to enjoy herself on her first trip out of the country since she had enrolled in law school.

She squinted as the sun came out even more forcefully in the sky. She reached on top of her head for her sunglasses; her fingers ran over her short natural without feeling the Prada shades Colette had bought her out of guilt.

Damn! She must have left them downstairs in the cabin. Erica pushed off the edge of the boat and turned to go back belowdecks. And bumped into something. A warm, hard something.

"Sorry!" She moved back automatically, bouncing off the firm chest she found herself pressed against. "Excuse me."

Hands clasped her upper arms, steadied her. "That's all right. It was my fault." The man's voice was low and deep.

His English accented not simply with Greek, but also a touch of British stiffness. *Odd. Interesting.* "I was moving too fast and not looking where I was going." Twinkling brown eyes looked down into hers. A megawatt smile flashed in his brown face.

"Ah…"

Erica caught her breath as she stared up into the most gorgeous face she'd ever seen. The man was young, maybe in his late twenties, and dressed in cutoff jean shorts. Nothing else. His chest rippled with muscle. His long thighs were thick and strong. An electric current of attraction jerked through her spine as his touch lingered on her arms. It had been months, her body abruptly reminded her, since she'd had a man in her bed.

She cleared her throat once, then twice. Then tried her voice again. "Please accept my apologies. I wasn't watching where I was going."

The stranger's hands fell away from her arms and she felt oddly bereft at their loss. "Now we're both sorry," he said. There was laughter in his voice and in his eyes, the impression that he saw everything around him as a joke. Another carefree pretty boy.

"Excuse me," she said. "Sorry again." Then she stepped away from him, past the built-in arrangement of padded benches and picnic-style tables, and went below to her cabin.

Away from his too-warm gaze, she pressed her hands against her face. Allowed herself a deep and admiring breath. That was a face that would drive a woman to sin. She found her sunglasses sitting on her bed, grabbed them and went back up on deck. A couple had taken a seat on one of the padded benches nearby and was sharing a pot of tea. The other bench had been taken over by a motley collection of bags.

The couple spoke what sounded like Japanese and wore matching wedding bands. They glanced at Erica as she claimed a seat next to them. She smiled at them in greeting, and they smiled back.

With the sunglasses covering her eyes, Erica looked around the boat at the other passengers. It was a nice multicultural gathering of people. A teak-complexioned woman with waist-length, straight hair and her two white traveling companions, both men. And there were three other black people in addition to Erica. One woman sat whispering to her white boyfriend. The other two looked like mother and daughter, with the same big wavy hair worn in matching ponytails, their brown faces wreathed in excited smiles as they looked around and made eye contact with everyone near them.

Erica was the only one traveling alone.

She casually regarded her surroundings, trying to convince herself that she was not looking for the bare-chested Adonis. That beautiful man who had made her feel the first touch of real attraction in almost a year. The last man she had allowed into her life had satisfied her in bed, but he had also been a cheat and a liar. Dropping hints that he wanted to marry her after law school while planning on leaving her for a pretty Spelman girl still in her junior year.

She rolled her eyes as Trevor passed through her mind. A waste of thought, energy and the nearly two years she had invested in the relationship. Good riddance.

With her elbows braced on the low backrest of the bench she sat on, Erica watched what was going on among the boat's small crew. There seemed to be at least five of them, a staff made up of two women and three men. They didn't wear any identifying clothing; it was simply how they looked as they walked around the boat, knowing and commanding. The magnificent view did not distract them as the boat sailed toward its destination.

A pretty blonde—the one who had taken everyone's tickets as they got on board—stood nearby with another member of the crew, a slim man with close-cropped hair and pale eyes, watching the passengers with a mixture of curiosity and contempt.

A movement drew Erica's eyes from the crew to the couple on the bench next to her. The woman stood up and gently placed her gigantic camera in her husband's hands. She walked to the back of the boat to the door leading be-lowdecks. As she neared the door, it opened. And Adonis stepped out.

A tiny butterfly fluttered in Erica's throat as she stared at the beautiful stranger.

He was just as breathtaking the second time around. He looked around the boat, eyes alighting briefly on her, before he spoke with the blonde. The girl nodded, and Adonis said something to her in return before walking away. Straight toward Erica.

He took the seat the Japanese woman had left even though her husband gave him a narrow-eyed stare. He was lean, and the energy of youth moved through him like electricity. His body radiated a tempting warmth as he sat close to her, his bare chest drawing her eyes with each breath he took. Her pulse thumped hard in her throat. She bit the inside of her cheek to stop herself from staring at him like an infatuated ingenue. But he was hard to ignore. Her eyes flickered down to his chest again.

"Were you just staring at me?" His voice was low and teasing; his accent made the words almost a song.

Something inside her jumped at the sound of his voice. Something primal and feminine. She pressed her palms flat onto the bench on either side of her thighs.

She noticed again that his eyes were a liquid brown, soft and full of laughter. Long and wild black curls were pulled back from his face into a messy ponytail, and one of his thick eyebrows had a slashing scar through it, dangerously close to his eye. He was a strikingly beautiful man whose darker skin and curly hair set him apart from the other crew members. Africa touched his full and curving lips, the generous width of his nose.

Erica had no idea there were men this gorgeous who existed in the world. She swallowed and tried to play it cool.

"Why would you ask me something like that unless you've been staring at me?" She raised an eyebrow in his direction.

His teeth flashed brilliant white against his skin. "It seems like we're at an impasse here." The laughter rolled through his voice like music. "I'm Nikolas." He held out his hand toward her, palm up.

Erica looked down at his hand, then into his brown face, browner than the people he worked with but a lighter shade than hers. She took his hand, squeezed it and bit the inside of her lips as another current of attraction moved through her. She told him her name.

"A beautiful name to match a beautiful woman," he said.

She chuckled in disbelief at the compliment, more than aware of her average looks. Her large eyes and lush mouth were her best features in a collection that was passable at best. People who thought they had the right often mentioned that her neck was too long, while more than one lover had complained that her breasts were too small or that she was too tall.

Erica leaned close to the man. "I bet you say that to all the tourists you're hoping to get into bed."

His head jerked back in surprise, and his eyes widened. If possible, he looked even more interested than before. "Not all of them," he finally said. "Some of them are not beautiful, but there is something special about all the women who interest me."

"That's honest enough," she said. "I think."

"Excuse me." A soft voice from nearby interrupted them. It was the Japanese woman whose seat he had taken.

"My apologies, madam." Nikolas leaped to his feet with a smile. "A thousand pardons. I merely wanted to speak to this woman who has so thoroughly captured me like a fish on a line."

The Japanese woman laughed, and Erica looked at him with a considering smile. The woman settled into her seat and cuddled up to her husband, watching Erica and Nikolas with curious eyes.

"Another time, my beauty," Nikolas said.

He bowed and left, gracefully making his way through the small gathering of travelers, some seated on benches, others standing to watch the swell of blue water under the boat. Nearly all the women, and even some of the men, watched him go. Erica chuckled, reminding herself to take a photo of him so Colette could see what she'd missed by not coming on the trip.

"I think he likes you," the Japanese woman said with a friendly smile.

"I think he likes women," Erica replied, then laughed at the look on the husband's face.

The couple introduced themselves as Ren and Kyoko, honeymooning from Nagasaki. After exchanging small talk with them, Erica settled back against the bench to watch the small islands pass by.

Some of them were shrouded completely in mist. Most had only the vaguest outlines showing of the craggy cliffs, white houses and churches perched on top of the black volcanic rocks. It was all so beautiful. So amazing.

A voice over the intercom pulled her from her musings.

"Excuse me, ladies and gentlemen," the accented female voice announced. "We must apologize to you because there has been a mix-up."

The woman, who had introduced herself earlier as Celandine, went on to say that the boat had gotten different orders from what was apparently on the passenger tickets. Instead of the three-day cruise that the passengers had paid for, the boat had been sent on a four-day tour, which included a visit to a goddess's temple and an abandoned castle. They would not be arriving back at the port in Thira until Monday.

Celandine apologized again, and added that the passengers could enjoy the fourth day at no additional cost since it was the tour company that made the mistake. Ren and Kyoko looked very pleased; they spoke to each other in a rush of Japanese punctuated with smiles and kisses. They weren't the only ones who seemed happy about this change of plans. But Erica was furious.

Chapter Two

Erica went to speak with Celandine. The woman traveling with the two men was already standing, also ready to talk with her. Erica waited until it was her turn, then approached the annoyed-looking blonde.

"Pardon me," she said to Celandine, who was holding a clipboard. "I have plans for Sunday evening. I can't stay out here until Monday."

"I am sorry, ma'am." The woman, who looked like she was in her early twenties, shook her head. Her ponytail wagged against her neck. "There is nothing we can do." She tucked the clipboard under her arm.

"That doesn't make any sense," Erica said, her voice rising. "There has to be something you can do to get me back to Thira on the day I initially arranged."

Celandine shook her head again, holding up her hands in a gesture of apology. She fixed an earnest look on her face. "Please, ma'am. There's nothing we can do."

Erica wasn't having it. If she didn't get back to Thira by Sunday, she'd never get the chance to see the film she wanted to see in the theater. She had gone to college with the film's director, and watching the movie at Kamari's outdoor theater was one of the things she'd been looking forward to the most on this trip. "I don't believe there's nothing you can do." She put a hand on her hip. "Let me speak to the captain. Maybe I can sort this out better with him."

"She is very busy," Celandine said. She took a breath. "Give me just one moment."

She stepped past Erica to grab Nikolas, who was passing by with a thick coil of rope over one bare, muscular shoulder. They spoke in Greek, the woman shaking her head while Nikolas looked over her shoulder at Erica, a tiny smile on his lips. Then he nodded and loped off toward the back of the boat. Celandine returned to Erica.

"Nikolas—he's another member of the crew—will better explain everything to you. He will be back in a few moments."

Erica frowned. "But he's not the captain."

"No. The captain does not speak very much English. Nikolas will talk with her and come back to tell you what she says."

How convenient, Erica thought. "Fine. I'll just wait here for him."

Celandine looked relieved. She wasted no time in getting away from Erica, ducking around the corner and out of sight. A few minutes later, Nikolas reappeared. His smile was wider, his steps loose and unhurried as he made his way across the deck of the boat. Overhead, the sails billowed in the breeze, their heavy cloth flapping like the wings of birds.

"Let me guess—the captain can't do anything for me," she said as soon as he reached her.

Nikolas stood near her with his legs braced apart, hands in the pockets of his frayed shorts. "The captain can't turn around the boat, no." The wind played with the ends of his ponytail, lashing the dark curls against the back of his neck. "But I can endeavor to make this trip a luxurious and extremely pleasurable experience for you."

The way he spoke, low and deep, had her mind going to all sorts of wicked places, imagining what pleasures he could provide. She curled her nails into her palms to distract herself from her sinful thoughts.

"I don't doubt your abilities." Erica fought to keep her voice calm. "But I also don't understand why you can't just drop me off on one of our stops." The yacht was scheduled to make at least one stop each day of the tour. "I'm sure another boat can pick me up and take me back to Thira."

"Why are you so anxious to get back to the port?" he asked with a small lift of his scarred eyebrow. "Is there some Sir Galahad waiting there with wine and flowers to sweep you off your feet and into his bed?"

"Hardly that." Erica laughed at his overblown language, his sincere tone. "I want to go to the movie theater."

"Come again?"

"The outdoor movie theater in Kamari. That's where I want to go. Sunday is the last-night showing for my friend's film. I wanted to see it under the stars on Santorini."

"Ah. That is a great disappointment indeed." He lightly touched her arm, and she shivered. "The stars here on the boat are just as bright," he said. "And you will be here with new friends, enjoying a delicious Greek meal while the ocean lulls you into pleasure. Doesn't that make up for your loss of the stars in Kamari?"

"Not really."

A smile flashed across his beautiful face. "You are a hard woman," he said.

"No. I just know what I want."

"It is possible to want and to receive many things," he said. "Please, we don't mean to trouble you with our little mix-up, but it really is not possible to do what you say. We need to follow the rules and the manifest." He touched her arm again, a light brush of his fingertips over her sensitive flesh.

Nikolas had to know what he was doing, his effect on her. But despite being aware of his ploy, Erica still found herself charmed by him, by his accent, his lean brown body close to hers and the smell of his clean sweat under the bright sun. She'd had no idea she was this much of a sucker for a pretty face.

"Okay," she said. "Fine. I guess I'll just have to deal with it."

Nikolas smiled again. "You will be offered even greater pleasures than those Kamari stars," he said. "I promise."

Erica laughed. "Don't make promises you can't keep," she said.

"I never do." A serious look settled over his features. His eyes drifted over her face, her throat, then the subtle swell of her breasts under the tank top. "Come—sit back here with me where you will have the best view of the sea and our entrance to the volcano."

He guided her to a high perch on top of the boat. It was the sundeck on top of the pilothouse, according to Nikolas. Two men already sat on the sturdy platform, arms braced on the wooden railing, their legs dangling above the deck at least fifteen feet below them. One was the crew member Erica had noticed earlier, the one with black wavy hair and pale eyes. The young men looked up when Erica and Nikolas arrived.

"Sit, please," Nikolas invited with a wave of his hand.

She sat next to the young men, who had resumed their conversation in Greek after acknowledging Nikolas. They looked down at the passengers on the boat and laughed. Erica could only imagine the things they were saying.

Nikolas spoke to the two men, gestured to Erica and said her name. The young men looked at her with speculation, sizing up the tank top and shorts she wore, her natural hair and the designer shades on her face. They seemed to miss nothing.

Erica noticed the second young man, who was short with black hair and eyes and skin almost as dark as Nikolas's, say something to Nikolas that made his companion laugh. Nikolas shrugged, smiled mysteriously, then said something that triggered laughter again and a round of hand slaps.

Yeah, boys and their games. Erica rolled her eyes.

He dropped down into a crouch next to her, filling her senses with his scent: salty sweat and sunscreen. "I have to go back to work for a moment, but enjoy the view. I will return shortly." After a brief nod and look that begged an agreement from her, he left.

Erica sighed, shaking her head. *What are you doing up here?* she asked herself.

As Nikolas walked away, the shorter man greeted her in English and introduced himself as Cyrus and his companion as Max. He then proceeded to flirt with her, telling her about all the secret places around the islands he could show her.

"Ease off, Cyrus. Don't push up on the girl. You know she belongs to Nikolas."

Erica looked up in surprise at Max. His English sounded French accented rather than Greek. His flat, pale eyes lightly touched Erica before lifting away to stare out to sea.

"I don't *belong* to anybody," she said.

"Good," Max said. "Because Lani would be pissed."

"Who would be pissed?" Nikolas appeared on the platform, stepping off the ladder leading from the deck below with the grace of a large cat, his wild curls blowing in the wind. His eyes moved possessively over Erica, reinforcing what his friend had said.

"Lani," Max said with a short laugh.

Nikolas winced and looked guilty for a moment, then shot Max the finger. He sat down at Erica's side, his sun-warmed body pressing against hers from shoulder to knee. Did he really have to sit that close? She shifted next to him, trying to ignore the sparks of attraction flaring between them.

Erica cleared her throat. "Who's Lani?" She met Nikolas's eyes. The longer she looked at him, the more uncomfortable he seemed. Then he finally shrugged.

"She's a woman on the boat. Another one of the crew."

Erica stared at him, not understanding. The only two female crew members were Celandine and the captain. Unless they had another woman stashed belowdecks someplace. Erica frowned. "Who are you talking about?"

"She tells the passengers to call her Celandine. You know, the woman you were talking to earlier."

Seriously? Erica bit the inside of her cheek to stop herself from saying something rude. "And you're…involved with her?"

Footsteps sounded above the noise of the breeze flapping through the sails; then the blonde appeared. Celandine. Lani. She swept a single glance at the scene on the platform and pursed her lips.

"The captain wants you, Niko," she said.

As the woman stood above them, with her tanned skin gleaming in the bright sun and her C-cup breasts straining against her pink V-neck tank top, Erica felt a fleeting bite of jealousy. Well, maybe not so fleeting. She could easily dismiss the blonde's looks as watered-down and uninteresting, but if this was what Nikolas liked, then why the hell was he interested in her?

Nikolas squeezed Erica's shoulder. "I'll see you soon." Then he got to his feet, preparing to follow after Lani, who had already disappeared down the ladder.

"Don't bother," she said coolly. "I think our little romance has already run its course."

The two men sitting near them laughed. The one who'd revealed Lani's significance laughed the loudest.

"So quickly, American Princess?" Nikolas's eyes sparkled with humor. "The guys will never let me live this down."

Erica didn't bother responding. She stood up, walked past Nikolas and left the platform, climbing carefully down the chrome ladder until she was dropping onto the lower level with the other passengers. The seat she'd shared with the Japanese couple was already taken, so she stood up near the side of the boat, holding on to the edge as the vessel bounded over the bright blue water.

Men. Everywhere they were the same. She seethed at the Greek man's gall in courting her when he obviously had another woman. And one on the boat at that. If nothing else, he had a lot of damn balls.

The boat slowed down as it made its way toward an island jagged with black rocks. The contrast between the shimmering water and the obsidian rocks was gorgeous. The rocks glimmered in the sun, both swallowing the light and reflecting it. She imagined they were hot to the touch, burning if she dared to get too close. Against her will, her eyes moved to where Nikolas had been.

A feminine voice on the intercom announced that the

boat was docking at the volcanoes, the first part of their trip. These were the remnants of the active volcanoes that had formed Santorini and created the scattered and beautiful set of islands that drew hoards of tourists every year. The voice advised everyone to carry water and to not lose their tour guide since there would be at least three other boats and six other guides giving a tour of the impressive island of volcanoes.

Erica went down to her cabin, put on her bikini under her clothes and packed her small backpack with everything she might need out there—water, two apples, sunscreen, lip balm and her camera. Before she went back up on deck, she retied the laces on her tennis shoes to get ready for what was sure to be a long and exhausting walk up the mountainside. She'd spent most of the past three years in classrooms and lecture halls at the university, not nearly enough of it in the gym. She just hoped she wouldn't pass out and embarrass herself.

The boat docked, and, in short order, all the passengers unloaded onto the weathered dock. There was already another boat there, smaller than the *Agape* but packed with three times as many people. Those people swarmed the dock, chatting in more languages than Erica could recognize.

She pulled her sunglasses from the top of her head. Already she felt a different kind of heat as she stood on the volcanic island with her fellow travelers. Lani stepped in front.

"Follow me, everyone. We go through those gates there." The blonde pointed to a narrow opening fitted with a turnstile and guarded by two people in khaki shirts and shorts. The opening was under a roughly built gazebo so the workers wouldn't die from sunstroke, Erica imagined. Damn, it was hot. And she wasn't even standing on the black volcanic rocks yet. A long line formed to go through the turnstile.

"The price is three euros, everyone," Lani said. "Get your money ready so we can get through the queue as quickly as possible."

Erica rummaged in her pockets for the money. People jostled her good-naturedly as she made her way through the line and eventually through the narrow opening where the attendant took her money. Finally, she was on the other side with the group from the *Agape*. Standing nearby and holding up a clipboard, Lani was waiting patiently for everyone else to catch up with her. Erica quietly brought up the rear; then they were off.

As she started walking with the group, someone bumped her shoulder. She stepped away to stare down at the gorgeous stretch of ocean and the boats lined up on the docks like beautiful handmaidens awaiting the hoard's pleasure. She moved to the side to give the person more room. Then she was bumped again. Irritated, Erica looked up with a sharp word ready on her lips. Instead, her mouth fell open. The person bumping into her was Nikolas.

Chapter Three

Erica almost swallowed her tongue. He was shirtless, and his muscled brown skin glistened from some sort of oil. From the scent, it might have been suntan lotion, but she wasn't sure. All she knew was that suddenly she was overcome with the urge to touch him, to run her fingers over the muscles of his chest, the rippled wall of his abs, to see if he was as hard as he looked.

Even as she watched him, she was aware of other women watching and appreciating him, too. The cutoff shorts hung low on his hips, showing off the hard V of muscle, the flat plane leading down into his shorts. The bulge at the front of the shorts was indecently obvious. And Erica wasn't ashamed to think about unbuttoning that single button and following the plane of skin to where it led.

She jammed her hands into her shorts pockets.

"What are you doing here?" she asked him. "Shouldn't you be on the boat bothering someone else?"

"You're the one I want to bother right now," he said, completely unrepentant.

Erica shook her head. "Just leave me alone, okay? I don't mess with other women's property."

"I belong only to myself, beautiful girl."

She rolled her eyes and walked away from him to follow Lani up the steep side of the black mountain. Was it her imagination, or did the Greek woman look at her with murder in her eyes? Erica made a dismissive noise and looked away from the blonde. As she walked, rocks tumbled under her feet, some sharp and dangerous-looking. Heat radiated from the dark rocks, washing over her skin, her face. Was this what people feared when they thought of hell? A sweltering landscape where a beautiful man tempted her with his nearness and his woman looked at her like she wanted to kill?

Lani was talking about the volcanoes, which one was active, the dates each one had last erupted, but Erica barely heard a word she said. Nikolas kept step with her, distracting her with his presence.

Compared with the current emanating from his body next to hers, the warmth from the rocks was nothing. She fumbled in her bag for a bottle of water, unscrewed the top and put the bottle gratefully to her lips. The water flowed over her tongue and down her throat like ambrosia. Fresh, faintly cool. Necessary.

Nikolas gestured to the canvas messenger bag slung across his shoulder. "If you run out, I have some here, too."

"No, thanks," she said. "I'll be fine."

He only shrugged, a smile on his face. Then he stepped even closer. Quiet time was over.

"So listen, American beauty." His voice was deep and rough, effortlessly seducing her. "I mean to keep my bargain with you from earlier. I promised this trip would be fun. You won't regret a single moment."

"I already regret meeting you," she muttered and looked up ahead to Lani, whose back was turned.

Her feet crunched over the dark rocks. To her left was a humbling view of the bright water, the boats and a steep drop down the black cliff. To the right, the high cliff and a view of one of the volcanic craters.

"You don't regret meeting me, Erica. No one ever does." His eyes sparkled with amusement.

He effortlessly climbed beside her, his feet clad in dust-covered tennis shoes keeping step with her own. She stumbled. Instantly, Nikolas was there. He caught her, set her upright and carried on as if nothing had happened.

"You may not believe it, but this is one of my favorite spots on the trip. Some people may think it would be the warm springs or even the visit to the Frenchman's castle. But I much prefer this."

He gestured to the wide black island and the crater releasing its steam into the air. "The intensity of it, you know?"

Erica turned away from him. But she couldn't help but consider his words. Yes, the part of the tour she had anticipated the most was the warm springs with the mud baths. The waters of the Aegean were cold, a chilly seventy degrees even now in the height of summer. She looked forward to swimming in warmer waters that did not make her teeth chatter on initial entry or make her nipples stiffen painfully under her bathing suit. But as she studied her surroundings, the sultriness of the island, the crunch of the rocks underfoot, the sun like an intent lover looming above, biting into her bare shoulders and back, she felt the intensity Nikolas talked about.

He looked down at her with wonder. "You understand what I'm talking about, don't you?"

She nodded. "I do."

But she didn't want to feel any sort of accord with him. She wanted to dismiss this would-be cheater from her life as if he'd never been in it. And that should be relatively simple, right?

You just met him five minutes ago! Her inner voice chided her for her weakness. But he wasn't easy to ignore by any means. Already, she felt affected even in the most simple and elemental way by him, by his passion for the volcanic island. By his incredible body. Erica stiffened her shoulders and walked on.

The path narrowed until everyone could only walk single file. The air crackled with the sound of shoes struggling for purchase on the rocky and narrow slope leading up. As she walked, she felt Nikolas's presence behind her, heard his breath, felt it at the back of her neck.

"Stop following me so closely!" she snapped.

But he only chuckled and seemed to stand even closer to her, his body a distraction, a furnace that she longed to press her face and entire body against.

Jerk.

She hated it when pretty people took advantage of their looks. And she generally didn't trust people who were so gorgeous that the whole world noticed and loved them. Nikolas was like that. No one could ignore a man with that face or that body. Even his personality bubbled hot and wild under those gorgeous looks, making him just about irresistible to anyone who liked men. Although Erica suspected that some lesbians might be tempted to test him just on sight alone. If he actually talked to them, tried to charm them, their sexuality would be questioned for sure.

Erica giggled at the ridiculous monologue going on inside her head. Then she realized that she might be suffering from the slightest touch of sunstroke. She slowed down. At the top of the hill, she stepped to the side and let the others pass by her. Her breath was coming quickly. Her head swam.

Nikolas was instantly at her side. He guided her to sit down on a rock jutting up from the soil. As she stumbled to sit down with his help, she noticed some people looking at her with vague curiosity, but all of them walked on.

"You probably should have worn a hat," he said with a faint smile.

"But you're not wearing one."

"Yes, because I have the stamina of a god." His face was serious as he rummaged in his bag for a bottle of water and a face towel. He wet the towel and patted her face with it, then draped it over her neck. Erica sighed with the simple pleasure and relief of the cool rag on her burning skin. Nikolas put the bottle of water to her mouth. As she drank, he hovered over her, his body providing shade for her face.

She breathed deeply as she drank, then forced herself to stop drinking the water. The last thing she wanted was to have to go to the bathroom on the hike up the mountain. She didn't remember seeing a toilet anywhere.

"Thank you," she said.

"You're very welcome."

She straightened on the rock and felt it poke her skin through her thin shorts. But it was better than passing out on the trail and rolling down the cliff to fall into the water below. Erica pressed the wet rag to her face and closed her eyes. Slowly, the light-headed feeling faded away. Her throat didn't feel as dry. Her gaze sharpened again.

"Are you feeling better now?"

"Much. Thank you." She glanced up the hill at the disappearing line of people. Lani and her fellow passengers were long gone. "I'm not sure I can go on, though."

"You don't need to go on. I can give you my own tour of the island." He shrugged, the muscles in his body moving in a mouthwatering symphony under his skin. "We can take it easy, not worry about the crowd."

She didn't bother agreeing or disagreeing on the personalized tour. She had the feeling he had already decided what to do. With her. And she was so annoyed with herself for her physical failure that she would let him.

"Okay," she said.

He chuckled, white teeth like lightning across his brown face. "Good."

They waited a few minutes longer for her to regain her equilibrium; then Nikolas took her hand and helped her up.

"I'm not an invalid. I can walk on my own." She pointedly waited for him to take his hand off her before making a single step. Her knees trembled, but she kept going.

"You would deny me the simple pleasure of touching your flesh?"

"Yes."

"A cruel mistress."

"I'm not your mistress at all."

"The morning is young, American Princess."

She rolled her eyes and made her slow way up the trail at his side. They walked behind a few stragglers who were either breathing as heavily as Erica had been or were taking pictures. A young couple, who looked barely twenty, took turns with the camera and taking photos of each other against the backdrop of the dark rocks, glinting sea and crisp blue sky. Between every photograph, they stopped and kissed, their hands groping at body parts in an embarrassing way.

Nikolas grinned. "Young love is beautiful—is it not?"

"Are they in love, or are they just in lust?"

"Does it matter?" Nikolas tilted his scarred eyebrow her way. "Even though one does not have to be in love to have sex, it's still an expression of love."

"Yeah, right," Erica said, sarcastically, although that was an assumption on her part since she'd never been in love. Her eyes jerked to Nikolas's face. "Are you in love with that woman? That Lani?" She could have slapped herself when the question tumbled from her lips.

"I'm not in love with anyone," he said.

"Ah." Maybe he was one of those men who didn't believe in love. One who would spend his entire youth and vital years chasing anything in a skirt just to squeeze the last bit of sexual enjoyment from life before dementia or a necessary marriage claimed him.

"I don't think you understand," he said.

"I understand more than you think."

"No. You make your assumptions about me at your own peril, American Princess."

"Peril?" She made a disbelieving noise. "I don't think so."

They continued their trek up the volcano, Erica's footsteps becoming more confident with each passing moment. Nikolas walked at her side, graceful and agile, his breaths steady, bare chest gleaming with faint perspiration under the golden sun. The wind toyed with his glossy curls.

"So, tell me, Princess, why are you traveling alone and not with your boyfriend?" Nikolas did not look at her as he asked the question; he kept his gaze focused on the path ahead. His lips twitched with a smile.

"There's no boyfriend," Erica said, finding herself amused at the transparent ploy to find out whether or not she was attached.

She told him about Colette and the trip they had planned together as a reward for graduating law school.

"Ah, so you're yet another rapacious American lawyer on the loose." A smile took the sting from his words, but Erica found herself defending her decision anyway.

"And you're talking about assumptions?" She gave him an arch look. "I'll actually be working with the Innocence Project when I get back to New York. I want to help change the system that too often wrongfully convicts innocent people and throws them behind bars."

He looked at her in surprise, his mouth curving with quiet appreciation. "Beautiful and a warrior, too. I think I've just lost my heart."

Erica kept walking. But she couldn't hide her own smile.

As they achieved the top of the mountain, the entire volcanic formation unfolded like a tapestry before them—the sparkling waves of the ocean, the jagged rocks. Across the cerulean water, Erica could see the white cliffs of a neighboring island and, on top of them, whitewashed houses, churches with their blue domes, the traceries of streets. A slow breath of wonder eased from her lips. She was a city girl through and through, but this natural splendor just about brought her to her knees.

"Amazing." She turned in a circle to take in the wonder around her. "Do you ever get used to the beauty of this place?"

His eyes did not leave her face. "Never."

She flushed and looked away from him, glanced around again, feeling for the first time the *rightness* of her taking this trip. It had not gone the way she'd pictured. Being here with Colette, exploring the islands together, laughing and sharing an experience neither of them would forget. But still it had been wonderful. Memorable.

Nikolas came closer to her, so close she felt him again, smelled the sun and whatever faintly citrus shampoo he used on his hair. He put a hand on her shoulder and pointed across the water.

"You see that church with the tallest dome there?" His palm burned into her skin.

It took a moment for her to focus on what he was saying. She wet her lips in reaction to his nearness, to the smell of him so full and delicious that she could bite into him and sate any hunger.

"Yes, I see it," she murmured.

"There, three buildings over, is where I live."

She shook herself out of her stupor and stared at where he pointed in astonishment. The house, tall and multiterraced with a series of bright blue doors, looked large even from where they stood. She could only imagine what it was like up close.

"I didn't realize crewing for a tour boat paid so well."

He dropped the hand pointing to his impressive house but didn't remove the hand from her shoulder. "It doesn't. I'm filling in for a friend who wanted to spend the week in his girlfriend's bed."

So not only was Nikolas gorgeous beyond comprehension; he was rich, too. Some people really did have everything. "That's very noble of you."

"Not really. He promised to show me pictures when he gets back." He chuckled, a soft breath of sound that brushed against her cheek.

Nikolas laughed at her shocked expression; then the mirth receded from his face for a moment. "I'm joking, Princess."

"Are you?"

He laughed again.

They stood quietly for a moment, admiring the sea,

the hills and sky. Erica allowed herself to sink into his warmth, to relax at his side and enjoy the uncomplicated pleasure of his presence.

"Every night," he murmured, "I go to the rooftop of my house and look out on this beautiful island. Sometimes it is easy to become blind to the beauty of a place, especially when faced with it every single day of your life, but I have not always lived here, among this beauty. I've lived in Athens, too, in London, for a short time in New York, where I went to university. I take nothing for granted. Life can end. Privilege can end—" he made a sharp noise "—just like that."

Erica wished she thought and lived as he did. Grateful. In awe of the world around him.

She had lived in D.C. for years. She'd worked in an area with some of the most beautiful buildings in the world, but she couldn't say that she had appreciated everything she had seen as much as she could have. She had been born in a city and visited many others on family vacations. It was the pastoral and the tropical that took her breath away. The cities simply had been everyday life. Even New York, where she'd spent the first eighteen years of her existence.

It thrilled her, though, the idea that Nikolas had, at one time, been in the same city as her, but it was now thousands of miles away from where they currently stood. It felt like a shared history. Something concrete.

"Where did you go to school in New York?"

"Columbia," he said. "I swear I have been to every bar within twenty miles of that university. It is a miracle I learned anything while I was there."

Erica smiled. "I'm sure you got what you needed."

"Yes," he murmured. "I did."

Erica looked away from the island across the sea to Nikolas's face. His eyes were serious but glittering with life and the wildfire of loving everything he did. She'd never met anyone like him before. Her eyes dropped to his mouth, the strong column of his neck, then his chest. Bare and muscled, hard in the sunlight.

"If you keep looking at me like that, I'll have no choice but to give you a more personal tour of the island than you intended." The corners of his mouth pricked up in a smile.

Erica's head swam with his exhilarating presence, his low and teasing voice. "And what would that tour entail?" She heard herself asking as if someone else had hijacked her tongue.

Nikolas's eyes widened. Then it was her turn to feel the burn of his gaze on her mouth, on the press of her breasts through the tank top.

"American Princess, please don't say these things unless you mean them."

Quickly regaining her sanity, Erica opened her mouth to recant what she had just said when he leaned down and kissed her. She drew in a quick hiss of breath, drew the taste of him more fully into her mouth.

He tasted like olives and red wine. Salty sweet. Intoxicating.

His mouth touched hers lightly, hands falling to her waist. Then when she did not move back or protest, his mouth settled more firmly on hers and his hands tightened. Delicious mouth. Senses swimming. His tongue licking the seal of her lips, then plunging inside, firmly stroking the hot interior until she gasped with the sudden sensuality of it. Her tongue, teeth, her palate felt the intimate touch of his tongue. The agile muscle caressing her as if he wanted to feel *everything* about her.

A fever flooded her face, her body. Her sex plumped between her legs, and her skin tingled from his touch even though it was through the thin tank top. The sun's burn was nothing compared to his caresses. She twined her arms around his neck, pressed herself against him, rubbing her suddenly aching nipples against his naked chest. A purr rumbled from her throat.

"Oh!" he groaned into her mouth. "You feel so good...."

Erica's fingers clenched at his neck, slid up into his hair. She panted as their kiss intensified, grew deeper. Harder. She'd never felt such a powerful attraction before. And from the one kiss, a single kiss, she wanted to fall to the ground with him, allow him anything he wanted.

His hands dropped away from her waist and grabbed her ass, pulled her firmly, rhythmically, against him until she was moving her hips, circling for pleasure, wanting even more of a physical connection with him.

She touched his chest. The big pec muscle jumped under her hand. Smooth skin. Lush warmth. The sensuous movement of him against her. He was hard to her soft, food for her hunger.

She burned for him. She was wet. Swollen. On fire for him.

His hand touched her breast, fingers squeezing her nipple through the shirt. Past the loud strumming of the blood in her ears, she heard the crunch of footsteps against the rocks. People. Erica shoved at his chest and wrenched her mouth away from his, breathing heavily. But he clutched at her ass, trying to keep her close, his mouth diving back for hers. She quickly drew back, blinking into the sun that seemed even brighter than before.

Nikolas made a rough noise. His hips surged into her hips, but she kept some distance between them, her hand pressed flat against his stomach, their foreheads pressed together as they both panted. Erica licked her lips.

She looked away from him and immediately saw the young couple that had been taking pictures before, the amorous ones she had been so contemptuous of. And now here she was making out with a guy she'd only just met, seriously contemplating ripping his clothes off and climbing on top of him, right there among the sharp bits of shale.

"Let me go," she breathed.

Instantly he released her. She stepped a few feet away, pressing her palms to her burning cheeks. The couple had already turned away, but she heard the high-pitched sound of their laughter. Remembered the camera the boy had pointed at them.

"Damn! This is so not me." She turned away from him, barely restrained herself from pressing her palm against the front of her shorts. She was so wet and wanting that in those few moments that Nikolas had held her, nothing else had mattered but satisfying the desire that surged between them.

"Damn," she said again.

Erica ran a hand over her face, squeezing her eyes shut. Then she turned to Nikolas. Which was a mistake. He was mouthwatering. Bare chest glistening in the sun, full mouth wet and faintly red from their kisses, curls pulling loose from the ponytail. He was still breathing hard, his chest and belly heaving from the force of his breaths. And his bulge pushed thickly against the front of his shorts. He made no effort at all to hide his arousal.

She quickly turned away from him. Temptation in the flesh.

"It's only a body, American Princess. Surely you've seen a man hard with desire for you before."

She felt him coming toward her, heard him, and she kept walking. Feet slipping across the rocks, hands shoved hard in her pockets. Yes, she had seen erect men before. But she'd never wanted one the way she wanted Nikolas. His body was perfect. His accent made her knees weak.

When he touched her, she wanted to abandon everything she'd ever learned about decent behavior and make love to him out in the open as if that were her birthright. She swallowed again.

"Stay away. Please."

His footsteps stopped. She walked until she rounded a corner on the rocky hill. Not too far off on another hilltop, she saw at least a dozen other tourists. They were laughing and taking pictures. Some tried to cool off by fanning themselves with their hands or their hats.

Erica leaned back against the rough surface of the cliff face, pushing her back into the jagged rocks to distract her body from its clamoring desire. Her palms itched to touch him. Her nipples were still hard and aching for his mouth. She took long and deep breaths. Clenched and unclenched her hands until she felt more in control of herself.

After long moments, she turned and looked around the corner of the rock face. Nikolas stood where she had left him. His head was thrown back, hair loosened from its ponytail as the breeze played in his long and thick curls. He was so beautiful it almost hurt her eyes to see him. As if sensing her gaze, he turned to face her.

"Are you ready for the rest of your tour?" he asked.

Either that or we're having sex right here, right now. Erica took another breath. "Okay."

Nikolas gave her a quick smile, throwing off the look of desire on his face. "Let's go then."

Walking side by side, they journeyed higher up the volcano. Up ahead, Erica noticed a splash of blood on the ground, probably from one of those girls she'd noticed earlier wearing open-toed sandals. When she had booked the tour, the woman behind the counter had cautioned her to wear closed athletic shoes to protect herself from the sharp rocks.

"They say that one day these volcanoes will come alive again and swallow all of Santorini."

They stood on the top of the undulating slope of black rock and miniature desert plants, looking out over the wide vista of rocks, ocean and other tourists clambering up the volcanoes in a winding trail of humanity.

"Doesn't that scare you?" she asked. The very idea of it terrified her, to be basically burned alive, her body petrified under melted rocks, magma and ash. Or maybe even asphyxiated by the gases belched from the crater.

Nikolas shook his head. "If it's not this, then it would be a gunshot or airplane crash or even old age. Death comes to us all, Princess."

Erica shuddered. She'd rather die of old age in her sleep, or even be hit by a runaway bus. Maybe that was one of the reasons she could never see herself living in Hawaii or even California with its notorious earthquakes. She could easily imagine falling into a crack in the earth and being swallowed alive into the planet's core, never to be seen again.

He laughed softly. "There are worse things than burning." He slid her a look full of passion and longing. And for a moment, only a moment, Erica agreed with him.

While everyone else followed the path staked out by some long-gone tour guide, he took her to the hidden paths of the volcano, down isolated trails on the island that showed little signs of human trespass.

"The active volcano is there. From here, you can see the steam rising and smell the sulfur." He took a deep breath of it and turned to her, smiling. "You like?"

"It's scary," she said. "But incredible. Like a sleeping dragon, beautiful and frightening at the same time."

"Yes, exactly." He nodded as if she'd just revealed that she understood all the secrets of the universe.

Across from the crater where they stood, she could see dozens of tourists, some pointing to her and Nikolas. She could almost hear their thoughts, wondering how she and the Greek man had made it to the opposite side from everyone else. She backed away from view, not wanting to compromise their relative privacy.

As if he understood, Nikolas held out his hand. "Come."

They left the quietly smoldering crater and wound down a lonely path toward the beach. As they walked, he kept his hand at the small of her back.

"In case you lose your balance," he said with a wicked grin.

She shook her head. If she lost her balance, she'd probably tumble headfirst down the gully and into the water. Although Nikolas looked very strong and capable with all those muscles, she doubted he would be able to protect her from herself.

But at one point, she did stumble over a jutting rock. Nikolas quickly brought her up against his side, easily lifting her off her stumbling feet and setting her upright before she could do more than cry out in alarm. Her arm latched around his neck. She panted in fear, staring down at the rocky beach that was still at least fifteen feet below the steep incline.

When she looked away from the frightening possibility of her fall, she found his gaze on her, his eyes on her mouth. Suddenly, she was aware that they were pressed close. His skin was warm from the sun. Slippery. Its softness and the hard muscles beneath made her curl her fingernails into his shoulder before she could even think about it. He smelled delicious. Sinful. The vague odor of sulfur and the salty air stirred around them. Erica bit her lip and deliberately stepped back.

"Thank you," she said breathlessly.

"My pleasure."

He released her but kept a hand on the small of her back as they continued down the incline. With each step, she was aware of his smell, the weight of his hand on her flesh, mere inches from the curve of her ass.

Erica glanced sideways at him. She didn't know it was even possible to be aroused by someone this much. Just him touching her back made her wet. Her pulse strummed in her throat.

It seemed like it took forever for them to make it down to the water. The air was much cooler with the waves rushing up onto the dark, rocky beach. The sea was clear and calm with not even a boat in sight.

"We're going there." Nikolas pointed to a piece of the cliff face jutting out over the sea. "Around that rock."

Again, he led the way, holding her hand as they tramped over the rocks that glimmered wetly from the waves washing steadily, then receding over them. Up close, she could see that the rock cut out even more sharply from the beach than she'd thought. They would have to walk out into the water—and a drop of over three feet—to get around the rock and to the other side. As he was about to step around the rock, Nikolas released her hand.

"Be careful," he said. "Step where I step. And although you have your shoes on, still keep an eye out for sea urchins."

He glanced down into the deep blue water that rippled in the sunlight and grew darker the farther out to sea it went. In moments, he stepped into the sea and disappeared around the rock's bend.

With him gone, Erica felt utterly alone. Although she knew there were dozens of tourists somewhere nearby on the island and that Nikolas was only a few feet away, the melancholy stirring of the breeze and the whispering emptiness of the sea made it seem as if she stood on the loneliest place on earth.

Then she stepped toward the rock, into the water. *Cool.* The sea was cool around her thighs, lapping around her bare flesh at the edges of her shorts. Goose bumps blossomed all over her skin. Because of the proximity of the steaming volcano, she'd thought it would be warmer, at least warmer than the sea outside her room on the yacht.

She waded through the water, staying on the lookout for urchins as instructed, stepped around the rock and onto another rocky beach. Then she almost lost her balance as she stared in surprise at what she found on the other side.

It was a private beach. An isolated circle hugged on both sides by tall black rocks sticking out into the water, a convenient shelter from prying eyes. The water was clear and shallow and incredibly blue; the little beach was no bigger than her living room back home.

Even the rocks that made up the beach were smaller than the ones she and Nikolas had walked over to get there. An oasis. The sandy bottom of the sea mated with the fine black rocks on the beach in beautiful, rippling patterns she could see through the clear water. And there were no urchins, thank goodness.

Nikolas already had a blanket spread out on the beach. He was sitting down, simply watching Erica as she made her way toward him.

"How did you even find this place?" she asked, stepping out of the water.

"Luck." He shrugged. "I take my boat out here sometimes to scuba around the volcano. One evening, I came out farther than usual and stumbled onto this."

"It's like your own piece of the volcano."

"The government wouldn't agree, but, yes, it is. And I'm sharing it with you." His smile was inviting, flirtatious.

Erica couldn't help the answering smile that took over her face. This man was a charmer. He had to know what he was doing when he made declarations like that. She shrugged off her backpack and sat down next to him.

"Are you hungry?" he asked.

"Yes, actually," she said, surprised.

She'd only had juice and honey-drizzled yogurt at her hotel before she'd left for the boat, and now it had to be well past noon. She reached for her backpack as Nikolas opened his messenger bag.

He pulled out a bottle of water, two oranges and two spinach pastries. "I brought enough for both of us."

"How do you know I eat spinach? I might be the type to hate my vegetables."

"No one hates spanakopita. It's a law of the universe." His lush lashes swept up, eyes capturing hers.

She chuckled, unable to look away from the bright beauty of his gaze.

Why was this man so compelling? It wasn't as if she hadn't known gorgeous men before. Even her ex-boyfriend Trevor, who had gotten through most of his life so far on his looks alone, hadn't affected her like Nikolas. No one had.

Erica drew back, took a trembling breath. "Thank you. I'll be happy to share your meal with you."

"Good." He separated the bounty into two neat mounds between them and pulled out two cloth napkins from his bag, a small bottle of wine and plastic cups. "And if you're interested in something a bit more stimulating…" He waggled his eyebrows at her.

He *had* planned on seducing her up here. Wine. Food. A lovely view. Like he had planned a panty-dropper of an afternoon all along despite the guided tour they were supposed to be on.

"I'm not having sex with you," she said.

"I don't want you to have sex with me," he countered with a smile. "I want to make love to you, and I plan on doing all the work." His voice was low and sexy, eliciting a shudder over the surface of her skin. Skin that suddenly felt too sensitive for clothes.

She swallowed. "Why are you so determined for this to happen between us?"

"I'm not determined," he said. "I'm hopeful." He uncapped his bottle of water and lifted it to his full lips, drinking deeply.

For a moment, Erica was mesmerized. She watched the seal of his mouth around the rim of the clear plastic bottle, the firm column of his throat, his Adam's apple moving with each swallow. Unable to help herself, she licked her lips, imagining she was that bottle, that he put his mouth on her, drank her up in such greedy and endless gulps. Erica flushed.

She was not the type to sleep with men she'd just met, but if she stayed next to him for a moment longer... Erica stood and walked to the water's edge. Splashed water on her face. She gasped at the cold shock of it. Closed her eyes as the cool droplets soothed her overheated face and neck. She thought she heard Nikolas chuckle behind her, but when she turned, she only caught him staring at her ass.

"Okay." She lifted her shirt to wipe the wetness from her face, ignoring his hungry look at her bared stomach. With a sigh, she sat down on the blanket once again, putting a few more inches between them. "You have to understand something about me," she began. "I don't mess around with men who have prior commitments."

"I don't have any prior commitments." He capped the bottle of water and dropped it on the blanket between them. The wind ruffled his long hair, tossed strands over his eyes.

"Does Lani know that?"

"She knows everything. I'm not her boyfriend. Never have been."

"Are you lying to me?"

He chuckled. "If I was lying, why would I recant and tell you the truth now?"

"Good point." She shook her head. "Just let me eat in peace for now, okay? You can try to seduce me later."

"Seduction and food go perfectly together," he said. "But I will wait. The anticipation will make it even better."

She bit into the spinach pastry, smiling in spite of herself. *Cocky bastard.*

They sat with their legs stretched out on the blanket, their feet planted in the sand. The sun was bright and gorgeous, shimmering over everything as far as Erica's eyes could see. Nikolas's face, the blue water, the stretch of black rocks surrounding the large cove and leading out to sea. The tiny swatch of beach was private in so many ways. A boat had to be already heading there and just about ready to toss down its anchor before anyone aboard could see them on the beach.

The idea of such complete privacy made her quiver just the smallest bit in anticipation. To distract herself, she inched even farther away from Nikolas. Then struggled for something else to squash her growing interest.

"Tell me about this girl, Lani," she said. "Does the rest of the crew think you and her have a thing?"

"Who knows what goes on in people's minds? I am certainly no mind reader." He chewed his pastry, his eyes twinkling in his brown face.

"Seriously, though."

"I'm never serious, American Princess. I'm surprised you haven't figured that out already."

"I doubt that's true. There's something else going on behind that pretty face besides jokes and good times."

"I think you give me too much credit, Princess. All I want is to have a good time on this trip, meet a nice girl or three. Enjoy myself."

But his words were not very convincing.

"If you say so," Erica said.

She shrugged as she finished the last bite of her spana-kopita. She drank nearly half the bottle of water before standing up and walking away from Nikolas. She felt his eyes on her the entire time.

The water before her was one of the most beautiful shades she had ever seen. Not the turquoise shimmer of the Caribbean, but a unique and captivating darkness that made her want to dive in despite its coolness. She looked over her shoulder at Nikolas. Yes, he was watching her. Not eating, not drinking. He was simply watching her with his dark eyes, his expression ravenous.

She dismissed him with a shrug, then pulled off her shorts and tank top. In her bikini and tennis shoes, she ran into the water, diving into the cool depths in one motion.

Erica gasped at the chill against her skin. Salt water flying up into her mouth, stinging her eyes. But, oh, it felt good. The warmth of the sun on her face and shoulders, her chest. The cool water rippling around her breasts, gently lapping at her belly. She shivered and dropped her head beneath the surface. Swam away from the shore.

She heard a splashing in the water behind her when she resurfaced. Nikolas. He swam lazily toward her. Droplets of water shimmered on his bare shoulders and arms. His head was as sleek as a seal's. She watched his smooth movements, hypnotized.

She dunked her head beneath the water again, need-ing the reassuring coolness on her skin. The worst—and strongest—part of her wanted to simply climb on top of him, kiss him again, share that heart-thudding desire that had moved like an earthquake through her on the volcano. But no matter what Nikolas said, he had a woman.

"Was that a challenge for me to follow you out here?" he asked.

The amusement was gone from his face. In its place was an intent and hard look; the angles of his face had transformed.

"I only challenge in the courtroom," she said with a slight shrug, sending ripples into the water around them.

"Liar."

He kissed her. The shock of it held her immobile for a moment. Much like the cold water had, stopping her breath, instantly stimulating her skin. Electric attraction jerked through her. She opened her mouth for him. Slid her hands into his heavy wet hair. Her tongue in his mouth. Him sucking her lips, licking the inside of her mouth until she loosened a noise, unable to keep quiet. From just that kiss, her bikini bottom suddenly felt too tight against her. She wanted to pull it off, she wanted to—

Her thoughts stuttered to a halt when he grabbed her ass and jerked her against him. Erica gasped. He was com-pletely naked. His body was hard and bare against her, smoldering iron under the cool water.

"Nikolas!" She pulled her mouth back from his.

But she felt her control slipping away. Her hips pushed back into him, her body practically purring from the large and solid feel of him.

"I love the way you say my name," he groaned, rolling his hips against hers.

She kissed and kissed him, her mouth opened wide

over his. He rubbed his tongue over the sensitive flesh of her lips while his hips moved against hers under the water, shoving against her, telling her what he wanted to do. She clung to his slippery shoulders, lost to the reality of wanting him.

Erica raked her fingernails over his chest, sighing in satisfaction when the prominent muscles jumped under her touch and he groaned into her mouth, moaning when she pinched his nipples. Both his hands were on her ass now, caressing her, slipping inside her bikini to grasp her rounded flesh, to squeeze and caress it. How did he know what would feel good to her? How? He pinched her ass as she pinched his nipples, like small stinging kisses lower and lower until his fingers slid between the thick globes and caressed her wetness.

"Ah, Princess…" He breathed into her mouth, his chest heaving and hard against her own. "I want you more than I should." He groaned out something in another language and kissed her harder. She joined him in the ferocity, teeth biting, breath huffing, until her lips felt wonderfully bruised and still wanting more.

"I don't…I don't…"

She thought she knew what he was trying to say. And she agreed completely. They couldn't do this in the water. Erica pulled back from him, breathing heavily, her breasts heaving. His eyes dropped to the front of her bikini and he reached for her again. She turned in the water and swam away, her body moving swiftly toward shore as if running away from her desire for him. But it latched more tightly to her than ever before, pulsing hot and hard between her legs. Her nipples were aching and tight with arousal, the breath rushing from her lungs.

She wanted him. She exploded from the water, struggling briefly over the slippery rocks until she reached the shore.

Nikolas was only a few feet behind her. The loud stumbling of him made her feel like a lioness in the wilderness with a potential mate hard on her heels in search of the satisfaction only she could bring. Her heart pounded. She dropped down to the blanket on her back, reached for him even as he was falling into her, his hips landing in the V between her thighs that she made for him. Her desire was more intense than any she had ever felt before.

The sun beat down on her face, burned into her skin as he kissed her.

"You taste incredible," he murmured against her mouth.

She met his lips, openmouthed, drinking in his flavor, the hint of pastry on his lips, the saltiness from the sea. Erica clasped his hips, surging up against the thickness already probing between her thighs. The blanket was soft, but she felt the rocks through the material, piercing into her back, into her ass. The discomfort felt strangely good. Grounding her in the *now* of the moment.

Here I am! she wanted to shout.

Yes. Here she was, twisting with a stranger under the burning Greek sun on the small beach, her heart pounding, his palm pressing at her throbbing clit. An odd and delirious ecstasy.

Nikolas lifted his head, dark eyes hooded and glittering with passion. His mouth red and wet. "Condom!" He gasped the word, his chest moving quickly against hers.

He lifted from her and grabbed his bag, his movements frantic and uncontrolled. His hand soon emerged with the prize. Erica watched as he rolled it on, wetting her lips as the clear latex covered every potent inch.

Nikolas was big, definitely not the biggest she'd ever seen but gorgeous. The head glistening and fat, veins roping the length like tattoos. His sack was heavy and tight. It made her even wetter to know he was the same deep copper color all over. She bit her lip in anticipation as he reached for her, then squirmed against the blanket, wet and dripping into the crotch of her bathing suit.

He covered her. All hot and slippery skin. His lips parted, hands tugging off her bathing suit. Nikolas cupped her, fingers combing through the dark hairs framing the heat of her.

He gasped something she couldn't understand, fingers moving through her wetness. "I love touching your pussy," he said. "I want to feel it on my face."

She bucked at his rough words, already imagining how his mouth would feel on her flesh. His fingers slid over her clit, provoking pleasure, a moan. Then he slid a finger inside her before pulling back, then diving in again. He actually licked his lips, as if he wanted to eat her more than he wanted to make love to her, as if the choice was a hard one. Want flowed through her. His desire, clear and undeniable, shook her even more. She'd never known a man who'd wanted her this much. Who showed his desire so easily. He withdrew his fingers, sucked them.

"Yes…you taste good everywhere." His eyes were glazed with want.

Erica's center tightened with a powerful desire.

Her hands gripped his shoulders even as her legs sprawled wider to receive him; her feet planted into the sand. She lifted her mouth to his, commanding his lips, dragging him back from the stupor he seemed to be in. Her tongue dipped into his mouth, caressing him, teasing him. She tasted herself in his mouth, and her eyes rolled back in her head.

Erica liked it when a man couldn't get enough of her taste, when he enjoyed that bit of foreplay almost as much as he loved sex. Nikolas seemed to be that type of man. She slid a hand between them, stroking his hardness.

Nikolas groaned into her mouth. A sudden frenzy. His hands roamed over her belly, burning almost as hot as the sun on her naked breasts. Fingers tugged at her nipples while she stroked him, luxuriating in his length, his width.

"Fuck me!" she breathed against his mouth.

She didn't wait for him. Erica guided him to her entrance. Then his hand curled around hers, and the head knocked at her entry. She felt him glide against her wet and swollen lips.

"I want to make this good for you," he said. He held himself above her, keeping his weight from crushing her body. The muscles of his arms trembled as he hovered over her. Sweat popped out on his forehead. Uneven breath rushed from him. He was fighting against simply taking her. "I don't want to hurt you."

"You won't!"

With a heavy groan, he sank into her. She caught her breath at the sudden fullness of him. A pinch of discomfort. Then the sweetness of being filled so completely. He positioned his hips between her legs, dipped his head to tongue her breast. Erica gasped again, this time in undiluted pleasure.

"I want to see," she demanded.

He lifted his head, and she propped herself up on her elbows. Nikolas shifted his hips so she could see how they fit together. His thickness sinking into her dripping center. Her juices matted her wiry black hair, mingling with his dark curls. The liquid suck and kiss of their bodies connecting. Pleasure skimmed over her skin, raising up prickles of sweat, her breath shivering in her chest.

Hair fell over his eyes. His body quivered on top of hers as if straining to keep the slow pace, the angle of his body. His sweat-slick hand squeezed her breast, thumb strumming her nipple. The action zinged straight into her clit. She bit her lip and moaned, back arching against the blanket.

His patience shattered.

"Next time I'll take it slow, I swear." Then he began to move at a more intense pace.

Plunging into her, angling to hit her clit with each powerful stroke. Her fingers curled into the blanket. Her head fell back. His fingers pulled at her nipple as he sank into her and stroked her with a hard sweetness that made her cry out. She locked her ankles around him, pulled him tighter against her. She panted. Her eyes squeezed shut to block out everything but the sensation of him inside her, his belly and chest moving against hers, the pebbles biting into her back, adding to her fierce and consuming pleasure.

"Look at me!"

Her eyes opened.

"I want to see when you come."

His eyes held hers as his face hardened even more with lust. He slammed inside her, gliding against her clit with each thrust. It felt like the sun was inside her, a glowing ball of light illuminating everything to a sharp and undeniable brightness.

Erica gasped under Nikolas, meeting his frantic thrusts with her own, twisting on the blanket. The sounds of her pleasure poured out of her throat and into the clear afternoon. The orgasm caught her unprepared. One moment she was riding a wave of pleasure, squeezing his thickness, her muscles gripping him hard, the heat a rich fullness inside her. Then feeling overwhelmed her. The orgasm brought her down like prey. She cried out, her nails scoring deep into his back. Shuddering. Her world a bright light. Blind to everything else. Her skin quivered from her pleasure.

"Nikolas!"

He growled something into her throat, his hips relentless as he poured more pleasure into her, his dick hard and firm and true. Nikolas threw his head back as wordless cries erupted from his mouth. Sweat dripped from his throat, and his body jerked into hers as he came. Nikolas panted.

Erica tilted her head back and stared up at the sharp blue sky. She slowly raked her fingers up and down the back of his neck as the after-tremors moved through her body. Her hips still moved, making unconscious circles on the blanket while her muscles clasped his softening flesh. She felt like purring. Her body hadn't been touched so well in ages.

"Damn, you feel better than any woman I've ever known." He murmured the words into her throat.

Erica stiffened at the reminder of his other women, specifically the other woman on the boat. Lani.

"Let me up," she said.

After a moment's hesitation, he did. She pulled away, disconnecting their bodies and not meeting his eyes. Afraid that one look from him would only make her want to feel him inside her again. The other woman was real. No matter what he said, the woman's feelings were still a factor in this. She pushed away from him, ignoring his puzzled look, and stumbled to the water to immerse herself and wash the sweat from her body. The water felt good on her skin, a cool splash to remind her that what she had done, what she was thinking of doing again, was completely wrong. She walked back to the sand with heavy steps.

Nikolas was sprawled on the blanket, watching her as she walked from the water, his eyes heavy on her breasts, her feminine curves.

"You are beautiful," he said.

But she didn't want to hear any more from him. Nothing about her beauty. Nothing about how he liked her more than other women he might be seeing. Erica didn't want to be just another girl in a long string. She quickly pulled on her clothes and shoved her wet bikini into her backpack.

"Shit!"

Her head jerked up at Nikolas's curse. He yanked on his shorts and stowed the bottle of water, his iPhone and the oranges in his bag.

"What's wrong?" She stared at him as he wadded up the blanket and quickly stuffed it in with the rest of his things.

"We have to go right now." He spared her a brief glance. "The boat is about to leave without us."

He didn't have to tell her twice. It was bad enough that she had to be stuck on the boat for a day longer than she'd planned, but she'd be damned if she got marooned out in the middle of nowhere with little food and no shelter with this insensitive tomcat.

She quickly followed Nikolas in the water and around the outcropping, gritting her teeth as she admired his taut backside in the cutoff shorts and the wide span of his bare, muscular back. This man needed to put on some clothes ASAP. If not to protect against skin cancer, then certainly for her sanity's sake.

They got to the other side of the rock. The water splashed their legs and thighs, and their sneakered feet crunched into the black rocks as they ran across the beach. Nikolas reached back for her, and she automatically grabbed his hand. It felt like forever, but soon they broke through the arid landscape and down to the docks. All the other boats were gone.

The only ship that remained was theirs. The *Agape* bobbed in the water, giving an air of impatience as it floated at the dock. Nearly half a dozen faces turned to watch them scurry down the mountain, some with curiosity, others with irritation.

As they ran down the face of the volcano, Max, the lone man standing on the dock, spied them. He shouted something toward someone standing out of sight on the boat, then crushed out the cigarette that he was smoking and dropped it in the small trash can near him. He jumped on the boat, leaving the gate swinging open for Nikolas and Erica. Nikolas waited for her to climb on the boat ahead of him before joining her. He slammed the small gate closed and latched it.

Most of the passengers on deck seemed relaxed, lying back with bottles of beer or glasses of wine. The mother and daughter couple faced each other over a board game and barely looked up as Erica and Nikolas stumbled on board.

Cyrus seared them both with a knowing look, his eyes lingering long on Erica. Lani was nowhere in sight. Did she know that Nikolas had been off with Erica? She wanted to not care, but she did. Her eyes skittered around the boat looking for the blonde.

After waving a quick goodbye to Nikolas, Erica ducked her head and went belowdecks to her cabin. A proper shower. That was what she needed. That and a healthy dose of anti-Nikolas. She'd always avoided drama like the plague. Even when Trevor had tried to pull her and the Spelman girl into a catfight, she'd merely turned her back and wished her ex well. Why now after a stellar twenty-eight-year record of being drama-free, had she come to Europe and lost her mind over a rock-hard body and a bold smile? It must be the sun. Erica stripped off her clothes and got into the communal shower.

She raised her head to the salty shower spray—recycled seawater, just like in her hotel—and closed her eyes. Memories of the beach came rushing into her mind. The hot slam of their bodies, the way he had moved on top of her and inside her, so well that her toes had curled.

He'd been so tender in moments and then so masterful, seeming to know just how to touch her. She remembered him caressing her, watching her face to gauge her reaction to each stroke of his fingers or tongue. Once he knew she enjoyed something, he did it again and again, teasing her until she was going wild. His hand between her legs. His eyes on her face as he touched her clitoris, as he slid seeking fingers inside her to check how wet she was. In the shower, Erica began to moisten, to get ready for him again. She shook her head, rousing herself from the intoxicating memories.

Okay. This isn't the kind of shower I need.

She picked up her washcloth and soap, finished cleaning herself and left the bathroom.

While the boat made its way to the next destination, Erica slept. She woke just in time for dinner. Then, wearing a simple white sundress and sandals, she climbed up on deck and found herself sitting with the young Australian trio traveling together.

The girl, Grace, was long-haired and charming, a gorgeous Aborigine with dark skin and gray eyes. The two boys traveling with her—blond Aidan and dark-haired Michael—both seemed infatuated with her. Even sitting at the table, they couldn't keep their hands off each other. Aidan rubbed Grace's back under her blouse while the girl linked her fingers with Michael's. Erica didn't doubt they were having a very fun threesome while everyone else was gawking at nature. Nice for them.

She enjoyed her moussaka and salad and indulged in a glass of red wine as she chatted with the Australians.

Grace leaned back into Michael as the breeze played in her loose dark hair. "So where are you from, Erica?"

"The States. Washington, D.C."

"Oh, cool." Grace looked genuinely interested. "I've never met anyone from there before. Usually Americans say they're from New York or Los Angeles."

"Or Texas," Aidan chimed in.

Erica smiled, toying with the stem of her wineglass. "I was actually born in New York City. I went to college and law school in D.C. I've worked there for a couple of years." She sipped the Shiraz, holding the faintly sweet flavor of the wine on her tongue before swallowing.

"Why would you give up the city that never sleeps for that dirty den of politicians?" Michael asked.

Erica didn't think he wanted to hear about her parents' expectations for her to continue the family tradition and attend Howard or some other historically black university. "It was a nice change from the hectic pace of New York," she said instead. "I'll be going back. A few days ago, I got an offer for a job in the city."

"Oh, good," Grace said with a wide grin. "I'd much rather come visit you in the Big Apple than whatever it is they call D.C."

Erica smiled. "The nation's capital."

"I'd rather bite the apple," Grace said.

Her two lovers laughed.

Their voices hushed in reverent silence when the sun began its descent toward the horizon. Oia's famed sunset blanketed the sea with deepest orange tones, ambers, spectacular shades of reds. The surface of the water glittered as if sprinkled with tiny diamonds. High up in the town set up on cliffs, she could see the hundreds of tourists who had gathered to watch the miracle of Oia's sun.

As she watched the gorgeous sunset, she couldn't stop

thinking about Nikolas and his kisses. His smile. All around her on the boat, the others were snuggling close together, cooing nonsense words as they watched the landscape all around them turn into gold. A few pulled out their cameras and took endless shots of the sky and the landscape.

It truly was beautiful. And for just one moment, she felt the prick of longing, the desire to share the spectacle of the sunset with the man she'd just met. And had sex with. Erica shook her head and shoved the longing away. It must have been caused by the lingering effects of her earlier sunstroke.

While she watched the sun and breathed deeply of the warm, salt-sweet air, she suddenly became aware of Nikolas on the deck. He was watching her. So she watched him. He was actually wearing a shirt for once; his body was clothed in a light blue shirt and faded jeans. His hair was loose and fluttered around his face in the wind. Her breath caught when the golden sun touched him. Gilded him.

Oh, damn...

She had never been one to believe in the power of instantaneous attraction. The few men she had allowed into her life and into her bed had cultivated the relationship they'd eventually formed with her. Erica's desire for them had grown over the course of weeks or months. This was the first time that her body was irresistibly drawn to a man, lusting after him with a strength that made her breathless and scared.

Erica forced herself to look away from Nikolas. She focused on the water, the cliffs, the golden sky. Anything else but his compelling presence on the other side of the boat. She lifted the glass of wine to her lips and swallowed.

Chapter Four

While the sun set over the Aegean, a few of the men jumped into the water instead of watching the sky. Erica was very aware that Nikolas was one of those men. He'd unself-consciously pulled off his jeans and T-shirt to show off his body, conveniently already wearing tight swim trunks. He glimmered like a god of old as he leaped off the boat, suspended for a moment above the water before arching into the sea with a splash.

Erica finished her dinner with the increasingly amorous threesome before making her excuses and heading to her cabin. Their happiness was beautiful to see. Still it made her lonely. Made her long for something, someone, she shouldn't want.

In the cabin, she put on her nightclothes, exchanging her dress for a tank top and loose pajama bottoms. She put her iPod on the speaker she'd brought and lay back on the bench with the pillows from the bed propped up behind her. Alice Smith sang from the speakers, infusing Erica's little room with melancholy and yearning. Beyond the porthole, the dark sea moved like a great beast around the ship.

Her eyes were beginning to drift closed when a knock sounded on her door. Erica jerked awake, not sure if she'd heard correctly or if the sound had been part of the music. Someone knocked again. She stood up, yawning. She pressed her fingers to her eyes and went to answer the door. It was Nikolas.

"American Princess," he murmured in his deliciously accented voice. "May I come in?"

Immediately, the tiredness fell away from her. Her entire body stood at attention, focused completely on him. The scarred eyebrow that should have been an imperfection but wasn't. His full and kissable mouth. The muscled landscape of his chest under the thin shirt. Erica gripped the handle of the door in her fist. "No."

"Don't be so uncharitable," he said with a smile. "I only want to talk with you."

"What, talk now and have sex later?"

"Or the other way around, if you want it that way." The humor vanished from his eyes. He took a soft breath and reached out a hand to touch her hip through her thin pajamas. "I was watching you earlier," he said. "You are so very beautiful." His voice was deep and low, rough as if forcing the words past a raw throat.

She shook her head, unable to think properly with his hand on her. "Nikolas…"

"I can't stop thinking about you." His fingers tightened briefly on her, a firm stroke through the cotton of her pajamas. "I can't stop thinking about the way you taste." He took a step closer. "About how you felt around my fingers." His hand slid under her tank top, lightly touching her side, stroking her skin. "Let me in, Erica."

The need rolled from him in scalding waves, brushing against her body. Her face. It grazed her nipples, which tightened under the thin cotton. Erica swallowed. Before she could think about what she was doing, she moved away from the doorway, retreating backward into the cabin. He followed with the heat of his body.

"Erica…"

Her mouth met his halfway. They came together like two pieces of a puzzle clicking tightly, belonging. Nikolas slammed the door shut behind him and pulled her tightly to him as Erica gripped his hair. They stumbled across the small cabin, discarding clothes as they went. His shirt. Her tank top. His jeans. Her pajama bottoms. They fell into her bed, Nikolas on top of her, falling between her parted thighs as if he belonged there.

"Wow! You feel good."

He devoured her mouth, sucking her tongue, his lips hard and firm on top of hers, conveying his desire, his want for her.

"I saw you in the sun this evening." He kissed her neck and her collarbone. "You were made to be in the light. So damn beautiful." He gasped the words against her skin as he moved lower, licking between her breasts, his breath skimming over her nipples, misting her ribs, teeth nibbling the delicate skin of her belly.

"Beautiful," he groaned.

He licked her hip bones, scraped them with his teeth. Erica jerked under him, her breath coming quickly as he kissed her, touched her. Nikolas pushed her thighs apart, his breath fanning against her hot and dripping spot. He kissed her.

"So good!"

His lips covered her throbbing clit, sucking it deeply into his mouth. She sank her fingers into his hair. The pleasure unfolded in her, fluttering over her body, renewing her like a summer rain. He groaned into her flesh, and the vibrations shuddered into her, bringing delight, pleasure, more wetness.

Between her thighs, his eyes lifted, compelling hers. While she watched, he parted her slick folds with his fingers, held her open, tasted her with long and luscious swipes of his tongue. Flames sizzled under her skin.

She couldn't look away from him. She felt that if she stopped looking at him, he would stop lapping at her. He ate her greedily, with a hunger that left her breathless. Her fingers flew away from his hair and twisted in the sheets; she was afraid she would hurt him.

His tongue thrust inside her, and she hissed at the thickness of it, so deep, so agile. Then his fingers. *Oh!* His fingers filled her. She writhed in the bed, gasped and moaned her pleasure and desire as his fingers stroked her deeply, pressing into her. She panted, wailed, cursed him as the sensations lashed through her.

"Oh, my God!" Her hips bucked under his mouth

He pinned her to the bed, loving her, plundering her wetness. Erica's thighs trembled. Her breath exploded from her lungs with each thrust of his fingers, each suck of his wicked mouth on her clit. He fluttered his hard tongue against her clit as she watched, his elbows pressing her thighs open, fingers holding open the wings as he teased her with his fingers and lashed her clit with his tongue.

The entire bed jerked with her tremors as she began to come, hoarsely shouting his name.

As he lapped at her, his hips thrust into the bed, the muscular globes of his ass making tight circles on the mattress. The sight of him taking his pleasure that way nearly made her explode. Everything about this man made her burn, made her drip, made her lose her mind.

Finally she couldn't keep her eyes open anymore. She flung her head back, squeezing her eyes shut. And screamed. Her throat was raw and hoarse from the scrape of his name as the tremors of orgasm swept through her.

He put on a condom and in one swift movement, rose up from between her thighs to shove himself inside her. He swallowed her gasp, his mouth claiming her completely. She moaned into him as he moved inside her, his hands firm on her ass, holding her to him as he moved his length with slow and thorough thrusts that she felt through her entire being.

Erica jerked upright in the bed. His body prevented the completion of the abrupt movement. Hard muscle. Sweat dripping from him. A haze of pleasure. The thrust of another orgasm exploding. Her shout. The sheets ripping in her fist. The bed rocking with each shove inside her. He grunted, and the mattress springs squeaked.

He moved inside her like a dream. Thick and hard. Rippling delight through her body with each thrust. Then she was coming again, body shuddering, her belly going tight as the orgasm rolled through her. Then another. And another. Her body and his a continuous loop of pleasure until she didn't know where his satisfaction began and hers ended.

He shouted into her throat. "So good!" His completion pumped hot and sweet between her thighs. The bedsprings wailed. Their damp flesh slid together.

Nikolas slowly pulled away from her, his gaze of wonderment on her. "I didn't think it could get better, but…I was wrong."

He gently caressed her hips as he pulled semihard out of her. He flopped over on his back to stare at the ceiling. At his side, Erica could only do the same. She licked her lips, unconsciously moving her thighs together, relishing the wetness between them, the soreness that already lay there. She turned to Nikolas. He was already looking at her. As she watched, his lashes slowly drifted down over his dark brown eyes, coming to rest against his cheeks.

Typical man, Erica thought. Just as she too fell asleep.

Chapter Five

She woke to the sound of his voice.

"This weekend I should have been in Athens with family friends, having a last holiday before I go to work with my father." The words were low, intent. He could have been sleep-talking. He could have been channeling another man, he sounded so different. This was the other Nikolas. The one who lived in a white palace at the top of a dark mountain.

"But you're here instead. Why?" she asked, deliberately keeping her voice low.

There was something almost magical about the mood between them. The music from the iPod was soft in the room, not shielding the hypnotizing sound of the sea. The boat rocked gently. All around, Erica felt the large boat humming with activity despite the lateness of the hour. And here, in her small room, sharing this night with her, was the sexiest man she'd ever met. She felt drugged with pleasure.

"I'm exactly where I need to be," Nikolas said.

"Shirking your duties on the boat just to have some fun?"

"Having fun with you is amazing," he murmured, his hand moving with hypnotic gentleness along the lines of her face and throat. Nikolas's lashes fluttered down over his eyes. "You make me want to say and do the most ridiculous things, jump from a cliff to catch an angel for you. Steal the breastplate of the goddess Athena herself. Make love to you all night and into the morning. Just to prove that I'm worthy of being here in your bed."

She stared at him in amazement. "Are you drunk?"

He laughed. "Drunk on you."

When he moved to gather her into his arms, she let him. Once sheltered in the crook of his arm, she sighed with the pleasure of it, wondering what had taken her so long to get there.

"My life is much too serious," he said. "My father would have me cut my hair and become just like him, take over for him at Andromeda Shipping tomorrow." Nikolas laughed without humor. "I am more than capable of the position I was born to fill. I am ready for it. But I will not be the type of executive my father is. His employees have never heard an appreciative word from him. He'd rather rule through fear than kindness and mutual respect. He doesn't know when work ends and living begins." He traced the bones of her fingers resting on his chest. "So when Christos asked me, I jumped at the chance to fill in for him this week. This is my last chance to do something completely for myself before I join my father and the board of directors in Athens next week."

"You act like you haven't had it easy your entire life," she said. "From what you've told me, you grew up with a silver spoon in your mouth. You can live anywhere in the world. You can buy or be anything."

"Easy is relative." His eyes darkened with emotion, but he said nothing else.

Erica lay still at his side, listening to the pain in his words. *Another poor little rich boy?* a snide part of her said. But he seemed so much more than that. And it wasn't just because he had a big dick and knew how to use it. She touched his chest, then lightly stroked the thickly muscled flesh.

"We all have things we have to deal with," she murmured.

"I'm hoping that one day you'll share your worries with me," he said softly. He touched her face, and she sighed. Her skin warmed and came alive under his seeking touch.

"You know that this is a vacation fling for both of us, right? There's not going to be anything beyond these four days." She felt she had to say it to take away the sting.

"Don't be so pessimistic." He kissed her mouth. "Spend some time with me after the tour is over so we can explore this thing between us." Nikolas brushed her nipple with his thumb. "Let us enjoy each other for as long as possible."

Could they? But what would that ultimately mean? Did he want…? Erica's train of thought tumbled off the rails as he caressed her. The slight flicker of interest became a flame as their kiss deepened. His tongue snaked against hers. "I want to make vacation love to you again."

She shuddered in pleasure at his words vibrating against her skin. His hands curved around her breasts; he hardened against her thigh.

"I didn't know talking about life made you horny," she murmured as he kissed her throat.

"Everything about you makes me horny." He slid seeking fingers between her legs.

Her nails dug into his back.

* * *

It was many hours later that he got up to leave her. Satisfaction sang through her body. Contentment in her very blood. He kissed her as he left the bed. She watched him as he pulled on his clothes in the faint light. His beautiful face, the wide and muscled chest, the narrow hips and the flaccid penis between thighs that she still wanted to bite and feel against her face.

"I have to get back to work," he said. His voice was heavy with regret.

She hated to see him go. Erica curled her hands in the sheet to prevent herself from reaching for him and tugging him into her bed. "Come back later." She grabbed his hand anyway, put it between her legs and into the wetness still there from their sex. "I'll wait for you."

Nikolas growled deep in his throat and sank his fingers into her, then pulled them back and licked them like they were laced with honey. "Hmm!" With his shirt gripped in one hand, he dipped back into the bed, kissing her mouth again.

"What are you doing to me?"

Erica smiled. "Come see me later." Then she put a hand in the center of his chest and pushed.

He allowed himself to be shoved away and pulled on his shirt as he stumbled from her cabin, eyes still dazed with desire. Once he'd closed the door behind him, Erica sighed and fell back into the pillows. She stared at the door where he had just disappeared, unable to believe she was indulging in the ultimate cliché. A vacation fling indeed. But damn he was so gorgeous and he wanted her as badly as she wanted him. She curled up under the covers.

Just as her eyelids began to sag, a knock sounded on her door. Erica smiled, anticipating Nikolas's arms around her again. She called for him to come in.

"Oh, good," she murmured softly as she sat up, allowing the sheet to fall away from her breasts. "You changed your mind."

But it wasn't Nikolas who stood there in the doorway. It was Lani. The girl stepped into the cabin and gently closed the door behind her. Erica stared at her, unable to believe she was actually in her room. Although swift color moved into her cheeks, she stopped herself from grabbing for the sheets to cover herself. Instead she leaned back against the wall and crossed her arms.

"What can I do for you?"

Lani stared at Erica's body, her face. "I wanted to know what he sees in you."

"Why don't you go ask him since you think the two of you still have a connection?"

The girl looked surprised at her response. Then her features hardened. "He only wants you because you remind him of his mother."

Erica raised an eyebrow. "That's not a very flattering thing to say about the guy you want back in your bed, is it?"

The blonde didn't blink. "You have that in common, you know. That dark skin and your Afri—"

Erica sat up abruptly in the bed, her eyes narrowed at the stupid blonde. "Stop right there before you say something you'll regret."

"The only thing I regret is you stepping foot on this boat." Lani clenched her hands at her sides. "Leave Nikolas alone. He may be half-black, but he's with his own people here and he's happy. Go back to America and stop confusing him. Stop trying to seduce him away from us with your black skin."

Before Erica could recover herself and say anything

in response, the girl walked out the door, closing it softly behind her.

Erica stared at the door, anger and disbelief warring inside her. Did she really come all the way to Greece to fight over some man?

Nikolas was an incredible lover, and he had been just what she'd needed to make her Greek vacation even more memorable. But was it worth all this? Erica cursed under her breath. She sat down at the edge of the bed and stared out the porthole at the dark and shifting sea.

Damn.

Chapter Six

Erica jumped off the boat with a wild yell. She dropped into the cool water in a bubbling rush. The wetness greedily swallowed her. Blue deep all around her. For a moment, she was suspended under the azure water, seeing the bottom of the boat, its anchor. The legs of her fellow passengers as they swam for the shore. A beautiful quiet that soothed her senses. Then she kicked her way back up to the surface. Breath held. Eyes open. She swam toward the brown water on the rocky shore.

The *Agape* was visiting the warm springs, a warm and sulfur-rich bay on one of the volcanic islands of Santorini. The bay was too shallow for the boat to dock, so anyone wanting to enjoy the warm, muddy waters of the springs had to jump from the boat and swim out to the rocky shore.

Erica hadn't seen Nikolas since he'd left her room the night before. She knew he probably wanted to talk to her, but she'd purposely avoided him, still rattled by her late-night visitor. Lani's desperate eyes and hunger for him had haunted her in her sleep. Was that how she seemed to everyone looking at her with Nikolas?

As she swam toward shore, she was strongly aware of Nikolas's presence nearby with a water rescue buoy in hand. He was watching the other swimmers, and watching her. With a few strokes of his powerful arms and legs, he was next to her in the water.

"Something is wrong," he said. He held on to the rescue buoy, his chest glistening, water droplets clinging to his thick eyelashes and dripping down his face.

The sea was already noticeably warmer around her, and she felt more buoyant. The warmth stroked her body, moving her toward Nikolas. The desire to wind her body around his, to kiss him and take his body inside hers, sparked her irritation.

"The only thing wrong here is you," she muttered. "Leave me alone and go back to your crazy ex. She's desperate to be your woman again."

Surprise flared in his eyes. "My woman?"

"I think he's drowning!" someone suddenly cried out.

Nikolas immediately dashed in the direction of the voice and the body flailing in distress. Erica stared in concern as he knifed through the water to reach the man thrashing uselessly and grabbing at his chest while his girlfriend looked on in fear.

Nikolas flipped the man onto his back, then grabbed his hands and fastened them to the ropes on the rescue buoy. The man wheezed as he clutched the bright orange tube, his chest heaving as if he was having trouble catching his breath.

"His asthma!" His girlfriend was in a panic. "The inhaler! It's in his bag on the boat."

Nikolas called out in Greek to someone on the yacht.

Seconds later, Max jumped into the water and swam toward them. He and Nikolas worked quickly, giving the ailing man his inhaler, which he gratefully grabbed and held to his mouth. Within moments, he seemed much better.

Everyone breathed a collective sigh of relief. With the man in good hands, most of the passengers continued on toward the shore. Only his girlfriend lingered with Nikolas and Max, staying with the men as they slowly made their way back to the boat.

Erica stared after Nikolas, noticing his effortless strength and the way he carefully handled the asthmatic man. Angry with herself for looking at him, she turned quickly in the water, splashing, to swim toward the other passengers. The cool water of the Aegean slowly warmed the closer she got to the rocky, mud-painted shore. As she swam, the water changed from blue to clay to a deep reddish-brown.

The warm springs. A small inlet where the water was heated by the volcanoes and turned a beautiful rust-on-copper shade, with mud underfoot that the guidebooks said was therapeutic and great for the skin. Erica's toes sank into the mud as she stood up in the waist-high water.

Grace and her two lovers swam happily nearby, splashing in the shallows while being careful of the rocks that became more plentiful the closer they got to the shore. Erica made her way toward them.

Once on the shore, she joined the other passengers in smoothing the mud over her face and body, surprised at the silken feel of it on her skin. She sat on a high rock, covered in mud, while the sun baked her. She laughed and joked with the Japanese couple and the three Australians. But she couldn't stop thinking about Nikolas. The look on his face when she'd mentioned his ex-lover.

With Nikolas on her mind, the pleasure of the warm

springs quickly faded. Erica was the first to swim back to the boat. She quickly changed out of her mud-stained bikini and showered, then went back on deck to grab a beer and lie in the sun.

Near her sat the asthmatic man, who had apparently recovered from his episode in the water. His girlfriend lay in the shelter of his arms; his sunburnt skin and her deeply tanned mahogany complexion contrasted as they reclined in the shade. Their fingers were linked and his head tilted down as he listened intently to whatever she was saying. Their happiness made Erica envious.

She exchanged a smile and a nod with the man, glad to see he was doing better.

On day three, the *Agape* sailed toward their next stop, an abandoned French castle on the other side of the island. According to local legend, the castle had once been occupied by a disgraced French *vicomte* who had fallen in love with another man's wife, kidnapped her and forced her to live out the rest of her days on the edge of nowhere.

In person, the castle was breathtaking. A high stone structure with an old system of drainage pumps that ran into the sea. It was a striking shape against the blue sky, a marvel of turrets and arches that had withstood the brutality of hundreds of years. But even after so long, an aura of despair still lingered around the castle.

The tour of the castle and the accompanying cliff-diving excursion lasted for the rest of the day. Erica saw Nikolas diving off the castle's high overlook, his body a sleek and glistening thing in the light before he plunged into the water forty feet below. She held her breath as she watched him, unable to look away.

At dinner that evening, she sat with the three Australians. Erica joked with them, did a few shots of whiskey and drank as much beer as her body could hold. She was determined to push Nikolas from her mind.

"I think that guy is looking at you," Grace said to Erica as they sat at the table watching the last of the sun bleed from the sky, their feet stretched out in Aidan's and Michael's laps.

"That guy" was Nikolas. Erica looked in the direction the other woman had jerked her chin to see him on the other side of the boat, watching her with an unblinking stare. When Erica looked at him, he dipped his head and flashed her a smile before making his way toward her. Her heart pounded in her chest. She swallowed heavily at the determined look on his face, the slim and gorgeous lines of his body in the faint light. Her breath caught. She couldn't breathe.

At the table, he greeted the Australians, politeness at its best. The wind ruffled his hair, tugged at his jeans and T-shirt.

"May I talk with you for a moment?" he asked.

"No." She leaned back in her chair, a bottle of beer held loosely between her fingers.

She felt her new friends' surprised eyes on her. Grace nudged Erica. "Don't be rude," she said. Then she lowered her voice, talking from the corner of her mouth in her version of a whisper. "He's gorgeous. What's wrong with you?" Everyone at the table heard her.

"Yes, Erica. What's wrong with you?" Nikolas tilted his head, charming and sexy at once. "Or is it me?" His mouth was full and hard in the light, his brown eyes bright with humor.

Through the haze of alcohol, Erica didn't see a damn thing wrong with him. He was beautiful. He was available to sleep with. He made her body feel incredible things. What was wrong with that? Absolutely nothing.

Nikolas extended his hand. "Come with me. Just for a few minutes."

Before she could speak, he took her hand and pulled her to her feet. Grace giggled.

"Have fun!" she called out as Nikolas drew Erica away from the small formation of dinner tables, past the Japanese couple sitting closely in a darkened corner, their bodies intimately pressed together. He guided her to the back of the boat, then up the ladder to the platform he'd taken her to yesterday morning. They sat down with their legs dangling over the water, arms braced against the railing separating them from the dark sea. The wind brushed against Erica's cheeks, pressed her shirt even more to her skin.

"Why are you avoiding me?"

With the wind buffeting them from so high, some of the alcoholic fog cleared from Erica's head. She leaned away from him. "Don't pretend you don't know why."

He made a noise. The light revealed barely a quarter of his face, his mouth and strong jawline, his eyes, the feathery weight of his lashes. "Pretend I have no idea what you're talking about. Pretend I'm an absolute fool."

She sighed and leaned back onto her straightened arms. For a moment, she couldn't even look at him. He was too achingly beautiful. The curve of his mouth only reminded her of last night, when he'd come to her cabin and nuzzled between her legs. Erica bit her lip as a fugitive electric current zinged in her belly. What the hell was wrong with her?

"After you left last night, your crazy ex-girlfriend came into my cabin to claim you. She was very out of line. I don't deal with that garbage, Nikolas. I don't put up with drama from anybody."

His jaw tightened in the half light. "I am no woman's man."

"Lani begs to differ." The anger bubbled up inside her again at the thought of the previous night. "It was my fault, though. Your friends told me you have a complicated situation here. I only have myself to blame for all this foolishness."

Despite her harsh words, she spoke softly. The blanket of night touched her with its delicate fibers and created an unbreakable intimacy between them.

"I am no woman's man," Nikolas said again. "Lani has no claim here. Believe me."

"Why is she acting like this if she isn't your girl?"

"Because her eyes are green...." Even in the dark, she saw the teasing arch of an eyebrow. The amused curve of his mouth. But she wasn't in a joking mood.

"You had sex with her?"

"Over six months ago, yes. But sharing sex is no declaration of a relationship."

Erica swallowed hard as she digested the truth that he and Lani had been together. There was no point in her being jealous. None.

"Did you ever think that having sex with you was an expression of her love?" She threw his words from earlier on the volcano back in his face.

"No." Nikolas shook his head. "Never. I was very clear with her in the beginning."

Curiosity needled her at his tone. She sat up to better see his face in the semidark. "You were clear about what?"

"I don't do relationships."

His simple declaration surprised her. But she had no idea why. Was there ever a man in the history of the universe who "did" relationships before being trapped by some enterprising lover? Nikolas was in his twenties. Very few men his age were into anything but indulging in as much uncomplicated sex as possible before marriage or death.

"Why don't you *do* relationships?"

She felt rather than saw his shrug in the dark, the warm movement of his body so very near hers, a whisper of his breath against her cheek.

"Did some girl break your heart?" She said it sarcastically, doubtfully.

He made a rueful noise. "There was no girl, just life."

As he spoke, he leaned closer and Erica detected the faint trace of alcohol on his breath. Not the beer or whiskey that she'd been drinking. It smelled like ouzo, that potent Greek liqueur she'd once sampled at a restaurant and that had knocked her on her ass until the next morning. But Nikolas didn't seem drunk, simply contemplative.

"What did life ever do to you, Nikolas?" Erica licked her lips, the taste of his name unexpectedly sweet. Like the whiskey she'd drunk earlier.

He laughed, not sounding the least bit amused. "It showed me that relationships end. There's no point in starting something that's just going to die. Is there?"

"That's ridiculous." She waved away his words with a dismissive hand, fingers slapping accidentally against the chrome railing. "Ouch!" She stuck the tips of her aching fingers in her mouth. "You might as well say every human should just kill themselves at birth since we're all going to end up in the ground anyway. I thought you were smarter than that."

"That *comparison* is ridiculous." A lock of his hair loosened in the wind and blew across the space between them to lap against her cheek. "We have no choice about being born," he said.

Erica caught the errant strands of hair and hooked them behind Nikolas's ear. She caressed his warm skin before pulling her hand back. "If you're choosing not to love, isn't it the same thing as suicide?" A devil suddenly pricked at her, taking over her tongue. "For all you know, Lani could have been the woman meant for you, but because of all this background chatter, you're letting her slip through your fingers."

She leaned her forehead against the railing with a low sigh. Her head was beginning to spin from all the beer and whiskey she'd consumed. As she briefly closed her eyes, the sea air lapped gently at her too-warm cheeks and throat.

"Maybe you're the one I'm missing out on," Nikolas murmured, moving close to her. "Erica. My American Princess." He sighed, his breath brushing her lips. "You're in my head, and I can't get you out. You make me feel things no other woman has."

She laughed weakly. "Oh, please." With a pang, she realized she wanted the things he said to be true. Who wouldn't want to be different for this man? But she knew he was just playing with her head.

Nikolas moved even closer. "Erica, I want to discover you. I want to touch and make love to you."

He trailed a hand down the length of her arm, and Erica shivered in reaction. Her skin felt feverish in the wake of his delicate touch; her body responded helplessly to him. He traced a tingling line into the center of her palm.

"May I, Princess?"

But he kissed her before she could answer. Erica leaned into him.

He nibbled at her mouth, licked her lips while his hand curved around the back of her neck, cupping the sudden heaviness of her head, filled with so much languor that she couldn't hold it up on her own. How did he know that? How had he known just how to touch her? Just how to—?

She gasped as his hand slid into her pants. When had he unbuttoned her jeans? Her fingers clutched his arm as his fingers slid into her panties, combed through the curly hairs on her mound. Then they moved lower. Nikolas moaned into her mouth when he finally touched her sex. Erica twitched, her legs falling open to accept the light stroke of his fingers.

My God! What was she letting him do?

His fingers slid over her clit, dancing over the sensitive bud, dipping into her to retrieve more moisture; there was an abundance for him to find. Erica shivered as he explored her mouth with his tongue, stroked her with his fingers. A soft noise escaped her as a lash of heat moved through her belly. She gripped his neck and slid her hands up into his thick hair.

"You're so amazing...so beautiful..." He tapered off into words she couldn't understand, seductive whispers against her mouth as his fingers worked their magic on her flesh. He tore his mouth away from hers. Yanked her legs up onto the platform. Jerked her pants down. She squeaked as the denim scraped her thighs. Erica was under him, the deck hard against her back, Nikolas's body hard at her front.

"Shh..." he murmured as his fingers returned to her hot and tingling spot. "Open your legs for me, Princess!" he gasped against her lips.

She couldn't have said no even if she'd wanted to. Erica fell back against the boat, a honeyed lushness invading her body, her nipples tingling against the thin material of her shirt. He must have felt it, too. He must have, because he pushed up her shirt, exposing her hard nipples to the sea air and to his mouth.

He sucked her breast, his fingers dipping inside her in search of her pleasure. And he found it. Lost in the haze of delight, her hips surging up against his hand, she heard the liquid kiss of his fingers inside her swimming wetness, felt the heat of his hand on her, his thumb on her clit, press-

ing lust into her until she was moaning his name behind
tightly closed lips. She didn't want to make any noise, but
her body was dangerously close to implosion. His thumb
flicked across her clit like a hummingbird's wing while
he curled fingers up inside her, stroking that sweet place
again and again.

"Hmm…"

Erica's body moved with the thrust of his fingers, with
the movement of his mouth on her breasts, sucking and
biting her sensitive nipples as he probed her deeply with
his fingers. The spring of desire tightened more and more
inside her until she couldn't hold back the sounds any longer. She whimpered as his fingers stroked her deeply, skillfully. Then the spring broke.

The orgasm washed over her, swept her away. It grabbed
the sound of his name from her throat, set her thighs to
trembling, her body completely at his mercy. She jerked
in the midst of an incredible satisfaction, gushing a thin
stream of wetness over his fingers. He was relentless, still
pressing her clit, still stroking her deeply as she gushed,
panting his name. Telling him to stop. Then don't stop.

Only when she slid bonelessly to the deck did Nikolas
relent. He raised his head to look at her, complete masculine satisfaction in his gaze. He lifted his fingers from
between her legs and put them in his mouth, sucking off
her juices glistening on them in the moonlight. Her clit
twitched at the sight.

She must be drunk. There was no other explanation for
the way she was reacting to him. None. But even as the
denial moved through her, she was reaching for his pants.

Although she wasn't sure if she could manage more
than a few strokes, Erica was willing to try and give him
even half the pleasure he had brought her. Her body felt
well and truly pleasured, weakened with bliss.

He kissed her mouth. Took her hand and pulled it away from his erection. "I don't need anything," he said.

"I like you," he murmured into her throat as he kissed her there. "I really like you."

Erica closed her eyes, inhaling his scent. And smiled.

Chapter Seven

Erica woke up with a raging headache.

She opened her eyes to the ceiling of her cabin, eyes tracing the familiar piece of slightly irregular wood overhead that led to the wall, then down to the porthole. She breathed in and out very carefully, taking care not to move around too much in the bed.

Bed. Sex.

"Oh. My. God."

Everything from the night before came rushing to her. Dinner and drinks with the Australians. Nikolas coming to talk with her. His complete seduction of her in the dark. How she had cried out his name as her body had gushed its pleasure all over the deck of the boat. All over her clothes.

"Oh, God…"

She closed her eyes at the memory. Her body warmed with remembered pleasure. And embarrassment.

A tentative glance at her watch told her breakfast time

was almost over. She blinked at the dial before slowly sitting up in the bed. On the small bedside table sat an unfamiliar silver tumbler. There was a note under the tumbler in an unfamiliar but masculine hand.

Drink this. It'll help with the stomach and your headache. It's a remedy my grandmother swears by. Without it, she would have never gotten out of bed to make Sunday breakfast.

He signed it with a simple *N,* although he hadn't needed to. Who else would come into her cabin, strip her naked and leave her a hangover cure?

By the time she felt human again and made it up on deck, it was well past breakfast. As she sat down at a table with Grace, who was finishing her meal, a hand slid a covered tray in front of her. She looked up in surprise as Nikolas flashed her a wink and kept going.

"If that wasn't an after-sex wink, I don't know what is." Grace giggled, leaning over to uncover Erica's platter.

It was her usual breakfast, Greek yogurt mixed with honey, thick slices of bread drizzled with olive oil and black pepper, a small bowl of dried dates. How did he even know that's what she normally ate? She looked up to find Nikolas, but he had already disappeared.

"Too bad the tour is coming to an end. Now that you two finally connected, it seems a shame not to be able to enjoy that sexy body of his some more."

"It is?" Even as she said it, Erica realized that Grace was right. This was the fourth day of the boat tour. The last few hours before they sailed back to Thira. She took a quick breath.

"Unbelievable!" Grace slapped a hand over her mouth. "You forgot, didn't you?"

She *had* forgotten. Erica looked around again for Nikolas as a heaviness settled in her chest.

Most of the other passengers were already preparing for the final excursion of the tour. Nearby, the mother and daughter pair she'd never properly met checked their backpacks, as if making sure they had everything, while Ren and Kyoko took photos of each other on every conceivable part of the boat. Grace's boyfriends and the other couple were nowhere in sight.

The end had come so soon.

Although she wasn't hungry, she forced herself to put something in her stomach and drink more water. As she ate, a small island formation came into view.

The rocks were dark and volcanic-looking, the hills steep and treacherous. On low land, she could just make out white marble, a statuary of some kind. Just as she began to wonder what it was, the intercom crackled to life.

Erica winced as Lani's voice spread through the air. The young woman quickly explained that this, their final stop on the boat tour, was the island of Kos, site of the recently discovered temple to Anahita, the Persian goddess of fertility and war, the patroness of women. The *Agape* was to spend three hours anchored on the island to give the passengers the chance to not only tour the temple, but also to take full advantage of the most beautiful beach in all of Greece.

Once the announcement ended, Grace quickly excused herself to finish getting ready. As Erica was finishing up her breakfast, a figure high up on the ship's main mast caught her attention. Nikolas.

He was strapped into some sort of a harness and had a bag draped across his shoulder and chest as he fixed something on the mast. His chest was bare, and the jean shorts hung off his narrow hips. She froze, watching the effortless beauty of the man, the way the sun burnished his skin, the faint sheen of sweat on his body. A lovely sight.

She remembered well the feel of that heated flesh under her hands and longed to touch it again. Erica didn't fight the craving this time, only allowed it to come, to fill her body with warmth and desire. She spooned a bit of yogurt into her mouth as she watched him, swirling her tongue around the spoon, imagining she was teasing him with her mouth.

"Lucky man."

She startled at the voice near her. It was Aidan, one of Grace's boyfriends. He sat down at her table, wearing his habitually happy grin, his blond hair in disarray.

"I wouldn't know a thing about his luck," she said with a smile.

"If I had a girl looking at me like you just did at that bloke, then I'd count myself real lucky."

She dropped her spoon into the empty yogurt bowl. "You already have that, in case you haven't noticed."

Grace looked at Aidan and Michael as if both men hung the moon and stars. As much as she loved men, Erica couldn't imagine sleeping with more than one at a time.

"Actually, about that." Aidan braced his elbows on the table and propped his chin up on his clasped hands. "Grace was wondering if you'd be interested in joining us this afternoon."

"For lunch? Of course. I'd love to."

"No. For sex."

Erica stared at him in surprise, not sure whether or not he was joking. "Isn't your bed crowded enough as it is?" Then she laughed before she could catch herself. "Don't answer that." She shook her head, still chuckling. "I—I'm very flattered, but I don't think so."

"Think about it." He grinned, apparently not taking offense at her rejection. "Grace would like another woman to play with. It's been a while for her, and you know Michael and I will take care of you." He licked his lips in an exaggerated way that left no doubt what he was talking about.

"I don't doubt your skill," she murmured, not hiding her smile. "But I just don't have any interest in sleeping with more than one person right now."

"Not even if we got your boyfriend to join us?"

He's not my boyfriend. The words almost fell from her lips, but then she thought of something else. "Did he agree to sleep with you?"

"No. Not yet. But you never know the answer to a question until you ask."

"Very true." Then she shook her head again. "I really thank you for the invitation to sleep with you guys. I'm flattered that you thought of me in that way, but I'm not interested right now, even if you get Nikolas to join in. I'm a little selfish where my lovers are concerned."

The Australian shrugged. "At least I tried. Thanks for at least hearing me out."

"No problem."

After he left, she looked up to the main mast, where Nikolas still dangled precariously. Was it her imagination, or did he just smile at her? She dipped her head, hiding her own smile.

The island of Kos was a place of simple charms. Its climate was similar to Santorini, arid and desertlike but with golden beaches that made it one of the most beautiful islands in all of Greece. Barely twelve miles long and five miles wide, it was home to little more than a hundred inhabitants, who mostly lived in houses built high in the mountains. The area around the low-lying temple was deserted, populated only by wild goats and olive trees.

Erica was one of the last to leave the boat, preferring
to find her way around the island with the rough map provided for each of the passengers instead of following Lani.
The girl and Max planned to lead the small group to the
temple, then up to the town in the hills, where they would
explore and have lunch before heading back down to the
beach for a swim.

Erica made her way slowly to the temple, deliberately
taking her time along the dusty, winding path so she would
miss seeing Lani. By the time she reached the temple, it
was deserted.

Ahead of her, the remains of Anahita's temple loomed
above the road. A stone wall. Four cracked marble col-
umns of various heights. A waist-high slab with a headless,
winged figure of the goddess. Her rippling, floor-length
dress left one breast uncovered, and she held the feet of
what seemed like two snarling lions in each hand. In the
bright morning, the goddess was beautiful. Around the
slab were the discarded remains of the temple. Pieces of
marble strewn here and there, and short brown grass grew
up between the ancient stone platform and through gaps
in the wall.

As she looked up at the goddess, the whispers of a conversation came to her on the breeze. Two voices, male and
female, urgently speaking Greek. The path leading to the
voices took her away from the main temple and toward a
high but crumbling wall, a place made for privacy. Erica
crept closer, chastising herself with every step for being
nosy.

Her sneakered feet crept over the dry gravel and through
the drifting white dust, making a crackling noise. At the
ruins of the wall, she poked her head around the corner.
And gasped. In the private arbor behind the wall, a surprisingly fertile area with lush green grass and a sprin-

kling of bright purple blossoms, two people stood nearly chest to chest. Nikolas and Lani.

Lani looked as ordinary as the first time Erica had seen her, blond hair straight and loose around her face, an overflowing bounty of breasts in her white tank top, pale yellow shorts clinging to her narrow hips. The couple stood in profile to Erica as they argued.

Lani had Nikolas's shirt gripped in her fists as she cried out to him. She pulled his face down to hers, but Nikolas turned away before their lips could connect. She stumbled back from him and pulled off her tank top and bra. Her bare breasts tumbled free.

Erica's hands gripped the edge of the wall, the stones digging hard into her palm. She stared at Nikolas's face. He was more serious than she'd ever seen him. His jaw was clenched tightly and his posture was stiff as he said something to Lani.

But she shook her head and grabbed Nikolas's hands. She dragged them to her breasts. After what seemed like an eternity to Erica, he pulled his hands away from the other woman's chest, put them on her shoulders instead and said something softly to her.

She reared back and slapped his face.

The sound of it was loud in the clearing. Abrupt. Nikolas's face hardened. But he said nothing. Lani raised her hand to slap him again, but he grabbed her hands and forced them to her sides. The girl pulled away from him, yanked on her bra and shirt and stalked off, walking toward where Erica stood, eavesdropping.

Erica ducked her head back around the wall and straightened from her crouch just as the blonde reached her. Lani's eyes widened at the sight of Erica, lips skinning back from her teeth.

"You bitch!" she spat. "I told you to stay away from

him. He was mine before you started wagging your fat ass in his face!"

Erica stepped back, expecting the girl to try to slap her. Instead Lani froze mere inches from her and started crying. The tears flooded from her wide blue eyes, and black mascara ran down her pale cheeks. "You two deserve each other!" the girl screamed, spit flying. "If he doesn't know a good thing when he sees it, then screw him." Lani jerked away from Erica and ran down the path toward the beach.

"Erica." Nikolas walked up to her from beyond the wall, shadows around his normally smiling eyes. "Did that entertain you?"

"I wasn't looking for entertainment," she said. "And I'm sure you know I don't speak Greek."

"You don't have to speak Greek to understand what that slap was about. Or those tears."

Erica shrugged. "You and her could have been discussing your recent engagement for all I know."

"Trust me when I say that's definitely not it." Nikolas sighed heavily. "Walk with me."

After a moment's hesitation, she fell into step with him. They walked gingerly down the path together and found themselves standing beneath the statue of the goddess. Nikolas sank down at the goddess's feet and leaned back against the marble pedestal.

The sun fell over him like a golden blanket, illuminating his smooth face, full mouth, the slumberous brown of his eyes.

"I've never understood the big deal about things like this." He gestured to the statue and the ruins of the temple.

"They represent history and give people something to believe in—like love. Everyone wants love," Erica said. "Some *need* it."

Nikolas shook his head, a tight smile pulling at the

edges of his mouth. "Everyone needs sex, maybe. Not love."

"Why would you say something like that, especially when sitting in the presence of the goddess?" She joked with him as she gestured up to the figure of the goddess, trying to distract him from the scene he'd just had with Lani.

"I think the goddess would forgive this nonbeliever."

She sat down next to him, leaned into the sun-warmed marble and tilted her head to look into his face. "I'm sorry about what happened back there. Are you going to be all right?"

For a moment, he glanced at her, a frown marring his smooth brow. Then he looked off in the distance, allowing the sunlight to move across the symmetrical planes of his face, his mouth and his neck.

"I mentioned before that I don't do relationships." The corners of his eyes tightened as he spoke. "The reason why happened a lifetime ago."

He looked so sad that Erica wanted to hold him in her arms until the smile she was used to transformed his face once again. She touched his knee.

"As if you're that old," she teased.

"I'm twenty-six years old." He said it as if he were Methuselah.

Erica rolled her eyes, keeping her hand on his knee. "And I'm twenty-eight. So what?"

"Are you really?" He looked surprised.

"Why? Does that mean you're not interested in my body anymore?"

"You know," he said, his eyes holding a faint teasing light. "I've always enjoyed older women."

Erica sighed with the beginnings of relief. He almost

sounded like himself again. Then he put his hand on top of hers, his palm radiating warmth into her skin.

"A lifetime ago," he said, "my parents were happy."

In a low and reflective voice, Nikolas told her how his father went to Zambia on a business trip and met his mother, Uzondile Kani. The pair fell instantly in love and married within a week. Their happiness in Zambia and then later in Greece was enough to make anyone who saw them envious.

Then, after twenty-two years and three children, Anatol Stephanides suddenly announced that he was no longer in love with his wife and wanted a divorce. He had discovered a passion for the twenty-five-year-old daughter of a business associate and wanted to start a new life with her. Despite what his father said, Nikolas had always suspected that it was Anatol's desire for the girl's money and status rather than her body that drove him from his family.

Nikolas's mother, a dignified and beautiful woman, accepted what her husband wanted and moved out of the family home. The three Stephanides children were devastated.

Uzondile moved to a smaller house on the island, a house with a swimming pool that she was always a little frightened of. One night, she ran out into the yard, chasing the small dog she had gotten to keep her company. It was dark. She tripped and fell in the pool. Drowned.

The security cameras caught everything on film.

Nikolas's voice broke. "My sisters and I thought father was joking when he told us. We could not believe it." Nikolas blinked as if walking through cobwebs. He looked up. "For a long time, I hated my father. If it had not been for him, she wouldn't have been alone in that house. She would be alive."

With Uzondile's death, Anatol rediscovered his love for his wife. He discarded the woman he would have put in her place. He moved her things back to the family home. But it was too late.

"One moment she was everything to him," Nikolas said. "And the next it was like she never existed. A relationship of twenty years and three children scattered like ashes. My mother dying alone in the dark." He refocused his eyes on Erica. "What do relationships mean when something like that can happen?"

For a moment, Erica said nothing. She sat next to the man she had come to feel so much for in such a short time, only able to imagine his pain. Her hand tightened briefly on his knee.

"Your father was having a midlife crisis," she finally said. "Don't allow what he did to ruin your chances at happiness."

"Other men have done similar things. Other women, too."

"So instead of being a better man, you're the one who plays around and discards your lovers' feelings?" She thought of Lani and the look on her face. The hurt and anger. Would that be her at the end of this trip?

"No. Never. Women have tried to change my mind, but they always know where I stand. I'm always clear that I just want sex." He dipped his head, glanced up at her through the thicket of his lashes. "You are the only one who has made me question myself…"

Erica's heart began a wild drumbeat at his words, but she forced a laugh. "Whore."

"Never. I'm much more discriminating than that." The smallest of smiles moved across his face. "Love is beautiful. I believe that anyone who wants it should have it, but it's just not for me." He looked at her defiantly.

She only shrugged. "Whatever you say, lover boy."

"You make me sound so unsavory."

"Never that," she murmured. "Because you are savory indeed, one of the best meals I've eaten in a long time."

Nikolas laughed as he threw off the last of his melancholy, reached out and drew her to him. "Every day, you surprise me."

His eyes looked deeply into hers. Erica felt every centimeter of his hands on her skin. Heard the far-off whisper of the sea rushing up to the sand. The breeze moving through the oasis behind them. Everything else disappeared except for his eyes and his touch.

"Are you trying to bewitch me?" she asked.

"Is it working?"

His mouth slowly lowered to hers. Nikolas took command of their kiss with a skill that made her thighs fall open. His hand at the back of her head guided her to his mouth. His tongue tested the pucker of her lips, tracing it before parting it, diving into her. A whine of sound escaped the back of her throat.

In the brightness of the day and with the alcohol gone from her system, Erica was better able to appreciate the sensations moving through her, the syrupy drip of arousal between her legs. Pleasure unwinding slowly in her from the caress of his hands on her back. He touched her belly through the shirt, making slow and languorous circles. Teasing. Aching. She pulled away from him, panting.

"I don't—" Her voice escaped her and she tried again. "I don't think it's a good idea to do what you're thinking."

"What am I thinking?" His voice was low. Rough.

At the touch of his hand between her legs, through her bathing suit, she hissed at the pleasure of it.

"I don't want to give people an eyeful out here in the open. Someone's going to see us!"

But she was the one who reached between them. She

was the one who unzipped his shorts. His dick sprang out, thick and hard in her palm. He swallowed thickly.

"Wow!"

They kissed again. A wild tangle of lips and tongues that caused an itch between her legs and made her heart pound viciously in her chest. The breeze blew over her skin, over her back.

"We can't," she said. "Not here."

"If not at the feet of the goddess, then where?"

His words were teasing, but his tone was urgent, hard. He pulled her into him, and the heat of his skin set hers on fire, made her nearly burst with the desire for him. She straddled him, and he rubbed against her through her bathing suit. Erica shoved aside her bikini bottom and gripped him in her fist. She thumbed the weeping head of his thickness, stroking him while the breath left him in urgent gasps.

"A condom!" she said. "Do you have one?"

He fumbled in his pocket, found a wallet, a silver packet. She ripped it open, slid it onto him. He groaned at the feel of her hands on him.

"I'm going to ride you." She whispered the words in his ear as she took him in her hand, touched it to her entrance and slid down onto him.

They both groaned.

"That was so easy, wasn't it?" He grabbed her hips. She undulated in his lap, gripping his fullness inside her wet and dripping walls, a hungry snake, swallowing him as she was absorbed in pleasure.

"The goddess would be pleased," Nikolas moaned.

Their eyes met and held as she moved on his lap. Her knees dug into the sparse grass. He adjusted his hips, moved so her knees wouldn't press into the slab at his back.

"Take off your shirt," she commanded as she moved on

top of him. Moments later, his chest was bare and glistening in the sun, deep brown flesh, defined pec muscles moving under his silken skin. She pinched his nipples. Erica gasped as he reached under her shirt and yanked her bikini top down and her shirt up. His mouth licked her nipple, a light feather's touch. Then he moved back, working his hips, inside her; then he licked her again. Erica twitched, the tease driving her wild.

"Suck it," she moaned.

He licked her nipple one last time, then latched onto it, pulling it hard into his mouth, laving it with his tongue. She bucked in his lap; her sex clutched at his hardness. Heat twisted in her belly. Flooded her.

"Nikolas!"

He hummed against her skin, his hands firm on her back.

The smell of the sparse grass around them was heavy in the air. Sweat dripped down Erica's skin as Nikolas thrust up inside her. He sucked hard on her breast, his tongue cupping her nipple, turning her entire body to liquid in his lap. Erica thrust her fingers into his hair, threw her head back to blink up at the heavens as the very sunlight itself seemed to pour into her body. Her heart thumped in her chest. Her hectic breath scraped her throat raw; her feet slid in the white dirt as she moved around. Lust was a wildfire in her.

She cried out his name again.

He grabbed her ass, slamming her down on his lap, and the sensations wrapped around her until she could barely breathe. Could only feel. His hardness full and thick inside her. The sun burning into her back. Sweat dripping down her skin. Heat. Her sex swollen with want for him. Wetness. Light. Lust.

Nikolas kneaded her breasts, squeezed her pebbled nip-

ples, growled in his throat as she rode him toward satisfaction. He burst inside her like sunrise. She gasped at the
feel of him jerking inside her. He clutched the back of her
head, fingers gripping her scalp tightly as his breath huffed
against her throat, as his body spasmed in its lust throes.

Shudders of satisfaction ravaged her from the inside out.

Erica held him to her as her heart calmed down. As her
blood settled. His hands were flat against her back, holding her tightly to him.

"Thank you," he groaned into her throat.

She lifted her head. Her neck felt almost too fragile to
hold it up. A weak chuckle left her. "I think this is your
doing." An after-shudder moved through her, and her core
tightened in response. A noise hitched in his throat.

He leaned his head back to look at her, the familiar
smile reasserting itself. "Every time we're together, I feel
like I should thank somebody. You're not like anyone else
I've ever met."

"Women like me are a dime a dozen in the States."

"I doubt that very much." Nikolas squeezed her waist,
kissed her throat. "I've been to your America before, and
believe me when I say, you're a rare flower among all the
rest."

Erica flushed at the compliment, sighed and pressed
her mouth to his. He returned the kiss with interest, stroking her tongue with his, their breaths weaving together,
lips caressing, mouths devouring. The feeling his kisses
evoked were like nothing Erica had ever experienced before. No matter how many times they touched, kissed,
made love, she felt utterly transported, her mind taken
to another place, her senses stimulated and retuned. She
moved in his lap, twisting her hips as new arousal moved
through her.

Nikolas made a low sound. "The spirit is willing, but

the flesh is soft," he murmured against her mouth, laughter in his voice.

Erica drew back, smiling. "I guess you're not Superman, then."

"In a comfortable bed, I could do a lot more with my hands and my tongue." He slid a hand between them and stroked her clit, sending a gasp rushing to her lips. "But this place is far from comfortable."

With a sigh of regret, she climbed from his lap, shifting her bathing suit and her shirt. She watched him tuck himself away, zip up his shorts, hungrily taking all of him in. The tour was coming to an end. This was one of the last times she would see him again. Sadness tugged at her. She swallowed.

"Are you okay?" He stood up, raking a hand through his hair.

"Yes. I'm good. Just thirsty."

"Well, I just happen to know a place where you can get a long drink of water and a few other things you might like." He gave her a wicked smile.

"Don't make me beg," she murmured.

"There's plenty of time for that later."

He took her hand and led her back to the boat, taking the relatively deserted route back to the dock. At his side, she felt everything. The breeze on her face, the heat of his palm against hers, the feelings he evoked bubbling inside her like lava. She didn't know what to do with those feelings. She barely knew what to do with him, this man who loved wearing a minimum amount of clothes, who loved sex and had the most wonderful laugh she had ever heard.

At the boat, only the captain had remained on board to enjoy a cigar on the deck. The weathered-looking woman with her long black hair braided down her back greeted Nikolas with a knowing grin and smiled at Erica. They ducked into her quarters with water, fruit and cheese he snagged from the galley. Then they ate and made love again, talked and made love some more until they were both too exhausted to do more than lie in the bed breathing each other's air while the boat rocked gently on the water.

"I wish I didn't have to go," Erica said.

She lay on her back while Nikolas hovered over her, leaning on his elbow as he traced a damp line down between her breasts, to her belly button.

"Ironic, since you were so hell-bent on leaving the tour early."

"That was before I knew what a great lay you are," she teased, running her fingers through his hair.

"Women always want me for my sex." He sighed in mock sadness.

"Once I'm gone, I'm sure Lani will be glad to have you back."

He shook his head. "I never go back, darling. It's a rule."

Erica hid her wince of disappointment, half acknowledging she'd had wild thoughts of coming back to visit Santorini next year, of hooking up with Nikolas again and reigniting their shared passion. But by then he would have moved on to another tourist, some other woman who would be the special one for the week or for the summer. She bit the inside of her cheek, saying nothing.

"You have the strangest look on your face," he said softly.

"Do I?"

"Yes. And don't try to deny it." He sat up in the bed, his hair falling around his shoulders, brown eyes drinking her in. "Enjoy the afterglow," he said. "Worry about life later."

"Is that what you always do?"

"Not always. But I try."

She reached for him, swallowing against the desperation squeezing the air from her lungs. "Help me, then. Help me forget about life one more time."

By the time the tour of the island was finished, it was time for Nikolas to get back to work. He had taken a shower in the bathroom near her room and gotten dressed in a new pair of shorts and shirt.

"Find me before you leave," he whispered into her throat just before he bit her skin.

She shivered in reaction. Licked her lips. She rolled her head back, allowing herself the pleasure of her hands under his T-shirt, his warm flesh against her palms. Erica ignored the sadness pulling at her. "Count on it," she whispered.

Chapter Eight

After Nikolas left, she sank down into her bed, trying to ignore the gloom threatening to overcome her. The past few days with him had been more than she'd ever dreamed. Erica had been drawn to him like she hadn't been to any other man.

Usually she preferred her lovers more solemn. Responsible. But it had been a pleasure to share laughter with Nikolas, to tease and be teased, relax in a way she hadn't done since she was a child. And then there was the sex. Her eyes fluttered closed as she remembered the incredible moments they had shared, their flesh pressed together, their breaths fierce in the air.

The *Agape* shifted beneath her. It was moving away from the dock and heading back out to sea. Above her, Erica could hear the faint sounds of footsteps on the deck, the clink of glass, feminine giggles. It was all happening too soon, this last day.

With a heavy sigh, she packed up her things into her

duffel bag. Combed her hair, washed her face, slid on her sneakers to get ready for her last hours on board. Then she went up on deck.

"Hey, there! We wondered where you'd gone off to." Grace, wearing a demure sundress and sandals, waved at her from across the boat. Erica waved back and made her way toward the girl.

"We didn't see you on Kos," Grace said.

Erica felt heat move under her cheeks, grateful that her deep brown skin hid the blush. "I met up with someone for a while, then came back to the boat."

"Met up, huh?" The girl pursed her lips, giggled.

"Yeah."

"Were you two messing around?"

"A little bit of that, too," Erica admitted. She leaned back against the railing next to Grace and braced her feet wide as the boat rocked to the rhythm of the waves.

For a moment, Grace looked at her with an odd expression, her gray eyes a little too intent. "You should have brought him along with you this afternoon. It would have been nice."

"Thanks." Erica didn't even know what else to say to that. "That is sweet of you guys to offer, but like I said to Aidan, I don't do that kind of thing anymore."

"Not even on a once-in-a-lifetime vacation like this?"

"Sorry," she said, although she wasn't. "You, Michael and Aidan are all wonderful. But I don't know you well enough to sleep with you." Even as she said the words, she thought about Nikolas, the stranger, who she'd had sex with more than once. The stranger who was never far from her mind.

Grace narrowed her eyes. "But you just met that guy. Don't tell me you knew him before you got on this boat."

Erica's face grew hot again, but she refused to drop

her gaze. "You're right. I didn't." She shrugged. "But I like him."

"Even though he's got a girlfriend?"

"Who told you that?"

"The girlfriend did." Grace looked away briefly before she defiantly met Erica's eyes again. "After you said no, we asked her. She said yes."

"Oh." Erica lifted her eyes, automatically looking for Nikolas, wondering if he would feel better or worse to know that his ex had ended up in a four-way with a group of strangers.

Then she came to her senses.

It didn't matter what Lani did. It didn't matter what Nikolas thought or felt about his ex. None of it was her concern. They were all strangers to her who would disappear from her life as soon as she left the boat. None of it mattered.

But she couldn't stop her gaze from moving swiftly across the ship, looking for him. She thought she saw him, a flash of his curly hair, the stretch of his brown arm, but when she focused her gaze, it was someone else.

Erica shoved her hands into her shorts pockets and deliberately looked away from the mirage. Grace was apparently waiting for her reaction to the news that Lani spent the afternoon in bed with her and her boyfriends.

"I'm glad you still managed to have a good time without me there," Erica said finally.

They shared a tight smile. Just as Erica was searching for something meaningless to say, she noticed Kyoko and Ren taking photos of the approaching port of Thira. She gratefully excused herself from Grace after exchanging email addresses and meaningless promises to keep in touch.

She hadn't seen the couple very much since the beginning of the trip; they'd been absolutely absorbed in one another.

Erica greeted them with a smile. "It's good to see you. It's been a while."

Kyoko blushed prettily. "Ren has been very bad, I'm afraid. On the last excursion, we didn't even get out of our cabin."

Her husband looked completely unrepentant, smiling warmly at Erica. "The sights below deck were much more to my taste," he said with a soft laugh.

"I'm sure."

The young woman blushed again. Then she stepped from the protective circle of her husband's arms. "Where is that man you met at the beginning of the trip? The one with the..." Her voice tapered off as she lifted her hands around her face to mime Nikolas's long curls. "He is very beautiful."

Ren excused himself, mumbling something about going to get them something to drink from the bar.

Now it was Erica's turn to look bashful. "He is beautiful," she said. "But I won't see him again after this." She shrugged.

"That is unfortunate. I see a spark of something very strong between the two of you."

"It was just our hormones going crazy," Erica said. "We get along very well when we're not talking."

"And when you *are* talking?" Kyoko's narrow brows rose as she smiled.

"Then, too." She remembered the good times they had shared, his way of making her laugh when she didn't even feel like it.

"Maybe the gods will let you keep him."

"I doubt that," she said with a grimace. "I go back home in a few days. He lives here."

"You know, we do live in an age of telephones and Skype."

"I know. But…" Erica shook her head, not believing for a moment that Nikolas would want to see her beyond their beautiful weekend fling. He didn't believe in relationships. If he was reluctant to start something long-term with an available girl who lived here in Greece, then he certainly wouldn't want anything to do with Erica and her American life.

She stayed for a few more minutes to talk with Kyoko, then she went belowdecks to be alone with her own thoughts. The past few days had been indescribably good. The sex, conversation, the islands, the sex. She was completely whipped. Dicklashed, as her friend Camille was fond of saying.

In the cabin that was hers for only a few more minutes, she repacked her bag and paced the small space, deciding and undeciding to find Nikolas one last time. Share a goodbye kiss and risk making a complete fool of herself in front of near strangers. Idiot that she was, she'd probably cry her eyes out.

In the end, she stayed in her cabin until the boat docked; then she slipped away without seeing Nikolas. The bus ride back to her hotel was a misery with her skin already yearning for his touch, her fingers longing to trace the muscles of his back, sink into his solid flesh. To cling and never let go.

For the first time since being on her Greek journey, Erica actually felt alone. Lonely. On the bus ride, she stared out the window as the lumbering vehicle made its way up from the pier, the engine laboring as it took the sharp and winding path up the hill. She was so caught up in her loneliness that she did not notice the beautiful landscape that had taken her breath away only a few days before.

That evening, she had dinner by herself at the outdoor

restaurant across the narrow street from her hotel. Grilled, fresh-caught fish on a bed of seasoned rice with a glass of white wine. A small band played traditional Greek music against a backdrop of purple bougainvillea and thick green vines while, all around the restaurant, patrons laughed, ate and enjoyed themselves. The sun slowly set around them, the sky turning to gold.

Nearby, a table of four women sipped from their glasses of red wine and shared dessert from two plates. They were Americans. Two of the women sat close together like lovers, one with her arm slung across the back of the other's chair. Her gaze would occasionally flicker to the other woman's face before going back to her companions. The strong Greek sun had darkened their skin. They looked happy.

Erica looked away from their table, fighting against the feeling of loneliness that sat like a heavy weight on her chest.

The waitress appeared at her side, elegant and solicitous, her black hair twisted at the back of her head in a tight bun. "Can I get you anything else?"

"Just the check, please."

As the waitress walked away, Erica noticed a man standing in the restaurant's arched entranceway. He had his back turned to her and was speaking in Greek to someone she couldn't see. The man wore an expensive-looking gray suit that fit well across his broad shoulders.

His hair was short, cut in a sleek style that showed off a strong, brown neck. There was something familiar about the way he stood, wide-legged, a hand in his pants pockets and his body absolutely at ease.

"Here you are, miss." The waitress returned to Erica's table. "Pay it whenever you are ready—no rush."

Erica pulled her gaze away from the man. "I'll pay now." She glanced at the total, quickly pulled out her cash and put the money, along with the old-fashioned handwritten receipt, into the waitress's hand. "Thank you."

The waitress smiled and walked away to get her change. When Erica looked back at the entrance, the man was gone. In the meantime, the sun had set. One by one, the lanterns hanging from the iron trellises overhead winked on, giving the restaurant a romantic glow.

"I'm glad you weren't hard to find."

Erica froze. Then slowly turned around and lifted her head. It was the man from the front of the restaurant. Her mouth dropped open as her heart did cartwheels in her chest. Nikolas.

He had transformed himself. A suit and tie instead of cutoff shorts and bare chest. His hair was nearly unrecognizable, clipped close to his head with only a hint of its curl. But his devouring brown eyes were the same.

"Nikolas?"

"Of course," he said, slipping into the chair opposite her. "Unless you were expecting another man for dinner tonight." He signaled the waitress with an imperious wave of his hand.

"What are you doing here?"

"You didn't say goodbye to me on the boat today." A corner of his mouth tilted up.

Erica stared at him in confusion. "I—"

Just then the waitress appeared. Nikolas ordered a glass of ouzo. He cleared his throat as the woman walked away.

"I— You're right, I didn't wait to say goodbye." She bit the corner of her lips, watched him tap long fingers on the table. "I didn't see the point." Even looking at him now, knowing he would get up and leave her life forever, felt like a pain, sharp and deep, she could do without.

"So now instead you've forced me to come hunting for you."

"But why?" She meant to be matter-of-fact, but the

words emerged with a sob, the pain inside her pouring out through her voice.

Nikolas's face looked stricken. He jerked a hand across the table toward her. "Erica…"

She drew away from him. "Why?" she asked again. "Tell me."

"Because I can't let you go." He sighed harshly, the breath whistling between his teeth. "It would be crazy for me to."

"Crazy?"

"Yes. I—"

The waitress returned with his glass of ouzo. Nikolas thanked her, quickly drank it down, peeled off twenty euros from his wallet and put the money on the table.

Was his hand shaking?

"I'm here to ask you out on a date," he said.

"What?" She felt like she had just been thrown onto a roller coaster. Her head spun. "Nikolas, what are you saying?"

"There's a movie showing tonight at the outdoor theater in Kamari." He named the film that she'd wanted to see, the one that had stopped playing the night before. "Would you like to accompany me to see it?"

She shook her head. "But—but it's not playing anymore. Last night was the last night."

"Actually, *tonight* is the last show," he said.

It took her a few moments to get his meaning. He'd done this. He'd arranged for the theater to play the show an extra night.

"Oh, my God, that's—"

"Amazing? Panty-dropping? Awe-inspiring?"

She laughed. Underneath the expensive suit and the sleek haircut, Nikolas was the same. Of course he was. A man couldn't change who he was in a few hours. No one could. And she wouldn't want him to.

Erica released a slow breath. "I was going to say that is really nice of you."

"That's all?" His scarred brow rose in a teasing arch.

She opened her mouth to reply with a flirtatious comment of her own but then pressed her lips together instead. "I can't do this, Nikolas," she finally said after a long moment. "I—like you too much. It's killing me to see you here knowing you'll be gone from my life again in a few hours."

Nikolas's face settled into grave lines. "I don't have to be gone."

Her heart stopped in her chest. Then started again. "What do you mean?"

"In less than a month, I take over as head of the U.S. division of Andromeda Shipping," Nikolas said. "I've spoken to my father and told him that I will run the division from the New York office, and I'll run it the way I see fit. All the Stephanides holdings on that side of the world are mine, Erica. But all that would mean nothing if you weren't in my life."

She stared at him in shock as he continued.

"I never expected to feel like this for anyone," he said, briefly looking at her, then away. "If I didn't know better, I'd swear you put a spell on me." He paused. "You didn't put a spell on me, did you?"

She shook her head. If anything, he was the one who had bewitched her. "Nikolas—"

But before she could say anything, he grabbed her hands and pressed them together between his.

"I'm no good at this type of thing." Nikolas looked away from her and toward the band, which was playing a lively song and inviting the restaurant guests to get up and dance. Then he turned his eyes back to Erica. "I've never been so captivated by a woman until you." He visibly swallowed. "I know if I let you walk out of my life today, I'll never see you again." Nikolas touched her face. "I don't want that."

Erica stared at him, unable to believe what he was saying. Her pulse drummed an excited tattoo in her throat.

Nikolas's hand fell away from her cheek. "If I'm alone in this, I'll take my foolish declarations and—"

She leaned across the small table and kissed him. He hesitated for a moment before he kissed her back, parting his lips and sweeping his tongue into her mouth. Erica trembled, her body warming for him as the arousal stroked between her thighs in a familiar and heady magic. Long moments later, they drew apart, both of them breathing heavily.

"You're not alone in this," she said.

Even in the darkening arbor of the restaurant, she could see the happiness flashing in his eyes, the fierce joy in his that echoed her own. They reached for each other again and held on tight.

* * * * *

LIQUID CHOCOLATE

Velvet Carter

Chapter One

"You like that, baby?"

"Oh…yeah," Mika exclaimed.

Mika couldn't hold back as Blaine flicked his tongue faster and faster, bringing her to a heated climax. Her back arched and her eyes fluttered closed as she surrendered to his oral magic.

Blaine brought his head from underneath the covers, and looked at her with her eyes shut. "Don't go to sleep on me. That was just for starters."

Mika glanced down at him and bit her bottom lip. He was so handsome—with caramel-colored skin, coal-black wavy hair and beautiful warm chestnut eyes—that merely looking at his face was a major turn-on. "Aren't you going to let a girl catch her breath?"

Blaine eased up, until his body was covering hers. He leaned on his forearms in order to considerately not put his entire body weight on her. "I'll give you a few seconds, and then it's on to round two."

"Only a few seconds?"

"One, two, three..."

"Wait a minute, you're counting too fast."

Blaine pressed his rising manhood against her groin. "You feel that?"

Mika swallowed hard. "Yes." She could feel his penis growing and the sensation was turning her on, causing goose bumps to spring up on her skin. There was no sense in trying to resist him. Her desire for him was too strong to deny.

"All this is for you," he said, pressing harder against her. "Can you handle it?"

"You bet I can." Mika opened her legs a bit wider, inviting him in closer.

Blaine took hold of her chin and softly kissed her lips. He then parted her lips with his tongue.

The moment Blaine's tongue touched hers, Mika took ahold of his head and gently pulled him in closer. Their tongues began dancing together, one exploring the other. Their passionate kissing went on for minutes until it was no longer enough.

Blaine roamed his hand over her taunt stomach, touching her smooth skin. He worked his way to the waistband of her thong and gently pulled it off. He reached between her thighs and found her moistness. He rubbed her clit with his index finger and didn't stop until she started to moan.

"Ohh...that...feels...divine," Mika said, the words coming out of her mouth in spurts.

Blaine kept his finger on her private pulse. At the same time he worked his mouth up her torso. He kissed his way between her breasts. He took her right breast in his mouth and sucked and kissed until it hardened. He then turned his focus to her left breast and sucked and licked until it also firmed from his efforts.

The sensation created from him sucking her breasts while at the same time giving her digital stimulation drove Mika mad. She whipped her head from one side to the other. She twisted and bucked from his delicious touch. Mika tried to hold back, but her orgasm was coming hard and strong. She bit her bottom lip, trying to stifle her screams.

"Don't hold back baby." Blaine increased the pace of his finger. "I know you wanna come, don't you?"

"Yes… Yes!"

Blaine slipped one finger passed her clit, into her wetness. He added more pressure and didn't let up until her warm juices covered his fingers.

"Don't stop… That's it… That's it!" Mika yelled out, no longer able to control herself.

"Oh…" She panted, trying to catch her breath. "You are a bad, bad boy."

Blaine flashed her a devilish smile. "Now you're ready for round three."

He reached across her chest, opened the nightstand and took out a condom. He then tore the foil wrapper with his teeth, and took out the extra long latex. He slowly rolled the condom onto his throbbing member. He then took hold of her leg and lifted it around his waist.

As he was guiding his manhood into her moistness, Mika heard a buzzing sound. She tried to ignore the annoying noise but it kept getting louder.

Mika popped open her eyes. She couldn't believe that her alarm clock had sounded before she and Blaine reached the pinnacle.

"Damn!" Mika sat up against the headboard. She unraveled the twisted covers from around her body. Mika was beyond frustrated. She was having the most erotic dream about the stranger. She had seen him on several occasions, committed his face to memory and longed for his touch. Though, she hadn't formally met him yet. But that didn't stop her from submitting to him in her dreams.

"Oh, well, so much for wet dreams." She climbed out of bed, padded across the carpeted floor into the bathroom. She showered and readied herself for work.

Mika stared at her reflection in the bathroom mirror. She secretly hoped that today would be the day she would finally have the courage to introduce herself to the man in her dreams.

Chapter Two

Delicious Chocolate Bar, a gourmet confectionary shop on Chicago's Magnificent Mile that catered to the residents and businesses along the Gold Coast, was abuzz with activity. Following the Christmas season, Valentine's Day was the second busiest holiday for the trendy adult candy store and bar. Customers who didn't live in the area came from far and wide to experience co-owner Mika Madison's liquid chocolate blends.

A trained confectionary chef, Mika had studied in France at Le Cordon Bleu, excelling in their Pâtisserie program. After graduation, she left the City of Lights for the Windy City—her hometown—and partnered with Fritz, her childhood friend, to open Delicious Chocolate Bar. Fritz was the business manager, and flamboyant host, while Mika donned her chef's jacket and toque, creating the unique chocolates—both liquid and solid form— surprising customers with the unusual combinations of roasted-pork-belly bon bons, chipotle-flavored peppermint patties, rose-petal chocolate crisps and lavender truffles to name a few.

Out of all the concoctions, her favorites were the liquor infused liquid chocolates that she made for the bar. Her flavored martinis ran the gambit, from white chocolate, to ginger infused dark chocolate, to chocolate pear, to raspberry chocolate, to chai-flavored chocolate. She hand made each flavor and infused the chocolates with vodka, rum or tequila. Mika loved spending time in her test kitchen concocting interesting combinations. Since she was both childless and man-less, she had plenty of time to devote to her craft. She often spent late nights at Delicious working on new flavor combinations for her cookbook, instead of going home alone to sit in front of the television mindlessly flicking channels.

"Two days and counting," Fritz announced, bouncing into the all-white kitchen. Fritz was openly gay and proud of it. He and his partner, Oskar, had been in a relationship for nearly eight years, and happily cohabituated in an opulent, Liberace-style loft.

Mika turned away from the industrial stove where she was stirring a kettle of dark chocolate with fresh mint. "Two days and counting for what?"

"You must really be in chef mode with your mind on cooking instead of on our first annual singles' Valentine's event."

"Oh, that," Mika said, without an ounce of enthusiasm. Mika was not looking forward to being alone on one of the most romantic holidays of the year. Normally, Sweetest Day and Valentine's Day didn't get to Mika, but this year was different.

Her best friend, Dana, was newly married. Once partners in crime, they had made a pact years ago to spend

Valentine's together if they didn't have dates. In years past, Mika and Dana ordered in pizza and watched old kung-fu movies. They were both Bruce Lee fanatics, and had seen every movie that the master of martial arts had ever made. Now that Dana was married, she and her husband were going to spend the evening together, leaving Mika flying solo.

"Okay, Debbie Downer, what's the matter?"

"Nothing."

"Oh, don't give me that. I can tell by your lackluster tone that something's up, so spill." Fritz was relentless and rarely took no for an answer.

Mika sighed. She wasn't the complaining type, but knew that if she didn't tell Fritz how she really felt, he would keep bugging her and she didn't feel like being hounded by him all day. "It's nothing really. I'm just feeling a bit lonely. This is the first Valentine's Day in years that I'll be by myself."

"But you won't be alone. You'll be here at the singles' party."

"Yeah, I know, but it's not the same. Even though Dana and I are just friends, it was still nice to spend the evening with someone who is special in your life. You probably forgot what it feels like to be alone, since you and Oskar have been together for so long."

"Oh, hon, I so remember all those holidays I spent by myself, longing for that special someone. I'm thankful every day to have Oskar in my life. I have my Mr. Right. Now we have to work on finding you Mr. Right, instead of Mr. Right Now."

"And what is that supposed to mean?" Mika asked, giving Fritz a quizzical look.

"Come on, missy, you know precisely what I mean. Remember, all those blind dates that I set you up with?"

Mika turned around to the kettle and continued stirring. "Of course I remember. Just about every good looking guy that came into the shop last year who wasn't gay or married, you somehow arranged a date for me. What are you trying to insinuate?"

"I mean you only went on one date with each of them. Let's see, where should I start? Oh, I know, I'll start with the handsome model from Aria Talent Agency. He was perfect. Tall, beautiful beyond belief, with the body of life. After the first date with him, you stopped taking his calls. That was Mr. Right Now, number one. So tell me what could have possibly been wrong with him?"

"He was as dumb as a rock. He was all brawn, and no brain. He couldn't even string two proper sentences together, let alone hold an intelligent conversation on world views. If I just wanted someone to look at, he would have been perfect. Does that answer your question, Mr. All Up In My Business?"

Fritz dramatically rolled his eyes toward the ceiling. "Okay, point taken, but what about Mr. Right Now number two?"

"Who, the commodities trader?"

"Yes, he was handsome *and* smart. So what was the problem with him?"

Mika turned the burner off, removed the kettle from the stove and poured the chocolate mixture into a stainless steel mixing bowl. She rubbed her hands down the front of her white smock and continued. "Yeah, he was smart all right, but he was also a prick. All he talked about was how much money he made on a daily basis. And that he was so rich, he could have any woman in the world. He said I was lucky that he wanted to spend time with me."

"He said all of that on the first date?" Fritz asked astounded.

"Yep, he sure did."

"Now I understand why that was your first and last date with him. I can't stand pompous men who think they are superior just because they have a ton of money." Fritz paused for a moment, and then said, "Hey, what about that guy who comes in every week and orders expensive boxes of chocolates?"

Mika knew exactly who Fritz was talking about. He was the man who starred in her erotic dreams. "That tall slim guy, with the caramel-colored skin and jet-black curly hair? What about him?"

"Yes, the good-looking one. I've seen you stealing glances at him from the kitchen door."

Mika didn't say anything for a few seconds. She had been busted. "Dang, Fritz, do you see everything?"

"I sure do, missy. Hey, why don't I invite him to the singles' event?"

"We know his name from the order forms. Other than that, we don't even know the man."

"So what? I've waited on him a few times. That should count for something," Fritz said, trying to justify his point.

"For all we know he comes in every week to order chocolates for his girlfriend or wife." Although Mika had fantasized about him, she wasn't the type to break up a relationship. "Please don't invite him on my account. Agreed?"

Fritz sighed. "Okay. But I still want you to find happiness. We're not getting any younger, and I don't want to see you grow old alone."

"Don't worry, I'll find Mr. Right. I still have time, it's not like I'm applying for my AARP card anytime soon."

Fritz walked over, gave Mika a tender hug. "Okay, whatever you say." He then went back to the front of the store.

Once he was gone, Mika sat at the long white counter

and thought more about their conversation. Although, she didn't want to admit it, Fritz was right. It was time that she found someone to settle down with. Fritz had Oskar, Dana had James, and she had…no one.

Chapter Three

As the owner of a boutique ad agency, charismatic Blaine Chess met beautiful women on a daily basis, as they came into the agency to audition for various commercials. Models strutted in with their portfolios full of glossy shots hoping to not only land a gig, but to also catch the eye of the handsome owner. Blaine had a strict policy of not dating the talent anymore. He had learned the hard way that mixing business with pleasure was a recipe for disaster. When he first opened the agency a few years after college—with a hefty investment from his mother—he used it as his personal playground. Blaine toyed with the models as if they were life-size Barbie dolls. He would have two to three dates a night with different women. He'd start off the evening with an early dinner with one woman, drop her off home and then pick up date number two. They would have drinks at some swanky lounge and if the chemistry was right they would end up in bed together.

If by chance he wasn't feeling her vibe, Blaine would take her home and call date number three. He thrived on the excitement that the variety of women brought.

After a year of burning both ends of the candle, Blaine began tiring of his playboy ways. Although the women were beautiful, they had no substance. Their entire conversations centered on advancing their modeling careers. Blaine finally broke off of his involvements with the models. The women seemed to take the news well, all except for Tanya, a fiery, six-foot redhead.

What do you mean it's over! Tanya had hissed one evening when they were having dinner at Nobu.

He had purposely taken her to the upscale restaurant so that she wouldn't make a scene, but his plan wasn't working.

Tanya, you know as well as I do that this *was bound to end.*

What do you mean by 'this?'

It's not like we have a relationship. We're just...

Just what? she'd snipped.

We're just, you know...friends with benefits, Blaine had said sheepishly.

Benefits? Seems to me you're the only one benefiting. I thought you were going to help me land a few commercials, but since we've been dating, you haven't hooked me up once.

Tanya, I never promised to help advance your career.

I just assumed since you were screwing my brains out night after night, you would at least book me for a few gigs.

Our involvement has nothing to do with the agency.

Why? You're the owner aren't you? she'd asked, pinning him with a serious look.

Yes, I own the agency. However, hiring of the models is left up to the booking department.

*That's not the impression you gave me when you ap-
peared in the audition room the first day we met. You
browsed through my portfolio and even commented on
how beautiful my pictures were,* she'd said, recalling her
first audition with his agency.

Blaine had done precisely what she said. Only he wasn't
present during the actual audition to make a decision on
hiring her. He was there to check out her swimsuit shots
and decide whether or not he was going to ask her out on
a date that evening, which he did. Now, looking back, he
regretted using the agency to meet women. He had acted
totally unprofessional.

*Tanya, I'm so sorry if you got the wrong impression.
I truly am.*

She'd leaned across the table and said between clenched
teeth. *You're not sorry yet, but you will be when I contact an attorney and sue you for sexual harassment in the
workplace.*

What? He was stunned.

Tanya then stood up, grabbed her purse off the table and
strutted out of the restaurant before finishing her meal.

Three days later, Blaine was served legal papers. After
looking into the matter, his attorney advised him to settle.
Tanya was smart and had copies of phone records and text
messages where Blaine had alluded to helping her with
her career. She even had a copy of her date book, noting
every time they had sex. Although their involvement was
consensual and he hadn't promised her any ad placements,
Blaine's behavior didn't look professional. His attorney
put together a settlement package, which included a non-
disclosure agreement. So the word wouldn't spread in the
industry that Blaine used models for his personal pleasure.
Tanya signed the agreement, took his money and moved
to Los Angles to start an acting career.

Blaine was thankful that that incident hadn't marked his career, and from then on, he never looked twice at a model that crossed the agency's threshold. That settlement was over five years ago, and he hadn't played the field since. He was a reformed man and now the only woman in his life was his mother.

Blaine's parents had retired to Florida three years ago, enjoying their time in the sun, until his dad passed away one night in his sleep from a massive heart attack. Now that his mother was widowed, Blaine doted on her, sending her weekly confections from the renowned Delicious Chocolate Bar, which was located around the corner from his agency.

He loved visting the chic candy store, which was decorated in cobalt blue with silver-foil wallpaper. Even the packaging was made of a rich azure satiny paper, adorned with a huge silver ribbon and bow. Blaine frequented the shop, not only for the delicious chocolates, but to get a glimpse of the woman in the chef's smock that sometimes appeared from the back. He didn't know her name, but admired her beauty.

She was petite with mocha-colored skin, almond shaped eyes and full, kissable lips. She wore her hair in a neat bun, underneath a chef's hat. Blaine tried to catch her eye a few times, but she always disappeared behind the double doors before he could say anything to her.

Today was Blaine's weekly visit to Delicious. Although he could have easily ordered his mother's chocolates online, he preferred the face-to-face interaction.

"Hey, there, how are you?" the man asked, standing behind the sapphire-blue quartz and plate-glass counter.

"I'm good, and you?"

"Couldn't be better. I've waited on you a few times

before, but we never exchanged names. I'm Fritz, the co-owner. What's your name?" he asked.

"Blaine Chess. I own an ad agency around the corner and walk over on my lunch breaks."

"Oh, I see."

Blaine attempted to avoid eye contact with Fritz who was looking him up and down. Blaine stood well over six feet with caramel-colored skin and jet-black hair, so he was used to the stares from either sexes. Especially when his face was cleanly shaven. Today he was neatly dressed in a cashmere sweater, a pair of jeans and a navy peacoat that showed off his slim build.

"So how can I help you?"

Blaine visually searched the display case, with its shelves of luscious treats. "I'll have the couture collection of lavender-flavored truffles, also I'd like to have them express-mailed to Florida."

"Good choice and those come with the chef's recipe for her signature chocolate martini. Are they for your girlfriend?" Fritz asked.

"No."

"Uh…" Fritz paused. "Are they for your wife, then?"

"No, I'm not married."

"Well, if you're free on Valentine's evening, my partner Mika Madison and I are having an intimate singles' soiree. You should stop by."

Blaine looked toward the back of the store at the double doors, hoping to see the woman in the white jacket, but she was nowhere in sight. He assumed that she was the master chef. He started to ask if she was going to be at the party, but didn't. For all he knew, she was in a relationship or married.

"That sounds like a plan. I'll try to make it."

"Great!"

Blaine gave Fritz his credit card and mailing instructions. On his way back to the agency, he couldn't help but think about the petite beauty in the chef's smock. She seemed the exact opposite of the models he'd once dated, and he was intrigued by her mystique. Blaine was no longer the playboy. He had mentally matured over the years and now wanted to be in a committed relationship. He hadn't met anyone who piqued his interest until now. As he walked along Michigan Avenue back to his office, he thought, *I wouldn't mind getting to know Ms. Chocolatier.*

Chapter Four

The day of the event had arrived, but to Mika it was just another work day. Aside from making her signature martinis, she wasn't putting any special emphasis on the soiree, since she didn't have that special someone in her life. Mika was in the kitchen preoccupied, working on her cookbook.

"Please tell me you're not wearing your chef's jacket and those jeans to the party," Fritz said, coming into the kitchen where Mika sat at the counter inputting recipes into her computer. She had on her usual uniform—jeans, T-shirt and white chef's smock, stained with chocolate.

"Well, hello to you to," she replied, flippantly.

"Hello, Mika, now please tell me you brought a change of clothes for tonight. I'm so excited. I've planned a special evening with a few interesting adult games."

"Oh, fun," she said, sarcastically.

"What's with you, Mika, why are you acting like a wet blanket?"

"What's the big deal? It's not like I have a date," she said, looking at her computer screen as she spoke.

"Actually…you just might have a rendezvous tonight."

She stopped typing and looked up at him. "What are you talking about, Fritz?"

He put his pinky finger in his mouth and nibbled on his fingernail. "Well…uh…I…"

"Come on, stop stalling. What have you done now? I certainly hope you didn't fix me up with yet another loser."

"I didn't officially arrange a date for you, but I did invite Blaine to the event."

"When did you talk to him?" Mika had usually caught a glimpse of Blaine whenever he came into the store, and was surprised that she hadn't seen him come in.

"The other day when he came in and ordered a box of truffles. I also asked if he was married, and he's not, nor does he have a girlfriend," Fritz said, sounding pleased with himself.

"My, my, aren't you the little detective?"

"Don't act like you're not glad I found out his status. I've seen how you stare at the man through the windows of the kitchen doors. Obviously you're interested in him. Am I right or wrong?"

She sighed, remembering her erotic dream. "Well, I wouldn't toss him out of bed." Fritz was right. Mika had secretly lusted after the handsome stranger from the first time she'd laid eyes on him.

"Speaking of bed, when was the last time you were tossed around in one?"

"I swear, Fritz, you are the nosiest person I know."

"Yes, I am nosy, and you've known that about me since we were in high school. So don't act surprised now."

"Let's just put it like this. I'm long overdue for some tussling and tossing."

"Well, Stella, if you want to get your groove back, you need to ditch the stained smock, put on a sexy dress and literally let your hair down," Fritz said, dissecting Mika with his eyes.

"It's not that serious. If he's interested, it won't matter what I'm wearing."

"Yes, that might be true, but it is Valentine's Day after all, one of the sexiest holiday's of the year. That's why I'm wearing my scarlet crushed-velvet dinner jacket, white silk ascot and crimson gabardine slacks tonight."

"Aren't you going to be a vision in red?" She chuckled, making fun of him.

"You're laughing, but guess who will be having red-hot sex tonight?" He pointed his index finger at his chest. "Yes…that would be me because I care about my appearance, and put effort into seducing my man," he said in an attempt to set her straight.

Mika stopped smiling. Fritz did have a point. He constantly thought of ways to make Oskar happy, and in turn, Oskar treated Fritz like a queen. They didn't take each other for granted. Mika wanted that same type of treatment, and realized that if she didn't put any energy into finding a man and having a successful relationship, then she would never have one. "I guess you have a point, but…."

"But nothing. Now go home and change before the event starts," Fritz said, sounding more like an overbearing mother than a friend.

"I don't have time to go home. I have to input these recipes into the computer." Mika had recently landed a publishing deal to write a decadent dessert cookbook.

"Aren't you going to Colorado so you can write?"

"Yes, and to ski. I plan to spend the mornings hitting the slopes and the evenings curled up by the fire working on my book." As an avid skier, she had been to some of the best resorts in the country—Heavenly Mountain in Lake Tahoe, Deer Valley in Park City, Utah, Whistler in Canada and Killington in Vermont. She was excited to hit the slopes in Vail and maybe take a jaunt over to Aspen.

"So what's the problem with putting off the writing until then?" Fritz asked, refusing to let up.

"My trip to Vail isn't for another few days. I've been on a roll lately, and don't want to stop."

"When is your deadline?"

"The manuscript isn't due for a few months, but I still have at least another fifty pages to go."

"Is that all? You'll have that book finished in no time. Mika, you can at least take tonight off and enjoy yourself. When was the last time you put on a dress and heels?"

"It's been a while. I didn't even bother dressing for my last date, since it was casual. To be honest, I don't have anything in my closet that I'd want to wear anyway, so what's the point in going home?" Mika wasn't very fashion-conscious. She preferred to spend her money on expensive cooking equipment and lavish vacations, instead of on designer clothing and shoes.

"Oh, I have an idea! Let's go over to the Water Tower and let me treat you to a new outfit."

"Fritz, you don't have to do that. I'm more than capable of buying my own clothes."

"That's not the point. You know I'm a shopping queen, no pun intended, and love putting together outfits. Come on, Mika, it'll be fun. Everything is all set for tonight. The assistant manager can hold down the fort while we run out for a few hours. Don't even try to say no. You don't have any more excuses left." Fritz stood in front of her with his hand on his slender hip, waiting on her reply.

Mika sighed. "Oh, okay. If I don't go, you'll just nag me to death."

"You know I will."

The possibility of meeting the handsome stranger tonight was motivation enough for enduring a shopping expedition. She saved the file she was working on and logged off the computer. Mika then took off her smock, put on a leather biker jacket, grabbed her tote bag and headed out of the kitchen arm in arm with Fritz. The more she thought about meeting Blaine, the more excited she became. She had spied on the man from the kitchen doors. Now thanks to Fritz she would finally have a proper introduction, and from there maybe her dream would become a reality.

Chapter Five

Mika and Fritz had spent the entire afternoon at Water Tower Place, shopping. They'd gone from one end of the luxury mall to the next in search of the perfect outfit. Fritz pushed for Mika to wear a fire-engine-red sequined dress with thigh-high slits and matching ruby stilettos, but Mika had in mind a more subdued look. She was the antithesis of the glitzy, glamorous type. Even as a child, Mika wore overalls, and played in the dirt, making mud pies. She didn't like playing dress-up like most girls. Her Easy Bake oven was her favorite childhood toy. She'd bake for hours, making miniature cakes for her friends and family.

After an exhausting couple of hours, Fritz and Mika had finally come to a happy medium regarding her look for the evening.

Back at Delicious, Mika had showered in her private bathroom and was now in her office getting dressed.

Fritz waited impatiently outside the door, ready for the big reveal.

"What's taking you so long?" he yelled at the closed door.

"Calm down. I'm almost finished."

"We're opening the doors in fifteen minutes. Hurry up!" Mika heard Fritz pacing in front of the door as if he were an expectant dad waiting on the delivery of his newborn child.

"Well…what do you think?" Mika asked, stepping out of her office.

"Oh, my goodness!" Fritz threw his hands up to his mouth and gasped. "You look like a supermodel. That dress fits you to a T!"

Mika wore a one shoulder, cherry-colored dress that stopped right above the knees, a pair of red, sling-back pumps and shoulder-duster rhinestone earrings. Her long hair was swept up in a French roll with wisps of hair loose around her ears.

"I don't look overdressed, do I? This dress isn't too short, is it?" she asked, fidgeting with the hemline.

"No, no, not at all, your outfit is perfect, if I do say so myself," Fritz said, grinning like a proud papa.

"I feel so uncomfortable. I'm going to change back into my smock." She turned around toward the office, but Fritz caught her by the arm.

"Oh, no, you're not! We spent too much time trying to find the perfect outfit. You're not wearing that smock tonight. Got it? Good!" Fritz took hold of Mika's hand. "Come on. Let's go up front and light the candles."

"Uh…okay." Mika reluctantly trailed behind Fritz, walking awkwardly in the high heels.

Fritz and Mika lit the candles that filled the shop. There were small tables for two lined up near the wall, which were dressed in crimson linen cloths with red taper candles in silver holders. Fritz had a speed-dating segment planned for the singles where they could get to know each other in a fun setting. Music played softly in the background, from a speaker connected to an iPod that was loaded with a selection of jazz and romantic ballads. As Fritz was attending to the final touches, Mika was behind the bar concocting a variety of chocolate martinis. She mixed vodka, her special blend of liquid chocolate in a shaker with crushed ice, and shook the silver shaker twenty times. She poured two drinks, and handed one to Fritz.

"I just want to say thanks for getting me out of my comfort zone. I'm glad you insisted that we go shopping. You were right. Tonight is special and I should look like the co-owner of Delicious instead of the hired help. It really doesn't matter if I have a date or not. I'm feeling festive," Mika said, raising her glass. "Cheers."

Fritz clinked his glass to hers. "Cheers." He took a sip of the martini. "Hmm, this is really good. What's in it?"

"A little of this and a little of that. It's a mixture that I blended especially for tonight. I call it the Two-one-fourtini."

"That's an odd name."

"Not at all. Two is for February, one and four are for fourteen, get it? February fourteenth, Valentine's Day," she said, taking a sip of her drink.

"My, my, aren't you the clever one? I hope you made enough of this love potion for everyone."

"Yes, I made quite a few batches. I also gave the bartender explicit instructions on how to mix the drinks."

"Good. I'm sure Blaine will love it."

"Why are you so bent on me meeting this particular guy?"

"I know I've been wrong in the past about the men I've

set you up with, but I have a feeling that Blaine is the perfect match for you. He's creative…"

"How do you know that?"

"He owns an advertising agency, so he must be creative, and so are you. That's something you two have in common, which is good for starters."

Mika sipped her drink, and couldn't help but wonder if Fritz was right. Suppose she and Blaine did share more commonalities. She didn't want to get her hopes up, but the thought of spending the evening with a handsome man was more than appealing.

As they were talking, a tap sounded at the glass door. Fritz waltzed over and opened it for his lover, Oskar.

"Hey, sweetums." Fritz greeted Oskar with a kiss on the lips.

"Hello, my love," Oskar replied. He walked in and surveyed the room. "This place looks fabulous. I love the candelabras on the counter. They're so romantic."

"Yes, the entire store resembles a den of inequity. I hope there're going to be many love connections made here tonight," Fritz commented, eyeing Mika as he spoke.

"I'll be right back," Mika said, heading toward the rear of the store.

"Where are you going?" Fritz asked.

"I forgot to put on some lipstick."

By the time Mika returned, the entire place was packed with singles hoping to make a love connection. The bartender was shaking and pouring martinis at a rapid pace. Servers were also on hand with trays of crab-stuffed shrimp, mini lobster rolls and tuna tartar.

"May I have your attention!" Fritz yelled. "We're going to play a getting-to-know-you game called Speed Dating. You will only have five minutes to talk, flirt or tell your innermost secrets before the buzzer sounds. At that point, men, you will switch tables, while the ladies remain seated. Are there any questions?" When no one responded, Fritz said, "Okay, let the game begin. Ladies, take a seat at the tables near the wall. The time starts now."

Mika watched as the men scurried to the empty chairs facing the women. From her vantage point at the bar, she couldn't hear the conversations and wondered what was being said.

"I'll have a martini," she told the bartender.

"Coming right up," he responded.

Mika surveyed the room while she sipped her drink. She was looking for the guy Fritz had invited, but didn't see him. She found herself checking the door every time someone walked in. *Why are you waiting on this man? You don't even know him.* Mika wanted a distraction, so she moved through the room toward the speed-dating tables. As she passed by, she overheard a guy asking the woman across from him a very personal question.

"So what's your favorite position?"

"On top," the woman replied.

Wow! That's pretty forward, but I must say, I like being on top, too, Mika thought as she giggled and continued walking across the room. When the buzzer went off, Mika turned and considered joining in what looked to be a fun time judging from the participants' giddy facial expressions. But all the tables were occupied, which was probably for the best, she thought. *I might as well go back to my office and work on my manuscript.*

"Hey, there, where are you going?"

Mika turned around, and there, directly in front of her, was the handsome stranger smiling, looking like a yummy piece of buttery caramel.

Chapter Six

Mika was rendered speechless. He was standing so close to her that she could smell his cologne, which had the scent of sandalwood, lavender and ginger blended together. Not only was his scent delicious, but his appearance was enticing, as well. He wore a black blazer, crisp white shirt, open at the collar, and a pair of black gabardine slacks. Mika swallowed hard. She didn't know what to say. They hadn't formally met, yet he was speaking to her as if they were friends.

"Uh… I was going in the back to work on a project."

"Whenever I get a glimpse of you, you're working. Do you ever take time off? Wait a minute…where are my manners? Here I am quizzing you and I haven't even introduced myself. My name is Blaine Chess and yours?"

"Mika Madison, I'm the co-owner of Delicious."

"Pleasure to meet you," he said, shaking her hand. "Your partner, Fritz, invited me tonight. Sorry I'm late, but I had a last-minute fire to put out at the office. I own an ad agency around the corner, and had to deal with a demanding client."

"Oh. No problem." *He's explaining his tardiness as if I'm his date,* Mika thought.

Blaine looked around the room. "You guys have a great turnout tonight."

"Yes, we do. People seem to be enjoying the speed-dating game. It's a real ice breaker."

"Isn't that a game where you have a few minutes to talk to the other person before a buzzer goes off?"

"Yep, that's the game."

"I, for one, would much rather have an intimate conversation without the pressure of a clock."

Mika felt the same way, but was too nervous to agree. She was finally face-to-face with the man she had admired from a distance for so long, and she didn't quite know what to say.

"Oh, I'm so glad you were able to stop by tonight," Fritz said, walking up to them.

"I am, too," Blaine replied, glancing at Mika.

"Where's your drink? Mika, you didn't offer Blaine one of your signature martinis? She makes the best cocktails in town."

"I'm sure she does. I would love to try one," Blaine said, smiling.

"Sure. Let's go to the bar." She turned to Fritz. "I'll talk to you later."

"You kids have fun." He winked at Mika. "I have to find Oskar and get ready for the next game." Fritz flitted away.

"Thanks again for the invite," Blaine said, and then followed Mika across the room. He sat on a bar stool and watched as she poured contents from a silver pitcher into a shaker, added ice and agitated the shaker vigorously. She poured the chocolate concoction into two martini glasses. The bar was abuzz with people chatting, drinking and munching on appetizers.

"Here you go," she said, handing Blaine the glass, "I hope you like it."

He took a sip and licked his lips. "Mmm, this is really good. I can't even taste any liquor."

Mika also took a sip of her drink. "Don't let the taste fool you. There's plenty of alcohol in these cocktails, and the effect will sneak up on you."

"I'm not worried about that. I'm a big boy."

You sure are! Mika put the glass to her lips and eyed Blaine over the rim as she drank. He was even more handsome up close. She hadn't kissed a man in a while, and had an impulse to lean across the bar and plant a juicy one on his full lips, but restrained herself.

"Excuse me," Fritz stood in the middle of the room and yelled over the chatter. "May I have your attention? The next game we're going to play is called Dim the Lights. The rules are simple. First, find a partner, and then have a seat. You'll have ten seconds to gaze into your partner's face. After the time is up, the lights will dim for thirty seconds. While the lights are dim, turn your back to your partner and take turns describing their best feature. Any questions?"

"Suppose you don't have a partner?" a guest asked.

"No worries. This game can also be played in groups," Fritz replied.

"Would you mind being my partner?" Blaine asked Mika.

"Uh…sure," Mika said, calmly. She downplayed her excitement.

"Okay, are we ready?" Fritz asked. When no one responded, he held a stopwatch and said, "The time starts now!"

Mika leaned her elbows on the bar and turned to Blaine. They gazed intently at each other. Mika searched his eyes, trying to see any hidden, undesirable flaws, but couldn't detect any. She roamed every inch of his face with her eyes. His skin was smooth, his lips were full and begged to be kissed. His eyes, which were staring back at her, were brimming with desire. She could feel a strong pull toward him. An intimacy was being created between them that couldn't be denied.

"Okay, time!" Fritz announced. "Now turn your backs. Oh…I forgot to add that you're to whisper this to each other." Fritz glanced over to Mika and Blaine, and said, "You two will need to sit together for the second half of the game."

Mika walked from behind the bar and without saying a word, sat on the bar stool next to Blaine. She then turned her back so that it was touching his. The moment their backs met, a warm sensation ran up her spine and she smiled slightly. This game had her totally intrigued and she was anxious to hear Blaine's assessment of her.

Once Fritz stopped talking, the lights dimmed, so that the only illumination was that of the candles, giving off a warm, seductive glow. The hum of whispers began filling the room.

"Where should I start? All of your features are perfect," Blaine began. "Your eyes are warm and kind. I know we've just met, but I can see that you're the type of person who loves deeply when you allow yourself to fall for a man."

Mika was astounded. He was absolutely correct. She wasn't quick to fall in love, but when she did, she fell hard. "I thought we were supposed to discuss features, not feelings," she whispered.

"I'm sorry if I offended you, but I just couldn't help telling the truth."

"No offense taken. Actually, I find your honesty refreshing."

"Good. Well, in that case, let me say that I'm glad we finally had a chance to meet. I find you extremely attractive and would love to take you out to dinner if that's okay with you."

"Yes, I would like that." Mika appreciated Blaine's direct approach. She wasn't one for game playing. She was becoming more and more intrigued with him. Blaine wasn't wasting any time conveying his interest in her. Sitting there with her back close to his, Mika could feel herself becoming aroused. This night was getting better and better by the minute. Suddenly, the lights came up. And unfortunately before Mika had a chance to describe Blaine's best feature.

"Ladies and gentlemen, that concludes the warm-up exercises for this evening. Hopefully, everyone has loosened up by now and you're no longer strangers." Fritz shot Mika another look. "Please eat, drink and mingle, that is if you haven't already found that special someone to spend the evening with. And to keep the mood festive, the lights will remain low."

"I like your partner's style. He really knows how to get the party going," Blaine commented.

"Yes, he does." Mika was grateful that Fritz had orchestrated the event. If she didn't know better, she would have sworn that Fritz had invented Dim the Lights in order to bring her and Blaine closer—which it did. She looked at Blaine's empty glass. "Would you care for another drink?"

"Only if you'll join me."

This time, Mika didn't walk behind the bar. Instead, she signaled the bartender and had him refill their glasses.

For the next hour, she and Blaine traded life stories, talking easily like they had known each other for years. They were both creative in their own rights and had similar life views of working hard and playing hard.

Time had passed so quickly that before Mika knew it, the event was over and people were filing out of the store. She was enjoying Blaine's company and didn't want the night to end. After talking for so long, both of their glasses were now empty again. The bartender was busy cleaning up, so Mika went behind the bar and poured them another round. Before she could walk back to the other side, Fritz and Oskar emerged from the back, strolling arm in arm.

"Well…I for one think tonight was a mega success," Fritz announced as he came closer to Mika and Blaine.

Blaine glanced across the bar at Mika. "I'll second that."

"Fritz, darling, you sure know how to throw an event. I just loved that Dim the Lights game. It really made people open up," Oskar commented.

"That was the point," Fritz replied, eyeing Mika.

She noticed that Fritz and Oskar had on their coats. "Are you guys leaving?"

"Yes, we are. The rest of our night needs to play out in private." Fritz winked. "Mika, the cleanup crew finished, and left by the service entrance."

"Okay, good night, guys."

"Oh, Mika, don't forget to turn the music off, and snuff out the candles before you leave."

"Okay."

"You guys have a great evening, and thanks again for the invite," Blaine said.

Shortly after Oskar and Fritz left, the bartender called out to Mika. "Hey, boss, I'm done. Is there anything else you need before I leave?"

Mika took a quick look around the store and everything

seemed to be back in order. "No, I'm good. Thanks for all of your help tonight, Frank."

"You got it. Good night."

Once the bartender left, Mika and Blaine were alone in the store, which was still bathed in candlelight with soft jazz playing in the background. Mika couldn't help but think, *it was the perfect romantic setting.* She sipped her drink, quietly contemplating what to do next. She was attracted to Blaine. But didn't know whether to step out of her comfort zone and make a move, or sit back and let the night unfold organically. After a few more sips, she decided to choose the latter.

"So tell me, what goes on behind the double doors?" Blaine asked, breaking the silence.

"My test kitchen and office are in the back."

"So that's where you make the magic? Concocting your unique blends of chocolate."

"It sure is."

"I've never seen a chef's kitchen before," he said, swiveling around on the stool and looking toward the back.

"Would you like the dime tour?" Normally Mika didn't allow strangers in her kitchen, but tonight she was willing to make an exception.

Blaine hopped off the stool. "I certainly would."

She led the way, with him following closely behind. When they reached the kitchen, the lights were off. Mika took a step toward the light switch, but Blaine caught her by the arm.

"Hey, where are you going?" he said, gently bringing her toward him.

Mika took a few steps until her breasts were touching his chest and she could feel his breath on her cheek as he spoke. His unexpected advance had taken her by surprise and now she was aroused with anticipation. He had taken the lead and his aggressiveness was a sure sign that he was interested.

"I was going to…"

She didn't get a chance to finish her sentence before he leaned in and kissed her mouth. Mika's lips met his and she wrapped her arms around his neck as their tongues danced softly together. He engulfed her in a tight embrace all the while passionately kissing her. Their first kiss seemed to last for minutes before they came up for air.

"I've been dying to kiss you all night," Blaine admitted.

Mika could only blush. She was rendered speechless.

Their arms were still wrapped around each other as he spoke. Mika thought about moving away from him, but she was too comfortable in his embrace. Their bodies molded into each other as if they were already lovers. Mika hadn't felt this excited about a man in a while and she planned to enjoy the moment.

Without another word, Blaine resumed kissing her. This time he reached down and began massaging her bottom.

Mika could feel his erection getting firmer and firmer. But she didn't shy away. She pressed against him and began slowly grinding her hips.

He slipped his hand underneath her dress and into her underwear. "You're getting moist," he whispered in her ear.

"And you're hard as slate."

"You've gotten me excited."

"What are you going to do with all of that excitement?" she tossed back, surprising herself.

"Should I tell you or show you?"

"Showing is so much better than telling, don't you agree?"

Blaine didn't say another word. He reached into his pants pocket, took out a condom, unzipped his pants and slid on the latex. He allowed his pants and underwear to fall to the floor. He stepped out of his clothing and then whipped Mika around so that her rear end was facing his pubic area. He gently bent her over and began massaging her female parts.

She spread her legs, took off her thong and welcomed his advance. He lifted her dress and entered her slowly yet purposefully. They immediately found their rhythm, bumping and grinding against each other. Their vertical dance lasted for minutes before they each gave in to an explosive peak.

Once they collected themselves, Mika whispered, "Blaine, I don't normally do this type of thing…" her words trailing off.

"Neither do I, but the chemistry between us is undeniable." He kissed her on the cheek. "Thanks for a wonderful evening."

"Yes, it was great." Mika wanted to ask if she was going to see him again, but didn't want to appear needy. "Well… I'd better close up. It's getting late."

"I'll blow out the candles," Blaine said when they reached the front of the store.

After turning the music off, Mika ran to the back to grab her belongings. Together they stepped out into the cold night air, and Mika then locked up the store. A bit of awkwardness lingered between them.

"Do you need a ride?" he asked.

"No, thanks, my car is in the garage across the street."

"Mind if I walk you to your car?"

"No, not at all."

Blaine took her by the hand and they made the quick walk to the garage. When they reached her car, Blaine took out a business card and handed it to her.

"Here's my card. It has my cell phone number, work

number and email on it, too, so you won't have any reason not to stay in touch." He smiled.

"I don't have any cards with me, but you know where I work," she tossed back with a sly smile of her own.

"Yes, I do. I will definitely call you tomorrow, that's a promise." He kissed her on the lips.

"Do you want a ride back to your car?"

"No, it's not far and I could use the walk. Good night."

Mika got into her car and watched as he flipped up the collar of his coat against the crisp night air and walked away.

When the evening began, she had no idea that it would end with her making love to the handsome stranger that she had admired for months. Mika didn't make a habit out of sleeping around upon first meeting someone, but there were exceptions to every rule. Their brief encounter was unexpected and now she wanted more of his brand of loving.

Chapter Seven

The following day was business as usual for Mika. Although she went about her normal routine, thoughts of sex with Blaine were ever present in her mind. His touch was firm yet gentle. He had turned her on, leaving her wanting more.

"And what have we here?" Fritz asked, standing in the doorway of the kitchen holding up a gold foil wrapper.

Mika turned from the stove. Fritz was holding up the condom wrapper from last night. She quickly spun back around without saying a word, focusing her attention on the pot of simmering chocolate, instead of answering what was sure to be an onslaught of questions.

"Oh, no, you're not just going to ignore me. Fess up, and don't leave a single thing out!"

Mika exhaled. "Who's to say that I know anything about that wrapper?"

"Don't get cute, missy. When Oskar and I left last night,

there were no prophylactic wrappers lying about. Oh, you naughty girl!" Fritz exclaimed, throwing his hand up.

Mika finished stirring the chocolate and turned off the heat under the double boiler. She walked over to Fritz, took the paper out of his hand and walked over to the trash can to toss it in the garbage. "Now, there's no evidence," she said dismissively.

"Look at you. Your face is glowing. He must have laid it on you really good."

"I'm glowing because I was stirring a hot pot of chocolate." Mika was reluctant to admit the explosive time she had with Blaine the night before. The morning had passed without a word from him. She thought that he would have called by now. But it was after three o'clock and there wasn't a peep. For all she knew, their encounter was nothing more than a one-night stand. Mika preferred to keep her emotions in check in the event she never laid eyes on Blaine again.

"Oh, don't give me that. You two were totally engrossed with each other last night. I haven't seen you that excited about a man in aeons. Did you exchange numbers, so you can stay in touch?"

"He gave me his business card with all of his information."

"Have you called him?"

"Of course not!"

"Why not? It's not the fifties, women are allowed to call men, or haven't you heard?"

"Who's being cute now?"

"If you want to talk to the man, call him. Don't sit around and wait for him to make the first move. When I met Oskar, I didn't waste any time calling him and letting him know exactly how I felt."

"I hear what you're saying, Fritz. But here's the thing,

I confess that we really, really, really had a great time last night. So good, in fact, that he should *want* to call me. Besides, he promised that he'd call today, and I want to see if he's going to keep his word."

"Maybe he just got tied up with work. Don't take him not calling you personally, Mika."

"Why are you trying to defend him, like he's your best bud?"

"Because I know how quick you are to dismiss a man and I want you to give Blaine a chance. Call it a hunch, but I think you two will be good together."

"You're right, Fritz. I break off relationships fast when I see a potential problem because I don't want to get hurt." Mika had learned early on that if she walked away before her emotions were vested in a relationship, she could leave with her feelings and pride still intact.

"All I'm saying is, don't prejudge the guy."

"I'll try not to."

"If he doesn't call you today, it doesn't mean he's not interested. Trust me, I know when a man is into you, and Blaine is totally smitten. It was all over his face yesterday."

Mika digested Fritz's words, and hoped they were true. "Last night was an exception. With the romantic setting and martinis, who wouldn't have been infatuated? Anyway, I'm leaving town for Vail the day after tomorrow. If I hear from him, great, and if I don't, great," she said, trying to sound as if it didn't matter one way or the other. But deep down, she wanted nothing more than to continue what she and Blaine had started. Their connection was beyond physical and Mika desired to spend more time with him.

"Just don't jump to any false conclusions."

"Okay, okay, I won't. Now will you please let me get back to work?"

Once Fritz left, Mika realized that maybe she was reading too much into Blaine's lack of communication. Before talking to Fritz, she had begun to regret giving in to her desires. She'd needed to hear Fritz's words of wisdom.

Mika busied herself with making her signature liquid chocolate, ensuring there was enough in stock while she was away. The hours ticked by and soon it was after six o'clock. There had been no call or visit from Blaine. A part of her was disappointed, however, she simply brushed it off, following Fritz's advice about not jumping to any false conclusions.

Chapter Eight

The past few days had been a complete blur for Blaine. After spending a surprisingly wonderful evening with Mika, he had planned to invite her to dinner the following day, but became consumed with work. One of his major clients had threatened not to renew their contract and take their business to a competitor. Blaine and his staff had to devise a new marketing campaign in fewer than twenty-four hours, to woo the client—which they did—meaning he had to work around the clock.

Now he was on a plane heading to Miami for his mother's birthday party. Being an only child, Blaine adored his mom and spoiled her on a regular basis, but more so after his father had passed away. Mrs. Chess was the reason Blaine had a successful advertising agency. She had given her son a hefty investment so that he could open the agency, and when his client list thinned out one year, she came to the rescue with another influx of cash. The Chess

Agency was now on solid ground and although Blaine had repaid the loans, he still doted on his mother and would do just about anything to please her.

When the plane touched down in Florida, Blaine called his mother to tell her he had made a safe trip, something she insisted on every time he traveled.

"Hey, Mom, we just landed."

"Oh, good. I was worried."

"Why? It's not like planes drop out of the sky on a daily basis." Blaine's mother had been overprotective all of his life. He equated her paranoia to him being an only child. Even though he was a grown man, in some ways she still treated him like her precious little boy.

"I know it's silly of me to worry, but I do. Some habits are hard to break. Anyway, I can't wait for you to get here. I have a surprise waiting."

Blaine's mother was known to shower him with unexpected gifts. Like the time she'd brought home a pair of lovebirds when he was seventeen and dating multiple girls at the same time. She'd told him that the birds mated for life and that he could learn a thing or two from them. His mother and father were high school sweethearts who married right after college. Mrs. Chess had told Blaine that she wanted the same type of long-lasting love for him. One day, she had blurted out, *Why can't you commit yourself to Ashley? After all you two went to junior prom together and made the perfect pair.*

Ashley was the perky cheerleader who lived a few doors down and had a major crush on Blaine. Ashley was always popping into their house visiting with his mother and helping her around the house. Blaine suspected that Ashley was hanging around to get a glimpse of him. He had liked her well enough, but he was young and didn't want to be tied down at the time.

He saw Ashley over the years when they were both home from college. One year they had a hot and steamy affair during Christmas break and nearly got caught by his mother who had come home from work early. Blaine thought that his mother looked pleased as she stood at the bottom of the stairs while they tiptoed down from his room, trying to not look guilty. In the end, nothing ever came of their affair. Though it didn't stop his mother from grilling him about Ashley every chance she got. The questioning finally stopped when Ashley married a doctor from Philadelphia and moved to the East Coast.

"What's the surprise, Mom? I hope it's not another pair of lovebirds." He chuckled.

"You'll see when you get here."

"Okay." Blaine disconnected the call. As he waited to deplane, he couldn't help but wonder what surprise awaited him.

Blaine rented a car and drove to his mother's home in Coral Gables, a posh community about thirteen miles from Miami Beach. Blaine's mother told him on more than one occasion that she loved living in Florida, and that she no longer desired the cold. She had been an avid skier, but recently put their winter condo up for sale.

When Blaine reached the two-storied white stucco house with the huge manicured lawn, there were two cars in the driveway that he didn't recognize. His mother's party wasn't until the next day and he wasn't expecting his mother to have any company. Blaine retrieved his duffel bag from the backseat of the rental car, and headed to the front door. He used his key and entered.

"Hey, Mom! I'm here, where are you?"

"Hi, honey, come to the kitchen!" she yelled from the back.

Blaine made his way through the massive living room,

which was decorated in all white with gold accents. As he passed through the dining room, he noticed that the table was fully set with china, flatware, crystal goblets and linen napkins. His mother loved decorating and kept a well-appointed home. Blaine often asked why she needed so much space. After his father had died, Blaine tried to convince his mother to move in to a condo, but she flat out refused, saying, "I just love rambling around in this big old house. Besides it gives me plenty of room for out-of-town guests."

Blaine pushed through the swinging door and stepped into the kitchen. He stopped in his tracks as he looked around the marble island where his mother and her two guests sat.

Mrs. Chess, a fit woman for her age, jumped up, trotted over and threw her arms around his neck. "Oh, Blainey, it's so good to see you," she said.

Blaine hugged her back, all the while staring at her guests. He didn't know quite what to say, so he held his tongue.

"Honey, let me introduce you to Seymour, the event planner for my party. He's fabulous. I'm getting old now and can't orchestrate a shindig like I used to."

"Oh, nonsense, there's nothing old about you," Seymour gushed. "Nice to meet you, Blaine. Your mother talks about you nonstop."

"I'm sure."

"Blainey, don't just stand there, go and say hello to Ashley. I told you I had a surprise, and here she is! Ashley's in town visiting her parents. I asked her to come over for cocktails, so you two could catch up. Doesn't she look lovely?" Mrs. Chess said as she gave him a slight push toward the marble island.

Blaine couldn't deny that Ashley was still a knockout.

Her once long auburn hair was now cut into a short pixie style. Her honey-colored skin looked soft and dewy and her hazelnut eyes were as piercing as ever. A knot formed in his throat as he approached her. Blaine hadn't seen or spoken to Ashley since they had made passionate love in his boyhood bedroom.

"Hey, Blaine, it's so good to see you!" Ashley exclaimed, getting up from her seat.

Blaine gave her a friendly hug. "Good to see you, too. I didn't know your parents moved down to Florida. Mom never told me," he said, looking suspiciously at his mother.

"They only moved here last year. They couldn't take the cold Chicago winters anymore," Ashley replied.

"So, are you still living in Philly? Mom told me you married a physician and moved east."

"Blainey, here, have a cocktail before you start quizzing Ashley," Mrs. Chess said, handing him a drink. "Take a sip and tell me if you like it. It's a chocolate martini. The recipe was in the last box of chocolates you sent."

As he sipped the chocolate martini, Blaine flashed back on his night with Mika and the fact that he hadn't called her yet.

"So how is it?" his mother asked.

"Good. I'll be right back. I have to make an important call." Blaine excused himself and went upstairs to the guest room where he normally stayed. He closed the door, took out his cell phone and called the candy shop since he didn't have Mika's cell phone number.

"Hello, Delicious Chocolate Bar. Fritz speaking. How may I help you?"

"Hi, Fritz, this is Blaine Chess. Is Mika around?"

"Oh! Hello, Blaine! How are you? I hope you had an enjoyable time the other night. I was just talking to Mika about you, and…" Fritz rambled into the phone.

"Uh… Is Mika there?" he asked again, interrupting Fritz.

"She's in the test kitchen. Hold on."

After a few seconds, she picked up the line and answered in a dry tone, "Hello?"

"Hey, Mika, it's Blaine. How are you? I'm so sorry I'm just now calling. The past couple of days have been crazy. How are you?" he repeated, sounding nervous.

"Fine."

He detected an attitude in her voice. "Mika, please don't be mad. I am truly sorry for not calling. I had an emergency at the agency and then had to fly out to Miami for my mother's birthday party." Blaine was speaking so fast that his sentences nearly ran together.

"Your mother lives in Miami?"

He could tell by the way she asked that she didn't believe him. "Yes. My parents relocated a few years ago, shortly before my father passed away."

"Oh, I'm so sorry to hear about your dad."

Blaine heard a softness in her voice. "Thanks. Can I take you out to dinner when I get back to town?"

"I'm going on vacation. I guess I'll see you around when we're both back in the city."

"Mika, I really enjoyed our time together and hope we can continue where we left off. You want to hear something ironic?"

"What's that?"

"My mother has made a pitcher of your chocolate martinis," he said, hoping to lighten her mood a bit more.

"Your mother? How did that happen?"

"The recipe was in the last box of chocolates that I sent her."

"Oh, you must have sent the couture collection of chocolate truffles. I had a copy of the recipe attached to the inside of every box as a little added bonus," she said, her tone sounding a bit brighter.

"Well, it's definitely a hit with my mom. Can I have your cell number, so I won't have to go through Fritz the next time I want to talk to you?" he said.

Mika laughed. "I'm sure Fritz wanted to quiz you when you called. My business partner is quite the nosy one." She gave him her number before hanging up.

"Okay, talk to you soon and travel safely," Blaine said.

"Thanks. You do the same. Goodbye."

Blaine sat on the bed after he hung up, and thought for a moment. He hoped that he hadn't blown the chance to get to know Mika better. Her cool aloofness intrigued him. Even after their chance encounter, she wasn't acting needy and desperate. Mika was someone he could see having a future with, but his past had mysteriously reappeared— compliments of his mother—and he wanted to know why.

By the time Blaine ended his conversation with Mika and returned downstairs, Ashley and the event planner had left.

"Blainey, how rude of you to stay upstairs so long. Ashley had to leave to make dinner for her parents. I wanted the two of you to talk," Mrs. Chess said the moment he stepped back into the kitchen.

"I had an important call to make. Besides, what was Ashley doing here anyway?"

"I invited her. I've always liked that girl. She's perfect for you." Mrs. Chess beamed.

"Mom, you ought to give it a rest. She's married, so even if I was interested, what's the use?"

"Well, Ashley is recently divorced and quite available. I think you two should go out on a date while you're both in town."

"That's not going to happen. I don't have time. After

the party, I'm flying out to meet with the potential buyer
for your condo. Remember?" Blaine had set aside a few
extra days in order to take care of his mother's business.

"Of course I remember. I'm old, but far from senile."
Mrs. Chess pinned her son with a serious look. "Blaine,
honey, when are you going to settle down and get married? I would love to spoil a grandchild or two before I
leave this earth."

Blaine's mind flashed back to Mika. "It might be sooner
than you think, Mom."

"Well, if I have anything to do about it, it surely will."

"And what does that mean? Mom, please don't try and
play matchmaker. I'm more than capable of taking care
of my love life."

Mrs. Chess just smiled.

As they were talking, Blaine's cell phone rang. He
reached into his pocket and retrieved the tiny gadget. It
was his office calling.

"Hey, Jacoby, what's going on?" Blaine asked his account manager.

"I hate to bother you, Blaine, but you forgot to sign the
new contract extension."

Lately Blaine had been multitasking at a rapid pace, trying so hard not to lose his major client that he overlooked
the most important element. "Can you fax it over?"

"Normally, I would, but you know the suits on this account are extremely finicky and want all original signa-
tures on the contract."

Blaine and his team had worked tirelessly to keep the
global cosmetics account. He had no intentions of blowing the deal now. He thought for a moment. "Jacoby can
you meet me at the airport in the morning? I'll change my
ticket, so that I can fly back into Chicago before going on
the second leg of my trip."

"Sounds like a plan. Let me know what time to meet you and I'll be there with the contract."

"Okay." Once Blaine disconnected the call, he phoned the airline and made the necessary changes.

Chapter Nine

Mrs. Chess's party had been a grand soiree. A jazz quartet played during the gourmet dinner of lobster bisque, chateaubriand with double whipped potatoes and grilled asparagus. Afterward, music was provided by a DJ who had the guests on their feet dancing and enjoying themselves until well after midnight. Well into the evening, Blaine finally had a chance to talk to Ashley.

"You know, you were my first love," Ashley admitted while they slow danced.

Blaine was shocked at her statement. "No, I didn't know that. Ashley, we went to junior prom together and only hooked up once while we were in college."

"Yes, I know, but I've been in love with you since we were kids. Why do you think I was always hanging around your house? I do adore your mother, but I was really there to see you. Meanwhile, you didn't give me the time of day," she said, with a trace of sadness in her voice.

Ashley was right. Blaine hadn't paid her much attention. He was too busy playing sports and playing the field. "So… why did you get a divorce?" he asked, changing the subject.

"The truth is, I never really loved my husband like a wife should. My heart has always been with you."

Blaine thought he had steered the conversation away from memory lane, however she was right back on the topic. Instead of saying that he didn't return her sentiment, he simply said, "I'm sure one day you'll find true happiness." He was too much of a gentleman to hurt Ashley's feelings.

She looked lovingly into his eyes. "I'm working on it."

After their dance and for the duration of the evening, Blaine steered clear of Ashley. He didn't want to send her any mixed signals. He escaped to his room before the party was over and prepared for his early flight.

Back in Chicago, after meeting with his account manager and signing the contract, Blaine boarded another plane, heading off to take care of his mother's business.

"First-class passengers are free to board at this time," the gate agent announced.

Blaine gathered his black leather duffel, moseyed down the ramp and onto the plane. As he was putting his bag in the overhead bin, a passenger bumped against his back. He turned around and couldn't believe his eyes.

"Mika?"

"Blaine?"

He immediately engulfed her in a hug. "It's so good to see you." He squeezed her tight. After letting her go, Blaine ran his eyes up and down her petite body. She wore a black turtlenecked sweater, black leggings and a crimson ski jacket. Her hair was pulled back into a ponytail and her face was free of makeup, except for a smear of red lipstick. Her ruby lips, made him want to kiss her right then and there, but he held back. "Wow, what are the chances of us being on the same plane?" When Blaine rearranged his flight schedule, he had no idea that fate would intervene and pair him and Mika together.

She looked at her ticket, then at the number on the row. "And what are the chances of us sitting together?"

"Here, let me take your bag." He placed her carry-on in the bin next to his.

Mika moved to the window seat and fastened her seat belt. "Are you a skier, too?"

"Yes, I've been skiing since I was a kid. My parents have a condo in Vail, which is on the market now. I'm going there to meet with a potential buyer."

"Oh, I see."

"I'm surprised you could get away from the shop. Whenever I've caught a glimpse of you at Delicious, you always seem so busy."

"Well, this is a working vacation. I'm writing a cookbook. In between hitting the slopes, I'll be sitting by the fire cranking out the last few chapters."

"I hope you won't be too busy to do a few runs with me… That is, if you can handle the Black Diamonds," he said, with a smile.

"What? I'm the mogul queen. I'll dust you on the slopes."

"Okay, Ms. Mogul, we'll see about that. My precision skis are at the condo ready to go."

"And I've reserved a pair of Fischer Racing Skis, which are waiting for me at the Ski Shop."

"Flight attendants, please prepare for takeoff," the pilot announced.

Once they were airborne, Blaine redirected the conversation. "Mika, I truly enjoyed our time together the other night."

A smile brightened her face. "I did, too. I surely didn't expect the evening to end with us—" she blushed "—being naughty in the test kitchen."

"What can I say? You brought out the bad boy in me. I hadn't done anything like that in years." He leaned over and whispered, "Sex with you was an unexpected treat." He then blew a seductive breath in her ear.

She exhaled and whispered, "You wouldn't be trying to arouse me, now, would you?"

"I sure would." He gave her a soft kiss on the cheek. "Is it working?"

Mika looked around at the other few passengers, who were absorbed in their own worlds, either watching a movie or reading. "Yes."

"Ladies and gentlemen, please return to your seats and fasten your seat belts. We're heading into a severe weather pattern and may experience some turbulence," a flight attendant announced.

Suddenly, the plane jerked to the right, and then to the left before plunging a few feet. The swift drop caused some passengers to gasp loudly. The aircraft gyrated and shook violently as if it were on an obstacle course. The turbulence let up for a few seconds only to start again. This time the plane rocked and bumped so violently that the air masks deployed. The yellow masks swung back and forth as the plane shook like a toy.

"Are you all right?" Blaine asked, with a sense of urgency in his voice.

Mika grabbed hold of his hand. "I'm scared. What if we crash?"

"We're not going to crash. We're just going through a

patch of bad weather," he said attempting to calmly reassure her. Blaine held tightly on to her hand as they rode through the storm.

Outwardly Blaine maintained calm, but inside he was a nervous wreck, as well. His mind flashed back on the conversation he'd had with his mother earlier, *It's not like planes drop out of the sky on a daily basis.* He had made that comment after landing safely. Now that he was in the eye of a storm, the likelihood of the plane crashing and dropping out of the sky was indeed a real possibility. He gripped Mika's hand tighter as the plane once again jerked back and forth.

There were now screams of panic as well as passengers reciting prayers, but Blaine and Mika sat in silence as the minutes ticked past. After what seemed like hours of pure terror, the plane leveled off.

"Ladies and gentlemen, we're now above the storm clouds and should have smooth sailing for the duration of the flight," the pilot announced.

"That was beyond scary," Mika said.

"You can say that again. Having your life flash before your eyes makes you realize that our time on Earth is short and you should cherish every moment." Blaine was still holding on to her hand as he spoke.

"I couldn't agree more."

"I think we need a drink after that experience." Blaine pressed the flight attendant's button and ordered them each a double shot of tequila on the rocks with limes.

Mika sipped her drink. "I'm feeling much better now."

"Do you feel well enough to, uh…"

"What?"

"Try a new experience," he whispered.

"Like what?"

"Like joining the Mile High Club?"

She blushed. "Are you kidding?"

"Nope. We could have crashed, and one item I would like to mark off my bucket list is making love on a plane," he said, looking into her eyes.

Mika cautiously looked around at the other passengers. Most of them were now having cocktails and consoling their travel companions. The flight attendants were busy moving back and forth into the galley kitchen. "Okay, but how are we going to do this without getting caught?"

"Part of the thrill is trying not to get busted. You slip in the lavatory first and I'll follow shortly thereafter."

"Got it."

Mika unhooked her seat belt, stood up, put her purse on her shoulder and made her way into the tiny bathroom. Once inside, she removed her leggings, along with her underwear and put them in her purse. She looked in the mirror at herself and smiled shyly. "What have you gotten yourself into," she said to her reflection.

A few moments later, the narrow folding door opened and in slipped Blaine. He didn't waste any time. He pulled her to him and kissed her ruby lips with heated passion. He wrapped her tiny frame up in his embrace, nearly lifting her from the floor. Their kisses grew more intense by the second. He abandoned her lips and trailed his tongue to her neck.

"Take that off," he said, tugging at her turtleneck.

Mika quickly lifted the sweater over her head and tossed it on the sink. She then unhooked her bra.

Blaine massaged her petite breasts before engulfing them with his mouth. He licked and kissed each breast with tenderness until her nipples firmed in his mouth. "Turn around," he said, taking her by the waist.

Mika did as instructed. She watched in the mirror as he removed a condom from his pocket, took off his pants and rolled on the latex.

Blaine rubbed his erect penis against her backside, teasing her with each stroke.

"You're making me so hard," he panted in her ear.

"And you're making me wet."

"Let me see." He reached between her legs and found her moistness. "Oh, yes."

"See what you do to me?"

"I can't hold back any longer. I want you so badly." He reached around to her stomach and brought her closer to him. He entered her from behind and slowly began pumping.

Mika matched his moves, rotating her rear end so that he could move deeper inside. She gripped the tiny sink and bucked back. "Oh, yeah, that's it!"

"Are you coming?" he whispered.

"Yes, don't stop, please don't stop."

Blaine increased the pace, pumping harder and faster until they were on the verge of an explosive ending. The tiny lavatory was filled with their essence as they gave in to each other. They panted, gasping for air as they recovered from the experience.

"I like the Mile High Club," Mika said, smiling. She maneuvered around him and dressed in the cramped space.

Blaine kissed her on the lips. "Membership does have its privileges. I must say that we created some turbulence of our own."

"Yes, it did feel like we were rocking the plane," she said, smiling.

They quickly dressed and Mika exited first. Once they were back in their seats. Blaine took her hand, brought it to his lips and kissed it. They spent the remainder of the flight gazing into each other's eyes enjoying the aftermath of their naughty little secret.

Chapter Ten

Mika had arranged to have groceries delivered to the condo in advance. She planned on creating new recipes for the cookbook, but now she had another use for the chocolate. Once they landed, she and Blaine shared a taxi. Ironically, his mother's condominium was in the same complex as her rented condo. After their near-death experience in the air and making love on the plane, neither of them wanted to leave the other's side, so Mika invited Blaine over to her place.

The two-bedroom condo was comfortably furnished with overstuffed sofas and a bearskin rug, which lay in front of a stone fireplace with fresh firewood on the side.

"Why don't you start a fire, while I whip up something to eat," Mika told him, once they had settled in.

"No problem. I'll have you to know that I'm a master fire builder."

Mika came up and kissed him on the lips. "You're a man of many talents."

"Yes I am and you've only seen a few." He winked.

"I can't wait to see them all."

He hugged her close, kissing her back. "You will, my dear. One at a time."

Before Mika made her way into the kitchen, she watched as Blaine took a few pieces of wood, layered them with newspaper and started a roaring fire.

In addition to her confectionary skills, Mika was a great cook of savory foods. In no time, she had prepared a light dinner of grilled salmon, sautéed spinach and orzo. For dessert, she combined dark chocolate with vanilla beans, heavy cream and honey. She stirred the concoction until it was creamy smooth, and then removed the pot from the stove.

"Hmm, something sure smells good in here," Blaine said, coming up from behind and hugging her around the waist.

She turned around and gave him a sweet kiss on the lips. "I hope you're hungry."

"Yep, hungry for you," he said, returning her kiss.

Mika wiggled out of his embrace and prepared their plates. As they ate at the black marble counter in the kitchen, Mika stole glances at Blaine. She couldn't believe that she was actually having dinner with him in Vail of all places. A few days before, Mika had resigned herself to the fact that she might not ever hear from him again. She had totally forgiven him for not calling the day after their first night together. Joining the Mile High Club had brought them even closer together. Everything was moving at such a fast pace. She thought about slowing things down, but after experiencing what could have been a fatal plane crash, Mika realized that life was too short to not enjoy every moment.

"Would you care for seconds?" she asked, once he had finished.

"No. I'm ready for dessert now." He winked.

"Me, too, and I have just the treat for us," she said, standing up and clearing the table.

"Is it a chocolate treat?"

"You'll see, but in order to taste this dessert, you'll need to wear your birthday suit."

"Oh, I like this treat already."

"I'll meet you on the bearskin rug in a few minutes."

Blaine went back into the living room, while Mika poured the warm chocolate mixture into a ceramic bowl. Before turning off the kitchen lights, she disrobed, put her clothes on the back of the chair and made her way toward Blaine.

The living room was aglow with shades of amber reflecting off of the cream-colored walls from the roaring fire. Mika could feel the warmth of the flames as she knelt down on the plush bearskin rug next to Blaine's naked body. He was lying on his side, and she could see the rippled muscles along his back. Clearly he worked out on a regular basis. "Hey, there," she whispered.

Blaine turned around to face her. "Wow! You're beautiful. The glow of the fire is making your skin look like chocolate. I just want to taste you." Blaine licked her taut stomach.

"Hold on. I'll taste even better with this." Mika took a spoonful of the mixture and poured some over her breasts.

Blaine stuck out his tongue and tasted her liquid-chocolate-covered nipples. He sucked them until the sweet confection was gone. "Hmm, I'm liking your version of dessert." He took the bowl out of her hands. "Lay down."

Mika stretched out on the rug and closed her eyes. She inhaled and exhaled slowly, anticipating his next move.

Blaine stirred the mixture with his finger before drizzling it down the entire length of her body. He then massaged the rich thick chocolate into her skin, starting with her breasts, down to her stomach and in between her legs. He leaned over and covered her most private area with his mouth and started licking passionately.

"Ohhh," she moaned.

"Does that feel good?"

"Ohh! Yess!"

Chocolate begin oozing down the inside of her thigh as he slowly kissed it off. Blaine then focused his attention on her lady parts and increased the friction of his tongue. He didn't stop until she yelled out in ecstasy.

"Ohh… You're going to make me come!"

Blaine didn't say a word, instead he continued passionately licking and sucking her clit.

Mika was on fire and couldn't hold back any longer. Although her dream of him performing oral sex was hot, the reality was even hotter.

Blaine didn't stop until her sweet juices released in his mouth.

"I'm coming. I'm coming!" she screamed out.

Blaine leaned up on his elbow and wiped around his mouth. "Mmm, you taste good."

Mika smiled giddily.

He smiled back. "I'm glad you enjoyed it."

"I truly did, now it's my turn," Mika said, once she recovered. "Lie on your back."

Blaine did as instructed. Mika picked up the bowl and slowly poured the remaining contents over his chest, abdomen and manhood. She then licked every inch of his body, stopping in intervals to savor the sweet chocolate. She took his erection in her mouth and sucked the decadent confection until there wasn't a single drop left.

"Hold on a second," he said, stopping her before he came.

Blaine stood up, crossed the room and retrieved a condom from his toiletry bag. He strolled back over to the bearskin rug and lay beside her. He then stroked her soft cheek. "You're so beautiful."

Mika blushed. "Thank you."

"Turn over on your back," he whispered. Blaine then covered her body with his. He rubbed his manhood against her clit, teasing her all over again.

Mika spread her thighs, welcoming him inside. Blaine lovingly held her head as he rotated his hips against her groin. Their sticky limbs were intertwined, her legs were wrapped around his waist, and his arms held her tight as they slowly and passionately made love.

"Now, that's what I call dessert," he said, hugging her closer.

They slept on the bearskin rug that night in total bliss, cradled in each other's arms, the crackling of the burning wood lulling them to sleep. Mika thought this was the perfect beginning to what was sure to be a romantic getaway.

Chapter Eleven

The following morning, Blaine and Mika awoke early. The logs were no longer aglow, however their afterglow of lovemaking was ever present. Blaine had an appointment with the potential buyer for his mother's condo, but he didn't want to leave Mika. He was still reeling from the previous evening of seduction, from the liquid chocolate to the cozy fireplace to the plush, bearskin rug.

"Can you come here, please?" he yelled from the bathroom.

While Mika was placing dishes in the dishwasher from their breakfast, Blaine was busy in the bathroom creating a romantic scene. He had run a bath with lavender-scented bubbles. He found candles underneath the sink, which he placed around the large Jacuzzi tub and lit them. He turned off the lights, so that the room was bathed in candlelight.

"Wow, what have we here?" she exclaimed, coming into the bathroom.

"After a night of smearing our bodies with chocolate, I think we need a proper cleansing," he said, sitting on the edge of the tub naked.

A broad smile painted Mika's face, as her eyes took in his muscular body. "Oh, you do, do you?"

"Yep." He reached out his hand to her. "Come here."

Mika moved toward him. When she was within inches, Blaine untied her robe and gave it a soft tug, causing the silk fabric to glide off her body onto the marble floor. He stood up, stepped into the tub and held her hand as she did the same.

"Mmm, this water is so warm," she said, sliding into the tub.

Blaine settled in behind her, straddling his long legs around Mika's body. He then took a large sponge, which was floating in the bubbles, and began rubbing her skin.

"Ohh, that feels good," she moaned, leaning back onto his chest.

"You deserve to be pampered after making a delicious dinner and a special dessert last night."

"I'm glad you enjoyed it."

"*Enjoy* is an understatement. I loved licking the liquid chocolate off of your body, and you devouring the decadent sweetness off of mine. Believe it or not, I've never done anything like that before."

"Neither have I. Even though I've created countless recipes for liquid chocolate, that was the first time I used it while making love. It was divine, but afterward we were a sweet, sticky mess."

"Now I get a chance to clean off what my tongue missed."

"I like the way that sounds," she said.

Blaine poured liquid soap on the sponge, and lathered

her body, rubbing her arms, legs, back and chest. Once she was clean, he released the sponge, took two handfuls of bubbles and began massaging Mika's breasts. He let his hands slide over her nipples while softly kneading them. Once they firmed to his touch, he moved his hands slowly down her stomach and in between her legs. He parted her thighs and found her pleasure point. Blaine rubbed her softness until she began moaning with pleasure. He added a little pressure and increased the pace of his fingers.

Mika closed her eyes.

"Hearing you moan really turns me on."

Mika eased her legs open as far as the tub would allow. "And your fingers on my clit really turns me on."

"I can't seem to get enough of you."

He increased the pace of his fingers. "That's a good thing." Blaine eased two fingers inside of her, while stroking her small piece of the pinkness. He wanted to please her and didn't stop until he heard her panting.

"I'm coming. I'm coming."

Blaine gave her a few more strokes, ensuring that she was completely satisfied.

"Wow! That was amazing. This gives taking a bath a whole new meaning," she said, opening her eyes.

"Just call me the Cleanup Man," he joked.

After their bath was over and they were dressed, they sat at the kitchen counter drinking coffee, savoring their last few minutes together.

"I hate to leave, but I have to meet the potential buyer at my mom's condo," Blaine told her.

"No worries. I need to stop by the Ski Shop and pick up my skis. I can't wait to try them out."

"Don't hit the slopes without me. I'm dying to see your skills on the mountain. The appointment shouldn't take long. Why don't you meet me at my mom's after you get your skis?"

"Okay. Sounds good."

Blaine gave her the unit number, kissed her goodbye and headed over to his mother's condo.

Mrs. Chess's unit was bigger and more grandiose than the one Mika was renting. The living room had picture windows that faced the snow-covered mountains. From that vantage point, skiers in brightly colored skiwear could be seen crisscrossing the slopes. The gourmet kitchen was equipped with Sub-Zero and Viking appliances. Lifelike silk roses in crystal vases accented every room of the condo, and Persian rugs decorated the blond wood flooring.

Blaine went into the master suite, put his duffel bag on the king-size sleigh bed and unpacked. He made his way to the expansive closet and chose a black, plum and white Descente ski jacket and a pair of black ski pants, with a plum turtleneck. No sooner had he changed clothes the the doorbell rang.

"Must be the buyer," he said out loud, as he made his way to the living room and opened the door.

"Hey, there!"

"Uh… Ashley, what are you doing here?" Blaine asked with shock registering in his voice. She was the last person he expected to see.

Ashley nearly bounced into the room, wearing a Black Diamond full-length mink coat, and carrying a brown checkered Louis Vuitton tote.

"How did you know I was here? Oh, wait… My mother told you." Blaine watched as Ashley strutted into the living room, settled on the sofa and made herself at home.

"Yes, Mrs. Chess told me that she put the condo up

for sale, and I'm in the market for a winter property. My divorce settlement left me well-off and I can more than afford the asking price," she offered without any prodding from Blaine.

"So you're telling me you're the potential buyer that I'm supposed to meet?" Blaine asked, astounded. He had half a mind to call his mother right then and there, but what was the use?

"Yep, I'm the buyer. Aren't you going to show me around?"

"Are you serious? Ashley, we both know you're not interested in buying this place. You only came here to see me." Blaine was upset that his mother had manipulated him.

"Okay, it's true that I wanted to see you again. We hardly had a chance to talk at the party. You disappeared shortly after our first dance. But you're wrong, I am interested in buying this place. Vail is so beautiful year-round and it would make the perfect second home." She stood up. "So give me the tour."

Blaine exhaled. He knew there was no arguing with Ashley, besides the quicker he showed her around, the quicker she could leave. He began walking toward the kitchen, with Ashley following closely behind, nearly stepping on his heels. "As you can see, all the appliances are high-end, including the wine fridge."

Ashley opened the well-stocked minirefrigerator, took out a bottle of Veuve Clicquot and set it on the white quartz countertop.

"What are you doing?" he asked, watching her open the champagne.

"Let's have a toast."

"A toast for what? We have nothing to celebrate."

Ashley opened an overhead cabinet. "Where are the glasses?" Before Blaine could answer, she opened another cabinet and found crystal champagne flutes. She poured them each a glass, and handed one to Blaine. "Come on, have a drink with an old friend."

Blaine reluctantly took a quick sip and set his glass on the counter, before continuing the tour. He had no intention of drinking the entire bottle of champagne with Ashley. He wanted to give her the tour and then show her the door. He had plans with Mika and wasn't going to break them for Ashley's sake. "The unit has three guest rooms, each with its own bath. All of the bedrooms have fireplaces, and…"

"Where's the master suite?" Ashley asked, interrupting him.

"Down the hall."

When they reached the bedroom, Ashley brushed past him and walked in first. Blaine turned his back to click on the light, but when he turned around Ashley was nowhere in sight. "Hey, where are you?" he called out.

"I'm in the bathroom."

Blaine exhaled. He wanted the tour to be over. He stood near the doorway and waited. The minutes ticked by, but Ashley hadn't come out of the bathroom. He walked over and tapped on the door.

"Hey, are you all right in there?"

"Yes, I'm fine. I'll be out in a minute."

"Okay."

Blaine went over to the window and looked out at the snow-covered mountains. He was anticipating skiing with Mika and was anxious to leave. Suddenly he felt a tap on his shoulder and turned around.

"What…the…?"

Ashley was standing in the buff, with the fur coat

draped around her shoulders wearing only a pair of thigh-high red suede boots.

"I want you, more than you know," she said, dropping the coat to the floor and moving closer to him. She then wrapped her arms around his neck and gave him a deep French before he had the chance to protest.

"Blaine!"

He broke from Ashley's embrace and whipped his head around. Mika was standing in the doorway with her mouth agape.

"Mika, it's not what you think. This is Ashley, an old friend," he said, stepping away from Ashley and toward Mika.

"Oh, and you kiss all of your friends while they're naked, wearing sexy boots!" Mika exclaimed, staring at Ashley as she spoke.

"I wasn't kissing her. She was kissing me," Blaine tried to explain.

"That's not what it looks like to me. You didn't have to lie and say you were meeting a buyer. Have fun with your—" Mika put her hands up in quotation marks "—friend. Goodbye, Blaine." Mika made a swift exit.

"Is that your girlfriend?" Ashley asked.

"Yes." Although Blaine hadn't officially asked Mika to be his girl, he felt as if they had committed themselves by their actions.

"Not anymore, I'm sure. Not after what she just walked in on," Ashley said, a sly smile spreading across her face.

"Nothing happened and nothing is going to happen between us. Please put on your coat and leave before I return," he said stridently.

Ashley reluctantly picked her mink coat off the floor and threw it around her shoulders.

Before Blaine gathered his ski jacket and left, he called a car service for Ashley with explicit instructions to take her directly to the airport. He hoped to find Mika so that he could explain. He didn't want to lose her over a silly misunderstanding.

Chapter Twelve

Snowflakes drifted from the sky as Mika wandered aimlessly through town. Vail Village was crowded with people browsing in and out of the quaint shops, and skiers carrying skis over their shoulders on their way to the lifts. Mika roamed without a destination, with her mind a ball of confusion. Blaine had said, *It's not what you think.* However, from what Mika saw before she busted Blaine—a bottle of champagne and two flutes sitting on the kitchen counter—it was exactly what she suspected. Blaine was on the verge of bedding another woman, shortly after he had made love to her. The thought sickened her. Mika couldn't believe how gullible she had been, thinking that he was single and free. Blaine was obviously in a relationship and had lied to Fritz.

Just when I totally open myself up without reservation, reality slaps me in the face, she thought as a single tear dripped down her cheek. Mika sniffled and wiped her face with the back of her hand. She was really enjoying Blaine and couldn't believe what a liar he turned out to be. The sadness she was feeling slowly began dissipating as anger and resentment took its place. Mika had a good mind to return to Blaine's condo and give him an earful, but she refrained. Instead, she took out her cell phone and called her business partner.

"Delicious Chocolate Bar, Fritz speaking. How may I help you?"

"You can help by never, I mean never, fixing me up again!" Mika ranted into the phone the second he picked up.

"Mika? Is that you?"

"Yes, it's me!"

"What's wrong? Why are you shouting? Is everything all right?" Fritz asked with concern in his voice.

"No, everything is all wrong!" Suddenly the onslaught of tears that she was trying to hold back came flooding out with a vengeance.

"Calm down and tell me what happened."

Mika found a coffee shop, went inside and took a seat by the window. She took a deep breath and told Fritz the entire story, from the airplane scare, to making love on the plane, to the morning after, to catching Blaine red-handed with another woman.

"How did you get into his condo?"

"When I reached the unit the door was ajar. I knocked but there was no answer. Blaine had told me to meet him there, so I just walked in, and that's when I caught him and his so-called friend."

"Oh, wow! I can't believe he would lead you on like that. But are you sure he's not telling the truth? Maybe the other woman was just a friend like he said."

"I seriously doubt it. You should have seen her standing there naked, pressing her body against his and kissing him as if they were long-lost lovers. I can't get that image out of my head."

"Oh, sweetie, I'm so sorry. I just knew he was the one for you. What are you going to do now? Are you coming back home?"

"No. I'm going to try and enjoy my vacation. I would go skiing, but I left my skis right outside of his door. I can't bear the thought of running into Blaine and his lady again," she said, sounding forlorn.

"Why don't you call the Ski Shop and ask if they can deliver a new pair of skis?"

"That's a good idea. Fritz, thanks for listening. I had to call and vent. I feel better now."

As they were talking Mika heard a beep in her ear. She looked at the phone's display. She didn't recognize the number and kept talking without clicking over.

"I'm glad. Instead of staying in alone tonight, why don't you treat yourself to a nice dinner? You deserve to pamper yourself after the ordeal you've been through."

"I really don't feel like going out tonight. Suppose I run into them? It would be awkward to see Blaine with another woman so soon after we were intimate."

"So what if you do? You don't have anything to feel bad about, you simply gave in to your feelings for him, there's nothing wrong with following your instincts. Hold your head high and keep it moving."

Fritz's words of encouragement were exactly what Mika needed to hear. "You're absolutely right! Thanks again, Fritz, for being such a good friend."

"Don't mention it. I'll always be here for you. And I promise, no more setups, no matter how many single good-looking men come into the shop," Fritz said with a giggle, trying to lighten her mood.

"Now, that's a deal. I'll see you in a few days."

"Okay, and remember, head high."

"Okay. Bye, Fritz."

When Mika hung up, she ordered a bowl of soup and a cup of herbal tea. The warm liquids helped to calm her even more. She sat in the café and people-watched as the snow began coming down faster. Through the glistening white flakes she caught a glimpse of a couple strolling arm in arm, laughing and talking, seemingly in love. A knot formed in Mika's throat, and she fought back tears as she mourned the future she could have had with Blaine.

Chapter Thirteen

After Blaine had called the car service for Ashley, he dialed Mika's number but got her voice mail. Blaine didn't bother to leave a message. He preferred to speak to her in person, instead of groveling on a recording. When he left his mother's condo, he noticed a pair of skis propped against the wall. *These are probably Mika's. She left so fast, that she forgot them,* he thought. Blaine picked up the skis, threw them over his shoulder and went across the complex to her condo. He knocked on the door and waited, but she didn't answer. He knocked several more times but there was still no answer. He put the skis by the door and jetted off to find Mika. Obviously, she wasn't on the slopes, so he decided to check out the shops in the Village.

The snow, which had been falling softly, was now coming down fast, creating a blizzard effect. Visibility was poor and Blaine was having trouble seeing in the distance.

He could only make out the people directly in front of him. He searched inside several boutiques, but no Mika. An hour and a half later, he still hadn't found her. Blaine was cold and weary. He dialed her cell number again, and this time left a message before returning to the condo.

"Mika, please call me back. I really need to talk to you. Call me back please!" he emphasized again before disconnecting the line.

By the time Blaine returned to the condo, Ashley was gone. He took off his snow-covered jacket and tossed it in a chair. He walked into the kitchen to get a bottle of water, and noticed a note on the counter. He picked up the piece of paper. "Blaine, I'm sorry if I caused trouble for you. I would have never come to Vail if I had known you were in a relationship. All the best. Love forever, Ashley."

He tossed the note back on the counter, took the water out of the refrigerator and went back into the living room. He plopped down on the sofa. He couldn't believe how fast everything had gone awry. Blaine believed that Ashley wasn't trying to make problems for him, but she had. If Mika had come into the room a few minutes later, she would have seen him refusing Ashley's advance.

He couldn't be too mad at Ashley. His mother was the one encouraging her infatuation. He took the cell phone out of his pocket and dialed his mother's number.

"Mom, what were you thinking, inviting Ashley to Vail?" Blaine asked, nearly shouting into the phone.

"Wait a minute, Blainey. I didn't invite her per se. I simply told Ashley that my condo was for sale and that you were going to be in Vail handling the showing. She jumped at the chance to meet you there. Honestly, I for one don't see what the problem is. You're both single, so why not spend a couple of days together in the snow?" Mrs. Chess said innocently.

Blaine shook his head. As much as he protested, he knew that his mother would always meddle in his love life until he settled down. "Mom, the problem is that I'm seeing someone else and now she thinks Ashley and I are an item, which couldn't be further from the truth."

"Who are you dating? You didn't say anything to me about a new girlfriend. Is it someone I know?" she asked in a flurry, nearly running all of her sentences together.

"Not directly. Her name is Mika Madison and she's the co-owner of Delicious, the chocolate shop that I order your truffles from."

"So, that's how you two met?"

"Yes."

"Oh, she's also there in Vail?" Mrs. Chess asked, sounding intrigued.

"Yes." Blaine was still a bit upset with his mother.

"Exactly how does Mika think that you and Ashley are an item?"

Blaine wasn't about to tell his mother that Ashley was standing in the bedroom wearing only a pair of boots, trying to seduce him. "Never mind how she got that impression. The truth is that I really like this woman, and need to straighten things out with her before we leave Vail."

"Where is Ashley now?"

"I sent her home. She's a nice person, she's just not the woman for me."

"Sounds like you're smitten with this Mika Madison."

Blaine couldn't deny his feelings. He and Mika had jelled together from the first night they officially met. "I think she's the one."

"Oh, Blainey, I've never heard you sound so sure about any woman. Are you positive she's the one? I've always thought that you and Ashley were meant to be together," she said, sounding disappointed. "Since me and your father met and fell in love in high school, I thought you would do the same."

"I was never in love with Ashley, but I've fallen hard for Mika."

"Blainey, all I've ever wanted was your happiness. If you're happy, then so am I. When do I get to meet her?"

"Don't be too happy. I haven't spoken to Mika since she bolted out of the condo."

"I don't know exactly what happened between you two. All I can say is, don't give up. Some women need time to process their feelings."

Blaine listened to his mother's sage advice, and then said, "I won't. Mom, I'll talk to you later. I'm going to call Mika again."

"Okay. Goodbye, son, and good luck."

Blaine felt a bit better after talking to his mother. He dialed Mika's number again, and again was met with her voice mail. This time he didn't leave a message. He disconnected the line and put his cell phone on the cocktail table.

Maybe Mom was right, maybe Mika needs more time before she talks to me.

It had been a trying day, and Blaine was exhausted. Even though it wasn't late, he moseyed into the bedroom and changed into a pair of flannel pajamas. The previous night, Blaine was being laced with chocolate, lying on a bearskin rug in front of a cozy fireplace with the woman of his dreams. But tonight, he was all alone. Blaine reached for a fluffy pillow and tucked it underneath his head. He stared at the ceiling, all the while hoping that he would have the chance to speak with Mika face-to-face. He knew that if she looked into his eyes, she would know that he was telling the truth about Ashley. Blaine drifted off to sleep with that thought in mind.

Chapter Fourteen

Once the snow let up, Mika left the coffee shop and headed to the condominium complex. She wearily climbed the two flights of stairs. She wasn't physically tired, but mentally drained. The first thing Mika noticed once she reached the landing was a pair of skis propped up beside her door.

The Ski Shop must have delivered my new skis, she thought, and then realized that she hadn't yet called them to make the request.

She walked closer and saw that they were the same skis that she had picked up earlier.

Blaine must have brought them over, she thought.

Mika unlocked the door, picked up the skis, brought them inside and placed them in the ski rack. She ran her hand over one ski, thinking about the playful ribbing she and Blaine had exchanged regarding competing on the slopes.

"I guess he'll never see how good I am, now that his girlfriend is in town," she said aloud.

Mika brushed off the thought, trying not to concentrate on what could have been. She took off her jacket, put her purse on the sofa and went into the kitchen. As she was opening the refrigerator to get a bottle of water, her cell phone buzzed. She went back into the living room, dug the phone out of her purse and saw that she had a few missed calls and one message. She dialed her voice mail and listened to the message.

It was Blaine. Mika didn't have his phone number programmed into her phone and had ignored the call earlier, thinking it was a wrong number. She pressed repeat and listened to his message again, trying to decipher the tone in his voice. Did he sound apologetic?

Mika scrolled to the missed call log, found his number and placed her finger on the button to call him back, but stopped.

What if it's really over between us, and he's calling to say goodbye?

She couldn't stand the thought of never seeing Blaine again. Mika felt like crying, but remembered Fritz's words of encouragement.

Mika went into the bedroom, took off her clothes and moseyed into the bathroom. One look at the tub, with the melted candles still sitting on the rim, and a flood of memories came back. Blaine had been so tender, as if she were the only woman for him. Mika shook off that thought, took a shower and dressed for dinner.

Sweet Basil was a well-known restaurant near the condominium complex. Mika walked briskly across the Village square, pulling the collar of her down coat around her ears, warding off the chilly night air. In no time, she was inside the restaurant talking to the hostess.

"Do you have a reservation?" the tall slim woman asked.

"No, I don't." Mika looked around and saw that the place seemed to be filled to capacity.

The hostess looked at the reservation book, and then back at Mika. "Are you dining alone?"

"Unfortunately," she said underneath her breath. "Yes, I am."

"I have one table left. It's near the fireplace. Is that okay?"

"Sure."

The hostess escorted Mika to the table and told her that a waiter would be with her momentarily. Mika took off her coat, sat down and scanned the room, making sure she didn't see Blaine and his girlfriend. There were plenty of couples in the place, but no Blaine. Luckily for Mika, she wouldn't have to sit through a meal staring across the room at them. As she waited to be served, she overheard the conversation of two older women who were sitting directly in front of her.

"I still can't believe we witnessed a young man proposing to his girlfriend right in the middle of the town square while people were standing around watching."

"And with the snow falling, it made the scene even more romantic."

The first woman then said, "Did you get a look at those red boots the young lady wore?"

"Yes, I did. Were they suede?"

"I believe so."

"Who wears suede in this type of weather? Back in our day, we only wore suede in the fall," the second woman replied.

At the mention of red suede boots, Mika's ears really perked up. She flashed back on Blaine's girlfriend, standing there naked wearing only a pair of thigh-high, suede boots. Suddenly, her stomach sank. Were the two women talking about Blaine and his girlfriend?

"Suede boots aside, I couldn't help but clap when he placed that beautiful engagement ring on her finger and…"

"And she agreed to marry him," the second woman said, finishing the other woman's sentence.

She began to feel sick. *How could I have been such a bad judge of character?*

"Excuse me, miss. Miss?" the waiter said, trying to get her attention. He had been standing at Mika's table asking if she wanted to order a beverage, but she hadn't responded.

"What did you say?" she finally answered, snapping out of her fog.

"I asked if you would like a glass of wine before dinner."

"No, thanks. I, uh…"

Mika stood up. After hearing the devastating news of Blaine's proposal, she no longer had an appetite.

"I'm sorry, but I have to leave," she told the waiter.

Mika hurriedly put her coat back on and rushed out of the restaurant. She nearly ran back to the condo as tears streamed down her cheeks.

Chapter Fifteen

The following morning, Blaine arose early. He looked on the nightstand for his cell phone, but it wasn't there. He then remembered leaving it on the cocktail table. Blaine yawned, stretched his long limbs and climbed out of bed. He made his way to the living room to retrieve his phone, hoping there was a message from Mika.

Blaine picked it up and looked at the screen, but there were no missed calls. He checked his voice mail, on the off chance she had called.

"There are no new messages," the automated recording announced.

Blaine realized that Mika might never call him back. But he was determined to straighten things out with her. He wasn't going to lose her over a silly misunderstanding. Instead of waiting on her call, he decided to go to her condo again.

"She's bound to be in now, it's so early," he reasoned.

Blaine quickly showered, dressed and headed out the door. Within no time, he was at Mika's door.

The first thing he noticed was that her skis were gone. Blaine panicked, thinking that maybe she had left Vail. He knocked on the door and waited, but there was no answer. He put his ear to the door, trying to detect if she was moving around inside, but didn't hear a sound.

Maybe she's on the slopes already.

Avid skiers loved fresh powder, and usually hit the mountain early before other skiers had a chance to pack the snow. Blaine rushed back to his mother's condo retrieved his skis and made his way to the lifts.

There were few people in line. He scanned the area but didn't see Mika. When the lift chair came, he slid on. As he rode to the very top of the mountain, he glanced out over the snow-covered peaks at a handful of skiers gracefully making S-shaped tracks as they made their way down.

Blaine adjusted his goggles as the lift neared the top. He scooted to the edge of the chair and waited to ski off once they reached the Black Diamond trail. Blaine remembered the crimson ski jacket that Mika wore on the plane and was on the lookout once he slid off the lift and began making his way down the mountain. The trail was littered with moguls, and he expertly managed each one, jumping, swerving and skillfully gliding over them.

Midway down, he looked in the distance and spotted a woman wearing a red jacket. Blaine picked up his pace, trying to catch up to her. His eyes were so focused on the red jacket that he didn't see the person skiing directly in front of him until they collided.

Blaine hit the snow with such force, that one of his skis popped off. After he recovered, he looked downhill and saw his victim was a few feet away lying facedown in the snow. He quickly put his ski back on and moved toward the person.

"Hey, are you all right?"

The person turned around and wiped the snow out of their face. "I think I…"

"Mika!" Blaine knelt down next to her. "I am so sorry. Are you okay?"

She looked up at him and paused for a moment. "I think I twisted my ankle." She tried to stand, but fell back down.

"Here, let me help you." He put his hand underneath her arm to give her support, but she snatched away.

"I don't need your help!" Her words were tight and measured.

"Mika, I know you're still upset about seeing me with Ashley, but she means nothing to me. I didn't even know she was coming to Vail, I swear!"

"Didn't you propose to her yesterday?"

"Propose! No way, I would never marry her! Ashley and I grew up together and she's always had a crush on me, but I never returned her feelings." Blaine was speaking in a flurry, hoping to explain away the problem.

As he was talking, the ski patrol came by. "Is everything okay here?" asked a big burly man in a yellow ski jacket and pants.

"No. She needs medical attention. Can you radio for a stretcher to take her down the mountain?"

"Sure thing." The patrolman took a walkie-talkie out of the breast pocket of his jacket, called the base patrol and ordered a stretcher.

"You don't have to wait," Mika told Blaine.

"I'm not leaving, so don't ask me to."

When the stretcher came and loaded Mika aboard, Blaine skied behind them all the way down the hill. He helped the patrolman take Mika off the stretcher and into the medic's office.

"What seems to be the problem?" asked the attending nurse.

"I twisted my ankle. I hope it's not broken," she said, taking off the ski boot.

Blaine stood silently against the wall, hoping Mika wouldn't ask him to leave. He wanted to hear the professional opinion of her condition.

The nurse examined Mika's entire leg, asking her to bend it in different directions, and then said, "Your ankle isn't broken, just sprained. I'm going to wrap it up and give you a few pain relievers. When you get back home, I suggest you see your primary doctor for a follow-up. I'll be right back with the pills and a pair of crutches."

When the nurse left the room, Blaine went over to Mika. "Sweetheart, I am so sorry about all of this. I was hoping to bump into you on the mountain, but not literally."

"Please don't call me sweetheart. Reserve that endearment for your girlfriend."

"For the last time, Ashley is not my girlfriend!" he said, slightly raising his voice. "What do I have to do to prove that I'm telling the truth?" Blaine thought for a moment. He knew the one person who could clear up this entire mess. He took out his cell phone and dialed his mother.

"Hi, Blainey, honey, how are you?" Mrs. Chess answered in a cheery tone.

"Mom, I need your help."

"What is it, honey? Are you all right?"

"Remember the woman I was telling you about?"

"You mean Mika?"

"Yes, Mika," he said, looking directly into Mika's eyes. "Can you please talk to her, and tell her about our conversation yesterday."

"Is this about clearing up that misunderstanding you two have?"

"Yes. Hold on." Blaine handed Mika the phone.

Mika was staring at him like he was crazy.

"Please take the phone, my mother wants to talk to you."

"Your mother? Why?"

"Just talk to her," Blaine said, nearly forcing the phone into her hand.

"Hello?" Mika said, hesitantly.

"Hello, darling. This is Blaine's mother, Mrs. Chess. He told me all about you. First, let me say thanks for making such delicious chocolates, and I especially love your chocolate martini recipe. Those martinis are a hit every time I make them." She giggled.

"Thanks, Mrs. Chess."

"Well, I know that Blainey didn't call me to talk about your martinis. He called yesterday and told me that you think that he and Ashley are an item. Dear, that couldn't be further from the truth. Ashley and Blainey grew up together, that's all. Blainey has never had eyes for Ashley, but I do understand that he cares for you very much."

"Oh, I see," Mika said, staring at Blaine.

"I look forward to Blainey bringing you to Florida so I can meet you in person and have you shake up a few martinis for me and my bridge club."

"That would be my pleasure. Goodbye, Mrs. Chess," Mika said, and handed the phone back to Blaine.

"Thanks, Mom. I'll talk to you later."

Blaine disconnected the call and turned his attention to Mika. "I hope that you believe me now. Ashley is just a friend and nothing more."

Mika hesitated. "Yes, I believe you." She smiled.

Blaine leaned down, hugged her and kissed her on the forehead.

"Here are your crutches and pain medication," the nurse said, returning to the room. "Are you taking her home?" she asked Blaine.

"I sure am."

For once his mother's meddling had paid off.

Chapter Sixteen

Mika's world had shifted yet again, this time for the better. She had thought that she had lost Blaine forever. The past few days had been pure bliss, with Blaine waiting on her hand and foot. He cooked breakfast, lunch and dinner while she lay in bed with her foot propped up on pillows. She used the downtime to work on her cookbook.

"Do you need anything?" Blaine asked, coming into the room wearing an apron.

"Hey, Blainey!" she teased.

"Don't call me that. Only my mother is allowed to call me Blainey. I've long since outgrown that nickname. When I was a boy, it was okay, but now I'm a grown man and—"

Mika cut him off. "Yes, you are a grown man. You're my man and I love every inch of you."

Blaine hadn't officially asked Mika to be his woman, but his actions spoke louder than words. "Yes, I am your man. Now what can your man do for you?"

Mika put her index finger to her chin and said, "Mmm. I can think of a few things."

"Like what?"

"For starters, take off that apron. Your kitchen duties are over. Now it's time for your night shift."

Blaine took off the apron, and began taking off his pants, but stopped. "Are you sure, you're up to a little hanky-panky?"

"Yes, I'm sure. It's been days and my ankle is feeling much better. Now get over here," she said, putting her laptop on the nightstand.

Blaine quickly undressed and got underneath the down comforter next to Mika. "You have on too many clothes," he said, taking his finger and sliding off the strap of her gown.

Mika kicked the comforter off with one foot, wiggled out of the gown and moved closer to Blaine.

"Come here, beautiful." He engulfed her in his arms and lay her down on the pillows. Blaine tenderly kissed Mika's entire face, saving her mouth for last. His lips touched hers with love. Blaine fed Mika his tongue, French kissing her with passion. His body was heating with desire with each passing second.

Mika wrapped her arms around him, hugging him tighter while at the same time exploring his mouth with her tongue. They kissed until they were on the verge of exploding, each wanting more.

"I should make some liquid chocolate," Mika said, coming up for air.

"We don't need it tonight. Tonight you are all the chocolate I desire."

Blaine began massaging her breasts, one and then the other. He trailed his massive hands down her stomach around her back and underneath her buttocks. The feel of her soft bottom in his hands made him even hotter.

"You feel so good."

Mika reached down and began stroking his manhood. "So do you. I want to taste you." Mika began moving down toward his manhood. When she reached his groin area, she kissed the tip and then wrapped her mouth around his manhood. He filled her entire mouth as she sucked and teased him with her tongue.

"Oh…baby…you're going to make me come," Blaine said in between breaths.

But Mika didn't stop.

"Hold on."

Mika stopped and met his gaze with a confused look.

"I want to make love to you." Blaine reached over to the nightstand, took a condom out of the drawer, opened the package and rolled it on his pulsating manhood.

He then covered her body with his, mindful of her leg and careful not to put too much pressure on her body. He slowly began grinding his hips.

Mika could feel him getting harder and harder. She wanted him in the worst way and couldn't take their foreplay any longer.

"Please make love to me," she whispered in his ear.

"With pleasure, my love."

Blaine inserted his manhood into her wetness and pumped slowly at first. Once they found their rhythm, he picked up the pace.

Mika wrapped her arms around his neck bringing him in closer. His member filled her up as they made love at a fast and furious pace.

"Oh, Blaine, I love you so much!" she exclaimed.

He held her head, and looked into her eyes. "I love you, too, Mika."

Sweat dripped off of their bodies as they rode the wave of ecstasy. Blaine felt his imminent release, but held back. He wanted to please her first. "Are you there?"

"I'm almost there…" she said, her words trailing off.

Blaine increased his pace, pressing farther into her.

Mika grabbed hold of his firm butt with both hands.

"Am I hitting the spot baby?"

Mika's eyes were clinched shut as she held on tight. "Ohh… Yeah."

Blaine rotated his hips harder and faster.

"Yeah…" she cried out.

Tonight, nothing stood between them and their shared passion as they came hard together.

Blaine rolled to the side and then pulled her to him. They lay in a cuddling position basking in the afterglow.

"That was beyond good," Mika said, after she had recovered.

"Yes, it was. We make a perfect match."

"I agree. When we get back home, I'm going to create a special chocolate blend just for us."

"I can't wait." He smiled.

"And I know just what I'm going to call the mixture."

"What?" he asked.

"Dim the Lights. If it wasn't for that game, we probably wouldn't have gotten so close, so fast."

Blaine kissed her on the lips. "You're right. No matter where we are next year, let's promise to dim the lights and expose our innermost feelings for each other. It'll keep our love fresh for years to come."

Mika snuggled closer to Blaine. After a litany of blind dates gone awry, she had finally found her soul mate and she couldn't have been happier.

* * * * *

HER WILD AND SEXY NIGHTS

Theodora Taylor

Chapter One

Don't cry. Don't cry. Please don't cry, Kayla Edwards said to herself as the plane took off. She turned to face the plane's small window and squeezed her eyes shut. But it was already too late. Tears spilled through her closed eyelids, despite the fact that she was sitting in a luxurious first-class cabin and was headed toward a dream vacation in Paris, France.

She couldn't help but blame the passenger who had taken the seat beside her. She'd been all right for the most part, besides the occasional feeling of sadness and anger, during the first leg of the trip from Los Angeles to London. But the seat beside her had been empty then. She'd just been settling into a good thousand-mile stare out the window when an English flight attendant had called out, "Hold it. We've one more coming down the ramp."

A few minutes later that empty seat made a heavy stretching sound as someone sat down. Though she'd done well up until then, the sadness of having that seat filled by someone other than Marcus rose to the surface so fast she barely had time to think. "No, don't cry," she whispered before the tears fell onto to the armrest of her white leather seat. And despite her best efforts, she couldn't make herself stop crying as the plane rose into the air at a forty-five-degree angle before righting itself into a straight line.

She took several deep breaths, trying to get her emotions under control. *He's not worth it,* she told herself. Marcus Thornhill wasn't worth a single one of her tears.

He hadn't been that great of a football player, a second-string kicker known more for his good looks than for his actual skills on the field. And he'd been an even worse boyfriend. Always broke because he spent most of the money he made on clothes, flashy cars and eating out at places purposefully chosen because of the paparazzi who hung out there. During the four years they'd been dating, he'd become increasingly obsessed with his "brand" to the point that he'd refused to go out with her if she wasn't dressed up with a face full of makeup and every hair on the weave he'd insisted she get in perfect place.

What if someone sees us together and takes a picture with you looking like that? he'd asked, completely serious. Though later, after the huge fight that ensued, he'd insisted that he just wanted the whole world to see how beautiful she was.

And fool that she'd been, Kayla had believed him. She still remembered him as the nervous boy with the Mid-western accent that had come into the Los Angeles Suns payroll office and asked if there was a place nearby where he could cash his check because he wanted to send money back home to his mama in Kansas.

Suzie, her boss and best friend, had warned against dat-

ing football players when she'd first started her job as a
payroll administrator for the Los Angeles franchise team.
"Their egos are like vacuums and it's a full-time job being
one of their girlfriends. Plus, most of them cheat like you
wouldn't believe."

But she'd thought Marcus was different. They'd had
so much in common, both being dedicated to family and
both having the same racial background—but actually now
that she looked back on it, she realized that was all they
had in common. And their differences had only grown as
the relationship progressed. Marcus's ego had indeed become one of Suzie prophesized vacuums as her own grew
smaller and smaller, until she was completely revolving
around her boyfriend, dressing the way he wanted her to
dress, going wherever he wanted to go.

But it still hadn't been enough. Two days ago she'd
used her lunch hour to make a packing list for a six-night,
seven-day grand-prize trip to Paris she'd won through a
fund-raising raffle for the school that Suzie's son attended.
It had been a trip Marcus had grudgingly agreed to take
with her, even though "They don't know anything about
football in Europe, and I'm not even on that *'Parlez-vous
français?'* tip." Still, she'd wanted to have both of their
bags packed early to help make the trip go as smoothly
as possible.

She'd also been hoping this trip would breathe new life
into their relationship, shake things up from what had become a rote routine of either going out to the hottest new
club or staying in at her condo and watching ESPN. She
was only halfway through the packing list for the trip,
when Suzie had called her into her office.

Girl, I don't want to show you this, Suzie had said after

closing the door behind her longtime friend, *but I'm your friend first, so I know I have to.*

She'd turned the monitor around to display the front page of a popular gossip website, dedicated mostly to giving snarky dissection of sports news and breaking scandals. Kayla blinked and leaned forward in the guest chair on the other side of Suzie's desk. Splashed across the monitor was a picture of Marcus with a woman she recognized as one of the new Suns cheerleaders, a buxom blonde barely out of college, who'd needed help filling out the simple direct deposit form. The headline of the blog post read Hot New Couple?

In the article, the writer supposed that Marcus Thornhill must have dumped his longtime girlfriend, Kayla Edwards, because he was seen the night before swapping spit with the cheerleader at one of L.A.'s hottest new clubs. And just in case Kayla had even been thinking for a minute that this was all made up by some shady blogger on a slow news day, there were several more pictures of Marcus tonguing down the cheerleader in the front seat of the Mercedes Kayla had paid the bill on last month because he had "miscalculated" some expenses.

Upon arriving home that evening, she'd immediately thrown all of the clothes Marcus had left at her place into the Dumpster outside her condo and gotten the locks changed. That meant she could just ignore him when he showed up at her door demanding to know why she changed the locks, then insisting that he'd been drunk and that the cheerleader had been all over him, then asking if he could at least get his clothes, then screeching like a girl when she told him exactly where they were.

She'd gotten the last laugh, but it hadn't been worth it because she was now the laughingstock of the entire Suns

office. She'd endured so many snickers and pitying looks
from her coworkers when she'd come out of Suzie's office on Friday that she'd skipped lunch just so she could
finish her work and get out of there as early as possible.

What an idiot she'd been. She angrily swiped at her tears
now. That empty seat had come to represent the four years
she had wasted on an empty person, and when someone
else had filled it she could no longer hold back her tears.

"Not a fan of takeoff either, hey?"

The man now sitting beside her had an English accent but not one of those nice, posh ones that the British judges on reality competition shows always seemed
to have. Rather, he had one of the grittier ones that made
her think of the violent English crime comedies that occasionally made their way to American box offices. He'd
dropped the *h* on *hey* and his deep voice sounded more like
an angry growl than the sophisticated dulcets she'd heard
coming off the other English passengers in first class.

He didn't appear to belong here either. Curious, she
turned to look at him and found she was right. His body
was roped with lean muscle, and he wore jeans and a plain
gray T-shirt. He wasn't bald, but his hair was shaved extremely close to his head. And even though he didn't look
to be that much older than she, his brutal face told a story
of way more life experience than she had. He had a crooked
nose that had obviously been broken at least once, presum-
ably in a fight, and piercing black eyes that stayed on her
with unnerving focus.

But none of this made him unattractive. In fact, he
oozed potent masculinity to the point that she could see
women throwing themselves at him, more than willing to
take a walk on his wild side.

"No, I actually like planes," she answered carefully,

wondering why a man who looked this dangerous would be making small talk with a woman in a modest broom skirt and Suns T-shirt who'd just had her weave removed in favor of simple twists that brushed her shoulders. A woman whose ex had described her as plain when she didn't wear makeup, like now.

He shrugged. "Well, I don't like 'em. Don't like to be driven around by other people 'less I'm on the ground and a lot of times not even then." He rolled his shoulders back. "I could do with a drink. You, too?"

It was technically a question, but his gruff voice made it seem more like a command.

"I don't think they can serve drinks before the fasten-seat-belt light goes off."

"No, it's all right," he assured her, waving down a flight attendant.

And it was. The flight attendant arrived two minutes later with two glasses of champagne for them. She seemed not only happy to do so, but also handed her seatmate his glass with a sexy wink.

Kayla was surprised by the obvious flirtation, but she didn't blame the woman. The man sitting next to her might not have been pretty like Marcus, but there was something übermasculine about him. The confidence that comes with being completely in control of one's world.

"You're one of those guys that's good at fixing things, aren't you?" she guessed.

With an amused look, he turned in his seat to face her. "I happen to come from a long line of electricians. Five generations for the power company, including me dad, me granddad and all me uncles. So say you had something sparking off in your flat, something that would be dangerous for you to manage by yourself. You could ring me, and I would most certainly come round and fix it." And just in case his tone wasn't enough for her to pick up on the sexual innuendo, he looked her up and down, his eyes going over her more thoroughly than an MRI. "Why? You have something that needs fixing?"

Her entire face burned as she answered. "No, I was honestly just asking because, quite frankly, I don't belong here—I won this trip, you see—and since you appear to not *belong here* either, I was just wondering about your background. That's all."

He looked her up and down again, obviously not convinced.

"Really," she added, feeling like he was dissecting her with his eyes. She raised her glass in an effort to change the subject. "Thanks for ordering us the champagne. I'm Kayla, by the way."

"I'm Mick." He clinked his glass against hers. "Yeah, cheers. Here's to moving on."

She took a sip but squinted her eyes at the unusual toast.

"That's what you're doing, right?" he asked. "Moving on from the last guy? Can only assume that's why you're crying into your window if you don't bloody hate planes like meself."

She hesitated, not wanting to divulge too much personal information. But why not? she thought. The champagne felt nice and warm in her stomach, and she'd probably never see this guy again after the plane landed. "Something like that. I was stupid enough to date a football player."

Now he squinted, obviously confused. And she remembered, "Oh, you guys call soccer football over here. I forgot. I meant I was stupid enough to date an American football player. Do you know anything about American football?"

"Only that I'm bollocks at it," he answered.

"Well, I work as a payroll administrator for this American football team called the Los Angeles Suns."

Again with that up-and-down look. "You don't look like any money person I ever met. Guy who does up the money where I work has a pocket protector and a terrible hairpiece."

She laughed. "We have a guy that looks exactly like that in our payroll office, too. It's actually a really unglamorous job, except that about ten percent of the people we cut checks for happen to be football players. That's how I met my ex."

The whole story came out then. She swallowed down the last of her champagne. "But you know, I've learned my lesson. No more liars—and no more football players! Not for me. Luckily, I won this trip for six nights in Paris—I really needed to get out of L.A."

She then realized that she'd been talking for a really long time. Mick, as it turned out, was a really good listener, which she wouldn't have guessed judging by his scruffy appearance or his unconcealed up-and-down looks. Not to mention his offer to fix whatever she had "sparking off."

But he'd seemed genuinely interested in the story and hadn't interrupted her once as it came spilling out. However, her monopolizing the conversation had kept her from finding out much about him, other than what he did for a living. "So how did you come to be in first class listening to me whine about my ex-boyfriend?"

"Won a trip, too," he answered with a shrug. "All expenses paid, including a room at the Paris Grand, but I only got four days, so you win," he paused, looking at her glass. "You're empty." He then signaled for more champagne.

Kayla was still confused. "Even I've heard of the Paris

Grand. That's one of the most expensive places in Paris. And you chose to take this trip alone? No wife or girl-friend?"

"Not one for travel companions. Learned to value the alone time early in life, you might say. I'll probably spend most of the trip in front of the telly, catching up on *Coronation Street* and whatnot." He stopped to study her confused face. "That's an English drama. I think you call 'em soap operas or something like that."

"But it's Paris. I can't believe you'd want to waste such a nice trip watching TV. In fact, just the thought of you spending four days inside your hotel room makes me feel really sad for you. I mean, there's so much to do and see."

"But no one to do it or see it with," he said, looking a bit thoughtful.

She sucked her teeth. "I'm sorry, but I find that really hard to believe. I mean, yeah, you're a little rough around the edges. Okay, a lot rough around the edges. But women really like that. Heck, from the way that flight attendant was flirting with you, I bet you could get her to show you the sights."

He lifted his eyebrows. "I don't want her to show me the sights." He leaned forward. "In fact, the only sights I want to see are right in front of me and currently all covered up," he whispered.

She stared at him for few seconds and then snorted. "You're not serious, right?" She felt a little rude for laughing, but things like this didn't happen to her. Yes, she was cute with some work. She knew that. Marcus had been forever on her about how good she could look if she just tried harder.

But even at her most made-up, she didn't look like the

kind of woman a guy like this would want to see naked. What else could she do but assume he was joking?

"I'm not kidding," he said, his voice suddenly serious. Very, very serious.

Her laughter died abruptly, replaced by shock and something else that had her raising her hand to her throat. His eyes were stuck there, and what she saw in them had her imagining what it would feel like to have his lips kiss her there.

"But we only just met," she whispered.

"Tell you what. You got six nights in Paris. Agree to spend the first of them with me and I'll make it the most memorable."

Her mouth parted on a silent gasp. Was he serious?

And again as if reading her mind, he said, "I'm completely serious. I want you, in my bed. Tonight. Say yes." His eyes bored into hers, making it impossible to look away.

Kayla had to wonder if he was hypnotizing her with those eyes because the next word she heard coming out of her mouth was, in fact, "Yes."

Chapter Two

The American had started having second thoughts as soon as she got off the plane. Mick could tell by the way she said, "Oh, oh, I should go to the bathroom before I go to baggage claim" at the very first airport toilet they encountered.

Also by the way she couldn't quite look him in the eye when she added, "Maybe I'll see you there?"

Mick, who hadn't picked up his own bags from baggage claim in more than a decade, folded his arms over his chest. "Yeah, maybe," he said. "But just in case we miss each other, remember I'm at the Paris Grand. Top floor. Penthouse suite. Only one of those at the Grand far as I know."

"Okay," she said as she backpedaled toward the toilet.

"Name's Mick—don't forget," he called out.

"What?"

"Mick. That's my name. And yours is…?"

"Kayla," she answered quickly, still refusing to meet

his eyes. He noticed she still didn't provide her last name either. "It was…um…nice meeting you."

His eyes stayed on her until she disappeared around the corner. He knew she wouldn't be coming out anytime soon and turned the rejection over again and again inside his head, wondering why it grated at him so much.

He supposed because he wasn't used to it these days. The five minutes he'd spent getting that original "Yes" out of her was about four more minutes longer than he'd had to spend on any other girl in recent memory. Probably wouldn't have taken that long if he hadn't been so thrown by her "No more football players" declaration, which wasn't the same as "No more footballers." Still, he'd suspected that letting the pretty American know he was one of the top soccer players in the English Premier League probably wouldn't help him in achieving his goal of getting into her panties.

A goal he hadn't been so serious about until she started going on and on about how sad it was for him to be sitting in his hotel room when there was so much to do and see and Paris. It had made him—well, actually want to do and see things. With her, the pretty little tourist, who was down about her breakup but genuinely excited about being in Paris. As any everyday person would be.

He supposed that was it. For the short flight, she'd made him feel normal. Normal like her. And he'd found himself wanting to bring her normal back to his hotel with him. Like something he'd ordered from the catalog in the seat pocket in front of him.

He tried to make himself be grateful that she'd reneged on her yes as he walked toward the first-class lounge, even though he knew that someone would be intercepting him before he got there. But he couldn't quite get himself there. A wave of now-familiar loneliness swept over him as he made the same trip he'd made at hundreds of airports around the world.

When the inevitable handler approached him, taking his leather duffel off his shoulder, he found himself saying, "Yeah, mate, when you go to pick up my stuff, there's this woman I'm traveling with. Kayla something or other. Can you have 'em pull her stuff, too? She's American. Hope that's all right."

If the French handler wondered why he would be traveling with an American woman whose last name he didn't know, he was professional enough not to let the confusion show on his face. "Why, of course. I will pull both your baggage and hers, personally see it through customs and have it delivered on to the Grand."

Mick nodded his thanks and tried not to think too hard about what he'd just done to ensure Kayla didn't get away.

"So who's the new girl? Doesn't seem like your usual type," Mick's sports agent, Gerald, said in reply to Mick's surly "What?" after he answered the phone.

Mick had arrived at the hotel more than an hour ago, and their luggage showed up soon after. But still no Kayla. Not even a ring up to the suite.

"What girl?" he asked Gerald, irritation over Kayla's absence prickling his skin. She wouldn't really go on without her bag, would she?

"The girl you were flirting with on the plane," Gerald clarified.

His focus immediately came back to the conversation then. "How'd you know 'bout that?"

"Somebody took a picture of you two chatting, passed it along to some gossip site and now it's all over the web."

"What? You're having a laugh," he said. "We only just got off the plane a couple of hours ago."

"Couple of hours is all it takes these days," Gerald informed him. "One of my other clients got caught giving it to a lady in the rear of his Jaguar after practice. Wife knew about it before he'd even gotten home for supper." Gerald heaved a weary sigh. "It's hard to do damage control most days. You'd want to pay these bloggers not to publish the racy stuff, but they put them up for the world to see before you can even ring in with a monetary offer."

Mick thought of what Kayla had just been through with her ex. He then thanked the stars she was American and would probably never discover her image currently splashed about European gossip sites. "Did they figure out who she was?" he asked, partly out of consideration for Kayla, partly because he was curious to know more about her himself.

"Not yet. That's why I'm calling you. I want to get a comment up."

"You want to leave a comment about the girl I was seen with on a plane?" Mick said, trying to figure out why Gerald would possibly want to do that.

"Yes, of course," Gerald answered, as if the logic of his request was perfectly clear. "You're in France to get wined and dined by a football club that's hoping to poach you, and your own football club has no idea you're even considering moving on. Can you tell me a better way to cover up why you're really there than with just this girl?"

Mick sighed. No, he supposed he couldn't, but he hated all the MI-5 level dramatics that came with playing footie. You'd think it was a matter of life or death the way people treated it, but it was just a game. One he happened to be bloody good at, but a game nonetheless.

"I thought you wanted the club to know Paris was interested."

"I wanted them to know in the midst of salary negotiations. Not a month beforehand when they still have time to replace you with two up-and-comers whose combined salary won't be nearly as much as what I'm planning to ask them for you. If we want them to give us what you're worth, we need an offer from France for them to top. But we've got to play this very wisely. No giving away the whole plot before we've even set down at the negotiating table. So her name, please."

Mick sighed. When he'd started chatting up the lovely woman with the soft voice on the plane, he'd merely been curious about why she was crying. But when he saw her face, those big, long-lashed eyes set off by creamy dark skin and a full mouth, he'd become curious about something else. What would it feel like to have her underneath him? Her skin creating a dark contrast against his as he moved inside her.

No more liars, she'd said.

He hadn't lied to her, he convinced himself now. Not exactly, because it was true—he did hail from a long line of electricians and he was handy around the house. He just happened to make a few million more pounds a year than an electrician, and he never had to fix anything in his mansion on the outskirts of London because he had people who handled that kind of stuff for him.

"I don't know her name exactly," he told his agent, once again choosing to tell only a partial truth. "She's an American."

"Ah. So she has no idea who you are," Gerald said, his voice laced with understanding. "Thinks you're some rough-looking bloke she met on a plane, and you figured, hey, why not take her on for a night."

When he put it like that, Mick felt like a predator who got off on converting good girls into bedpost notches, though he supposed that wasn't too far off from the truth. "Something like that."

"In that case, why don't you expand that nighter to the length of your trip? You can have some fun off the field, and she's a great cover story."

"Gerald, I'm not even sure if…"

He was going to say he wasn't even sure if he could make the one night even happen, given how they'd parted. But then the suite's doorbell sounded, and when he opened the door, he found Kayla standing there with Jacques, an older gentleman in a neat red suit who had earlier introduced himself as his personal concierge for the length of his stay.

"Mick? Mick?" Gerald said into his ear.

"I'll call you back," he said and quickly hung up the phone.

"I know this is highly unusual," Jacques was saying, "but you asked that she be sent up, and you dismissed your butler, so I had no choice but to escort her myself."

Apparently in Jacques's mind sending a guest up by herself wasn't an option that existed within the reality of luxury hotels that assigned butlers to their penthouse suites.

Mick's eyes went to Kayla, and her hands moved up to cling to the strap of her large, practical purse as if she was prepared to bolt at any moment. But she stayed where she was, even after Mick dismissed Jacques with a thank-you.

"So you took my bag?" she asked when Jacques had left.

Mick wasn't trying to make her any more skittish than

she already was, but he couldn't resist taking yet another long, dragged-out look over her curvy, petite body.

"You said yes," he said, trying and only slightly succeeding in not feeling like a perv when he reminded her of her earlier choice. Nearly any other girl in England would have happily come back to his room, he told himself. "And as far as I knew, you were planning to keep your word. So I got your bags sorted, assuming you'd be coming back here with me. But if we're being honest, I was beginning to think you'd never show."

She winced. "If we're being honest, I almost didn't come. I'm a practical person. I've had a regular nine-to-five since graduating college. I live below my means, I drive a Camry and I pay all my bills on time. I've only done three impractical things in my life. One was dating a professional football player, and that was only because I really did believe he was a normal Midwestern boy at heart. The second thing was taking this trip, and that was only because I won it. I never would have done anything like this, especially on my own if I had to pay for it out of pocket…"

She trailed off into nervous silence.

"And what's the third thing, then?"

She peeked up at him. "Saying yes to you."

Mick didn't know whether to be insulted or amused that she was fighting herself so hard about sleeping with him. Sure, she didn't know who he was, but it wasn't as if he would have had a hard time pulling women if he didn't have the professional soccer thing going for him. "You didn't believe I could make coming here worth your while."

She put a hand on his arm and shook her head, like an adult reassuring a child whose feelings she'd hurt. "No, I'm sure you have skills. You look like the kind of guy who has them. I'm just trying to explain that going back to some random guy's hotel room is way out of character for me, and I'd had two glasses of champagne. So I did the practical thing and stayed in the bathroom for a while, then after I discovered you'd taken my bag, I went to my hotel to rest. It usually takes an hour for each glass of alcohol to wear off, you know, and I wanted to make sure the champagne wasn't making me stupid."

Mick prepared to respond to her explanation with grudging respect, even as he braced himself for the letdown. He'd never met her before, but he was beginning to recognize her from his past. He'd known girls like this back when he was just Mick Attwater, the unfortunate son of his town's two most notorious drunks. Girls who never got in trouble for hemming up their uniform skirts, girls who kept their hair pulled back in neat ponytails, girls who would go on to sixth form and eventually university, girls who came from homes with two stable parents who didn't drink themselves into screaming arguments near about every night until they either passed out or the police were called round by the neighbors.

Happy, well-adjusted girls who didn't give guys like him from sad, ill-adjusted homes the time of day.

"So you only came here because the alcohol wore off."

"And I didn't want to leave my suitcase. It's got all my clothes, and I hear Paris is pretty expensive, so I didn't know if I'd be able to afford a whole new vacation wardrobe. Also, my e-reader's inside of there, and even though I was planning on sightseeing, I'll need a good book to get to sleep—"

He held up a hand to stop her rambling explanation. "So your answer's changed to 'no' now? You're just going to tail it back to your room and read a book, that it?"

Her eyes widened with surprise. "Oh, no, the answer's still 'yes.' I mean, I'm not that brave. If I had decided against sleeping with you, I never would have come here. Also—"

He cut her off again. This time with a kiss, dragging her body up to his and finally letting himself have a taste of her full lips. She tasted like the bowl of fruit she'd eaten on the plane, plus the champagne. Sweet. Just like he'd known she would.

To his immense satisfaction, after a moment of surprise, she wrapped her arms around his neck and kissed him back so fervently his cock swelled against her stomach. He found himself having to drag his lips away before he lost control and took her right there outside his hotel room.

But at least he no longer had to wonder if they'd be any good in bed together. He knew right then…they'd set it on fire.

"I think you had better come in," he said.

Chapter Three

Kayla's mouth fell open as she took in Mick's penthouse suite. Blue-and-gold Oriental carpets adorned the floors and went perfectly with the red and gold-trimmed baroque furniture. The vanilla walls featured oil paintings so finely rendered that even an art history know-nothing like Kayla could tell they were genuinely old and probably had a price tag to match.

She couldn't stop gaping as she followed Mick into the suite's main room. It looked more like a magazine spread than an actual place where human beings were expected to live, even for a short time. The view of the city beyond the floor-to-ceiling windows on the side wall looked like nothing short of a postcard, with the Eiffel Tower all lit up in seeming greeting. She could barely believe it was real.

"Wow, your prize package is a lot better than mine. My hotel room's like a coffin."

"Yeah, I guess it's all right," Mick said, walking over

to a full-service bar with a stock of high-end liquors and a selection of red wines she had no doubt hailed from the finest vineyards in France.

Kayla goggled at the backlit bar. "Yeah, your prize package is waaaayyyy better than mine."

"They put some champagne in the fridge. Want some?"

She came over to stand on the other side of the bar. "No, don't open anything. Do you know how much they charge for that stuff?"

"No," he answered as he grabbed the bottle of Krug Brut from the fridge and popped it open anyway, smoothly catching the liquid that came spilling out in one flute, which he handed to her. "Do you?"

"Well…no, not exactly," she admitted. "But I'm fairly sure it's a lot."

He shrugged. "Don't worry about it. This hotel's so posh, it's probably lumped with the rest of it, innit?"

She frowned, the numbers girl in her finding it too hard not to speak up. "I'm pretty sure it isn't. That's not how fancy hotels work."

He leaned forward then, placing his elbows on the bar. "Are we or are we not on holiday?"

"Yes, but—"

"Good, we're agreed. Drink your bubbly."

She took a sip of champagne, partly because she didn't want it to go to waste now that it was already open. But also because it gave her something to do now that she was actually in an insanely fancy hotel room. With a stranger named Mick. Preparing to have sex with the first person other than Marcus in four years.

Thinking of Marcus caused a sudden shadow to fall over her heart.

"Tell you what," he said, coming around the bar with

his glass of champagne. "If you're going to think of some other guy every time I give you champagne, we're going to switch this out for a couple of pints."

"Pints of what?" she asked, her thoughts of Marcus dissipating as she watched his lean body come toward her with athletic grace. Strange because the way he walked reminded her of some of the quarterbacks she'd seen.

"Beer," he answered. "That's my usual. But in my experience, girls don't like it."

She screwed up her face. "I hate beer."

"Proving me point. And I don't mind champagne, so a compromise we can all live with, right? Except you're looking like you're about to start crying again, and I can't have that. Not only does it kill the mood, but it's also a waste of nice champagne, innit?"

As sad as she'd been mere moments ago, she found herself fighting back laughter now. "Why are you laughing?" he asked. "I'm serious."

"I know you are," she said. And on an impulse, she stood on her tiptoes and tentatively kissed him.

She'd meant it as an innocent peck, but when she came back down to the heels of her feet, his whole face had changed, and what was burning in his eyes wasn't innocent at all. The look he was giving her now was steady and primal and made her think of the kiss in the doorway, the way his rigid length had pressed against her stomach, scaring her and thrilling her at the same time.

"All right then," he said, taking the glass of champagne back from her.

He tossed both of their glasses seemingly without a care for where they landed in the opulent room. She heard two thunks in the distance, and then Mick had enveloped her in a clench that seemed to be both a kiss and a method of clothes removal. His lips barely left hers, but before she knew it, her top had gone the way of her champagne flute and her broom skirt was in a cotton puddle on the floor.

But then he stopped and stepped back, his eyes taking in her kelly-green underwear and the matching bra. Self-consciousness began to douse the heat from their second kiss. It was excruciating, watching him observe her like this, and her arms came up to cover her chest.

But he knocked her arms back to her sides and gently kept them pinned there as he continued to stare. Then they just stood like that, his large hands on her wrists, his dark eyes on her body.

"Wall or floor?" he asked.

"Excuse me?"

"We're not going to make it to the bed." He finally took his eyes off her body and repeated. "Wall or floor?"

Kayla swallowed. She was not the kind of girl who had sex on the floor or up against walls. "How about the couch?" she asked.

He gave her a very feral smile. "So you want me to make the decision for you, do ya?"

"But the couch is right there—"

Her back hit the nearby wall, and his lips were once again on hers. And also once again, his kiss was hot but multipurpose. He took out his wallet and pulled something out of it before tossing it aside. Vaguely she realized it was a condom as he pushed down his jeans and boxer briefs. She soon felt the hooded tip of him press against her stomach but only for a few tantalizing seconds before he was sheathing it in thin plastic.

After that piece of business was taken care of, he cupped his hands around her nape and pushed his tongue deeper into her mouth, effectively short-circuiting every practical thought in her head. There was no room to think about anything but him. One hand came down from her neck and slipped inside her panties to find her core. Then two of his fingers were pushing inside of her like his tongue was pushing inside her mouth. It felt so good to have him touch her like this, and she felt herself clench hard around his fingers as he moved them inside her with a few strokes.

But then he broke off with a curse. "You're already wet."

She blinked in confusion. Was that a bad thing?

"I promised you a good time, but I'm not going to be able to…" He pulled his fingers out of her and stroked her nape. "I'll make it up to you later tonight, baby, I swear."

Make up what to her? She was ready to ask when he jerked down her panties and thrust himself inside of her with a forceful stroke that moved her entire body upward. It should have hurt, there'd been barely any foreplay beyond kisses, but he'd been right about how wet she was, and despite the thickness of his length, which stretched her wider than she'd ever thought possible, he felt right inside of her, like he belonged there. She welcomed every inch of him, her core pulsing with the pleasure of his invasion.

She might be a prim-and-proper payroll assistant, but at least one part of her was a very bad girl. She couldn't wait for him to start moving himself inside of her, the way he'd moved his fingers there earlier.

However, Mick shut his eyes and held himself very still, almost as if he was overcome by something…or trying to get a hold of himself.

"Mick?" she said. She'd meant it to be a question, like "Are you all right?" But her womanhood was clenching around him, trying to compel him to start moving. So what was meant as a question came out with a moan attached.

That was it. Mick picked up both her legs and placed

them around his waist before pinning her hips to the wall with his hard strokes, so rough and fast she had to cling to him, feeling as if she'd topple sideways if she didn't hold on.

But then Mick dug in deeper, pressing the rough sandpaper of his five-o'clock shadow into her chest as he drove into her, again and again, relentless in his attack until she exploded, the pleasure so overwhelming her entire body seized up.

The land mines inside of them seemed to be connected because Mick came just seconds after her climax hit, as if he'd been holding himself back, like a dog on a chain, so that she could come first.

He surged inside of her, yelling out as he released inside the condom. He cursed again. But this time Kayla knew it was because he was surprised by how impassioned and all-consuming their coming together had been and not because he was displeased.

She knew because she felt the same way.

Chapter Four

Mick knew he was making Kayla nervous as he sat across from her eating the veal chops he'd had sent up. If he'd been even half a gentleman, one of those guys who'd been raised to treat a woman nice and proper, he'd have attempted some small talk or at least answered her questions about his "prize package" with something other than "Yeah," "No" and "Not sure."

But the truth was, he was rattled. He'd thought he was the one roping the skittish American into his web, but now it was him feeling unnerved as he tried to work his mind around what had happened between them.

What the bloody hell was wrong with him? He'd meant to show her a good time, give her a story to take back to her friends. Instead she'd kissed him once, and it had been enough to make him lose control, taking her against the wall like a rutting beast. As opposed to an international soccer star who'd slept with more than his fair share of women.

What must she think of him now? Mr. Big Talk about how he would do her in bed turning out to be little more than an animal who could barely control himself.

Maybe it was her body. He'd not known what to expect, given the bulky nature of her orange-and-yellow American football T-shirt. But he'd found lovely and large breasts, Greek goddess hips and a derriere so expansive it could barely be contained by the boy shorts she was wearing. The perfect package, all wrapped up in a bright green underwear set.

It actually made him angry when she tried to shield herself from his eyes. Because why would any woman with a body like hers ever want to cover themselves up?

If he hadn't been so baffled by how fast things had gone between them, he wouldn't have let her put the T-shirt and skirt that had done her assets such a disservice back on. As it was, he wanted to burn the clothes she was wearing and then engage a barrister to sue the companies that had made them for defamation.

He also wanted to see her naked again. He could barely eat, could barely let her finish eating before wondering what her breasts looked like under the bra. His urgent need to be inside her hadn't let him remove it before taking her against the wall. Again, what the bloody hell was wrong with him?

Suddenly she was getting up, placing her cloth napkin down on the table.

"Where are you going?" he asked.

"I'm sorry I've overstayed my welcome," she answered. "I mean, when you ordered dinner, I thought, I don't know, that you actually wanted to have dinner with me. But you're barely talking, and I can see now you were just being nice and that I should have left after…" She didn't finish her sentence. Instead she rubbed her hand over her forehead. "I'm sorry. I haven't dated in a really long time—not that we're dating. Oh, God, I'm so not good at this. I'm sorry. I'm just going to go, okay?"

He caught her by the wrist and stood. "What do you want for breakfast tomorrow?"

She shook her head as if his question had only mortified her more. "You don't have to offer that just to be nice, and I should probably be getting back to my hotel anyway," she said, trying to tug her wrist away.

But he held on to her tighter, feeling along the lines of a kidnapper, but he was unable to physically let her go. "What just happened against the wall—we were both there, right? Do you really think there's any way in hell I don't want that to happen again?"

The urgent desire he was feeling at that moment must have translated onto his face because she stopped trying to get her hand back.

"But you were so quiet during dinner…"

"…because I knew you were probably hungry after that. Because I was holding myself from sweeping the table and taking you again on top of it. Because I'd rather be talking about how to make you come than just about anything else right now. Finish that sentence any way you want to, Kayla. But know that it's not because I don't want you here."

He pulled her to him and shuddered when her soft breasts pressed against his chest, even though they were covered up by that crap T-shirt. "I more than want you here. I can barely think, I want you here so bad."

He brought the hand he had trapped to the front of his pants and pushed it down past his waistband, where the beast he'd been trying to keep at bay all through dinner resided. "Feel for yourself what you do to me."

Her eyes widened, and he thought she might snatch her hand away and accuse him of being a pervert for making her touch him this way. But instead she gave it a squeeze, almost exploratory in nature, before running her hand up his entire length. But she stopped at the hooded top, running her thumb over its hole.

"Something wet's coming out, but it's not…" Her face scrunched up with curious confusion. "What is that?"

He unzipped his jeans, not only to give her more room to keep doing what she was doing, but also so she could see what was coming out of the head of his penis.

"Pre-cum. Means I'm excited. Real excited," he answered, battling with himself to stay still. He had thought she might stop if he didn't keep still. "You've never had a man want you so bad, he starts leaking like this when you touch him?"

She shook her head. "There weren't a lot of guys before my ex, and he never…."

He immediately knew that her ex was either gay or stupid. Probably both. But one thing was obvious—Kayla, a fantasy come true in just her bra and knickers, was wasted on a knob like that. Mick could only steal glances at her dark hand, stroking his pale flesh, without fear of coming quickly and helplessly like a schoolboy.

"You can keep on doing that," he told her, "but if you do, it's going to be more than pre-cum. You're going to get the real deal—my spunk all over your pretty little hand."

She looked away from him then but she didn't stop. And soon his dick spasmed in her hand.

He moved his head in front of hers, only to have her look to the other side. But she kept on stroking. He once again placed his face directly in front of her, and this time when she tried to turn her head, he gently grabbed her around the nape so she had no choice but to look at him.

"I like this," he told her. "I like you."

"I believe you," she whispered. "I like you, too."

I like you, too. His dick contracted with almost painful tightness, and he threw back his head before geysering, as promised, all over her hand.

When he opened his eyes he smiled. Not just because this sweet girl had given him the best hand job he'd ever had the pleasure of experiencing but because at least one of his wishes had just come true.

"Looks like I ruined your shirt," he said with no apology whatsoever in his voice. "We better take it off."

Chapter Five

Kayla might have thought the hand job would slow Mick down, but there was only a moment of calm before he slammed into her like a Mack truck. His lips smacked into hers and she had no choice but to stumble backward as he pushed her toward what she guessed was the bedroom. Her clothes went flying in every direction as he stripped them off of her, and she soon found out that she'd guessed right when he tossed her completely naked onto a bed covered in a billowy white comforter and several plush pillows.

The bed was so soft that it felt like landing on a cloud. Cloud nine, with a chorus of heavenly music going off in her head as she thanked her lucky stars that she'd taken Mick up on his offer.

But the man standing above her, yanking his T-shirt off over his head, was no angel. He'd already taken off his pants, and Kayla sat up on her elbows to stare at the long rod of flesh between his legs. Even spent, it was pretty intimidating, and she was glad the first time had happened so fast because she might have backed out if she'd had a chance to observe it beforehand.

After he got his shirt off, his eyes went to her uncovered breasts, studying them as if they were a work of art. A work of art he was very interested in possessing. To her surprise, his cock rose all the way up to full mast, pointing in the direction of her womanhood like an erotic arrow. She remembered how it had felt to have him moving inside her, filling her up so thoroughly, and her whole body tingled with sweet anticipation.

This time he seemed to be in no hurry. His eyes stayed on her breasts as he leaned over and put one of the orbs in his mouth. His lips encased her entire areola as his tongue pulled on her nipple. One of his hands reached down and cupped her down below with a casualness that belied how profoundly erotic it felt to have his hand down there while his mouth worked her breast.

But just as she was starting to squirm from the sensations he was giving her, he let go of her breast. "Almost forgot. I promised to make it up to you, didn't I?"

Oh, she'd say he was more than making it up. But he stood and parted her thighs, running his hands down the soft and sensitive insides. His eyes then swept down to the triangle between her legs.

When she realized what he was about to do, she quickly sat back up on her arms, slightly alarmed. "Oh, you don't have to do that. I'm fine with just— Oh!"

He wrapped his hands under her thighs and pulled her toward him with a rough jerk. And before she could protest any further, he was sucking the bud between her legs into his mouth liked he'd sucked on her breast just moments earlier.

Only this time he tugged harder. A shock wave of concentrated pleasure zapped her so hard that her hips bucked underneath his face.

"Shh…" he said, his mouth staying on her despite her sudden movement. He placed a heavy arm over her pelvis, effectively pinning her there while his tongue assaulted her with pleasure. For several minutes there was nothing but the sound of him sucking on her most sensitive part, of his tongue lapping the insides of her wet folds.

"Stop! Stop!" she called out, her hands fisting in the sheets as the top half of her body rolled and twisted on top of the comforter. "I can't take any more. It feels too good—"

The orgasm split her in two, and this time even Mick couldn't hold her down when she arched off the bed. But he didn't seem to mind. He kept his mouth on her, following her into the air and delving even deeper into her core. He plunged his tongue in and out of her, prolonging the orgasm until every nerve in her entire body was lit up with the sensation of coming.

Tears sprang to Kayla's eyes. She had never felt anything like this in her entire life. Not with Marcus. Not with anybody, and it was hard to believe that she had gone her entire boring life without knowing this feeling. The tears took on a new dimension then, and no matter how hard she bit down on her lip, she couldn't stop the sob that escaped. Or the complete collapse into tears that came after that.

That was when Mick finally stopped. He set her down carefully, and she rolled onto her side.

"Please stop crying," she heard him say above her. He sounded both distressed and angry.

"I'm trying to. I'm sorry. I'm so sorry," she said, her voice breaking on the apology.

She curled into a fetal position and tried to quell her emotions. But she just couldn't stop crying, no matter how embarrassing it was to be doing so in the bed of a sexy stranger who had just given her more pleasure than she ever thought possible.

The bed depressed beside her. "Seriously, baby, I can't…"

"I'm trying to stop," she nearly yelled, she was so upset about the situation and utterly embarrassed.

The next thing she knew, she was being pulled out of the fetal position and into Mick's strong arms. He lay down with her on the overly pillowed bed and held her tight against him, stroking the back of her head as she sobbed. And for minutes on end she continued to cry, her tears falling onto his bare chest.

"I tell you what—this does not make a lad feel great about his performance," he said when she finally calmed down.

She shook her head against his chest. "It wasn't you. I mean it was you. You made me feel good. Too good. I've never… Marcus only ever did that for me on my birthday, and even then he was reluctant. I thought maybe I tasted bad—I actually went to the doctor a few of months ago just to make sure I didn't have anything."

"That's his name, is it? Marcus?"

She nodded against his chest.

"Sounds like a wanker."

"I'm not sure what that is, but if it means asshole, then yes, he was one of those and a liar. I was an idiot for staying with him as long as I did."

"Tell you what, I'll come to the States and take him out for you. Punch to the nose, kick in the goolies, head butt. You name it, and I'll do it to this wanker right good. But just so you know, I've been told my head butts are particularly impressive."

A soft laugh escaped her throat then.

"Why are you laughing? I'm serious."

"Electrician from London, and you want to take your first trip to America just to beat up my ex and probably get arrested right after that?"

"I could find the dosh somewhere, and I'm good at talking the other guy into hitting first. If he hits first, it's self-defense—saw that on an old episode of that *Law & Order* show."

Earlier it had been tears, but now she couldn't control her laughter.

"I'm sorry," she said when she finally got over her fit of giggles. "For crying. But thanks for making me laugh. I needed that."

"It would probably only make you laugh harder if I told you at no point today have I actually tried to make you laugh."

He let her go and reached over to the nightstand to turn off the lights. She watched his sinewy body framed against the Eiffel Tower's light as he threw what had to be at least a dozen pillows off the bed before tucking a medium-size white one beneath his head. "I'm knocking off."

Her laughter instantly subsided. Was he going to kick her out? But before she could contemplate leaving, he hauled her right back up against him again. They both settled into a new position—him on his back, her tucked against his left side, her head lying on his chest.

They lay there like that in the silent room, the sound of Mick's heartbeat, calm and steady against her ear, for a long while. So long she thought he had fallen asleep.

"How long?" His voice was quiet and more subdued now.

She didn't pretend that she didn't know what he was talking about. "Four years," she answered. "We were together for four years."

"That's a long time," he said. His voice was monotone and she wished she could see his face to observe how he felt.

"Yeah, I know. It's a long time to go out with someone without getting married."

"Long time for any kind of relationship. Don't even have mates I held on to that long."

"Maybe because you keep head-butting them."

He laughed. "Yeah, maybe. Truth is I do have a few fights on my record, but the boys in the big offices had me do one of 'em anger-management courses."

"And that worked?" she asked, thinking of the many Suns football players who'd been forced to take a few classes after game fights or charges had been filed. Nearly all of them had gone on to rack up even more game fights, criminal charges or both.

"Sure," he answered. "Maybe because I wanted it, too, though. After a while all the fighting's not so fun anymore. Now I got mantras and such to keep me from blowing the lid of m' pot. But still don't have many mates. Guess I got used to going about in the world on my own."

"Seriously?" she asked, thinking of Suzie and all of her friends and family back in Inglewood. "I've known some of my friends since before kindergarten. My boss went to high school with me. She was president of the math club and I was the treasurer. And our moms have been friends since they were in high school."

"That's nice." His voice seemed a little distant now. "You have roots."

"Nice and not nice," she said, stroking his chest. "They

were more than a little impressed about me dating a football player. The Suns are a big deal in Los Angeles, and my boy cousins think Marcus hung the moon just because he gets to wear the uniform on game day. I'm sure they think he cheated on me because I wasn't sexy enough and didn't dress like all the other football player's girlfriends. A lot of them were TV stars and models, and I tried, but at the end of the day, I was just…well, me."

He sighed and shifted her off of his chest. She immediately realized her mistake. "I'm sorry. I'm sorry," she said for the umpteenth time that night. "I shouldn't have brought him up again."

He turned on his side toward her, his hands finding her shoulders. "Listen, I've run into people like Marcus. I know the deal with them. The crowds build them up, right? Make them think they're better than everyone else, yeah, just 'cos they can handle a ball. They start to think they're the soddin' queen of England. But I tell you what, at the end of day, it's people like them who're the idiots and people like you who…"

He stopped.

But she had to know. "People like me who what?"

"Never mind," he answered, turning back over on his back. "Let's knock off."

"No, I want to know."

"Conversation over, Kayla." He seemed almost angry with himself as he folded his arms over his chest.

Kayla sighed and settled in on her own side of the bed, feeling a chill pass over her now that she didn't have his body heat to keep her warm.

She sat up and to her surprise, he sat up, too. "What you doing?" he asked.

"I'm cold."

"And…"

"And so I'm getting under the comforter," she answered carefully. "Which is what people do when they're cold, especially when they're not wearing any clothes."

He seemed to consider that. "I'm not wearing any clothes either. How about if I get cold? I'm a big guy but I'm just as susceptible to a middle-of-the-night chill as the next bloke. Nobody likes to wake up freezing, but it feels like you're setting me up for just that scenario, don't it? So, Kayla, what if I wake up freezing. What then?"

She bit her lip, determined not to start laughing again. "Then you get under the covers, just like I'm about to do."

"Or…"

Even in the dark, she could make out that he was beckoning her to lay back down with him.

She happily came back to his side of the bed and settled into the position they'd been in before. For a little bit.

"Or maybe we should both get under the covers."

"Shh!" he answered.

"I mean, it's the most practical thing to do."

"Trying to sleep here," he said, drawing her in even closer.

So that's what they did, as Kayla thought that she would have never guessed that the dangerous-looking, sexy man she met on the plane that afternoon would be such an avid fan of cuddling.

Chapter Six

For as long as he could remember Mick had had trouble sleeping. When he was young, it was the raging arguments his parents would get into, often right after he'd put himself to bed. He'd wake up in the middle of the night to absolute quiet and become convinced that his parents had killed each other in an alcoholic rage, as they'd both been threatening to do while he'd drifted off to sleep.

He'd go downstairs, find them both passed out like boxers after a knockout fight and go back up to his room. Then he'd be unable to get back to sleep, and so it went—until he got signed for Bristol United's Youth Training Scheme. He had been able to leave his parents behind at the age of seventeen.

But he still hadn't been able to sleep all that well after that. At first there had been parties, living it up, enjoying the life of a young footballer. Then when he got older, sick of the parties and the never-ending stream of women willing to go off with him because of who he was, he'd wake up in the middle of the night feeling lonely.

He'd find himself seething with jealousy toward the guys who had married their secondary school sweethearts. The ones with kids, the ones who didn't have to come home to a gorgeous but empty multimillion dollar home every night.

The truth was that more than a decade after escaping his parents' house he still yearned for the same thing he had wanted when he'd lived there. A normal life, a normal family. But normal girls didn't exactly run in his circles.

Even the ones he encountered, the ones from upstanding families, the ones who had no idea what it felt like to have the police come round to your house at three in the morning and congratulate you on your last game as they took your father away to sleep off his drink in the local hold-up. Even those good girls turned out to be more interested in the flash life he could provide them than the star player, who used to average at least five fights a season and had never managed to posh up his accent.

So no, sleep had continued to be something he struggled with every night. Until he had managed to fall asleep easily with Kayla in his arms. That night he slept better than he could remember without the aid of the pills the football club's doctor had prescribed him. But this had been better than that drug-induced blackness. This had been a peaceful, deep sleep, one accompanied by dreams of the sexy American riding on top of him, her hips undulating as he played with her heavy breasts.

He hadn't been surprised to wake up from that dream with a tent in the sheet, which she'd apparently put over him some time during the night. But he had been surprised by the time—it was after nine in the morning. Even when he took an Ambien, his body usually jerked awake before six.

He checked his phone. Three missed calls from an unknown number with a French country code and six from Gerald, probably wondering why he hadn't shown up at the French team's practice facilities yet. They could wait he decided, dropping the phone back on the nightstand.

First, he wanted to see about making that dream come true with the woman who had been responsible for his first good night of sleep in years. But he rolled over to find nothing but white bed linens. He sat up in bed, his eyes immediately going to the corner where he'd left her suitcase. It was gone.

He cursed. She'd done a runner, and he couldn't blame her. All that pillow talk last night, him confessing his fight history and that he had no real mates right before he insisted on snuggling with her because he liked the feel of her body and also because he didn't want her to cover it up—he must have come off like a right mad nutter. No wonder she'd run the first chance she got.

Just then the door flew open, and Kayla came through, carrying a cardboard cup holder with two coffees and a bag with the name of a patisserie written on it in refined blue letters.

"Sorry for the door bang," she said. "I got us some croissants—or I guess I'm supposed to say *croissant*. Then it took forever to find coffee because every place I went acted like they didn't even understand the concept of a to-go cup. *Then* I could barely get to the front lobby because there were all these men with cameras outside." She set the coffee and croissants down on a nearby table. "Can you believe they started taking my picture and asking me all these questions in French? Only thing I understood was 'What's your name' and that's because it's all over my French phrase book."

His heart froze. "What did you say?"

She grinned as she tore the tops off two packets of sugar and poured them in one of the cups of coffee. "I told them my name was Beyoncé. I mean, obviously they're not used to seeing black people go into an expensive hotel, so they'd probably thought I just had to be famous."

Relief coursed through Mick's entire body. "Maybe next time you leave, you should go through the garage entrance. Jacques, the concierge, said that's what all the famous people do."

"The real famous people? Not the ones just claiming they're Beyoncé?" she clarified with an impish smile.

He couldn't help but smile back, albeit weakly. "Fake famous people can use that entrance, too. 'Cording to Jacques, a lot of paparazzi hang around this place, so sometimes it's the only way to avoid them."

It was true that a lot of paparazzi hung out outside the Paris Grand, but it was also true that if there were really as many as she'd described, they were most likely here because they knew he was staying here, and she'd probably caused a frenzy when she'd come in the hotel with breakfast.

Though he was having a hard time getting overly worried about that because the fact was she'd left, but she'd come back. And to him, that was all that mattered at that moment.

"Are you okay?" she asked, probably a little perturbed by the stupid grin on his face. Her eyes then went down to the sheet she'd thrown over him and her full lips formed into an O in surprise.

"I'm sorry—I didn't realize you..." She stammered

some more, but she didn't take her eyes off the tent in the sheet. Finally she bit her lip and asked tentatively, "Do you need help with that?"

His erection pulsed underneath the sheet. "Know what," he said. "I'll take any help you're willing to give."

She put down the coffee she'd been about to sip. And he watched as she pulled off her Suns tank top, uncovering a cherry-red bra with pink piping around its edges. Next came her Bermuda shorts, which revealed a matching pair of bikini briefs. She looked like a boring girl with a boring job through and through on the outside, but she knew very well how to dress underneath. The cherry-and-pink ensemble displayed her heavily rounded breasts and ample backside perfectly, like dessert.

A dessert he wanted to lick all over.

He liked watching her, wanted to see what she would do next. So he leaned back on his forearms and forced himself to wait for her to come to him.

She walked to the bed and removed the sheet. Then her eyes widened when she saw his erection, standing straight up and throbbing like a wild thing. A wild thing only she could tame.

She studied it like a math problem that needed solving. "I could…"

She took him in her hand and worked it up and down a few times before she shook her head and said, "But no, I already did that."

Truth was, he wouldn't have minded another hand job. His body had thrilled at her touch, then ached when she'd stopped. But that was before she crawled onto the bed and positioned herself between his legs.

He drew in his breath with a sharp hiss when she took

him in her mouth. And a bolt of red-hot pleasure pulsed through his shaft as she worked her lips down it.

Usually this was the part where he closed his eyes and concentrated on the sensations of being attended to in this way by whoever was down there. But this time he couldn't take his eyes off of Kayla. Her gorgeous ass in the air, her eyes looking up at him while her head bobbed up and down on his manhood.

"Baby…" he said. Mesmerized by the delicious picture she was making, he reached down to grasp the back of her head, guiding her into a nice rhythm.

That was a mistake because it soon became too much, and he pulled himself out of her mouth with a curse.

Kayla looked distressed. "Did I do something wrong?"

"No, I just…" He reached into the nightstand and grabbed a condom. He was so close it was a wonder he didn't come in his own bloody hand before getting it on. But the promise of what was awaiting him if he held out got him through. Moments later he was hauling her into a sitting position. He placed her legs around his waist and pulled her cherry-red underwear down just enough…then he was exactly where he wanted to be. Inside of her, pistoling up into her, even as he unhooked her bra and threw it to the side. An action that allowed her magnificent set to rub against his chest as she rolled her hips to meet his thrust.

The slap of their bodies was the only sound in the room as they both sought out an unnameable thing in each other, using gravity, friction and whatever physics were required until they came at the same time. Her with a happy cry, him with an urgent groan.

Only then did Mick close his eyes, convulsing into her and shuddering to a conclusion with his arms wrapped hard around her soft, beautiful body.

They breathed hard, clinging to each other as they came down.

"Did that help?" she asked against his shoulder. She was joking, of course, but he could already feel himself growing harder inside her.

"Only a bit, I'm afraid," he answered, dropping a kiss on her shoulder. "I might need your help again in just a few minutes."

Chapter Seven

Kayla was trying hard not to get used to this as she and Mick sat in the bathroom's blue-lit, rectangular Jacuzzi tub, covered in bubbles. Thanks to the half a bottle of perfumed bath soap he had spilled into the bath after not one, not two, but three bouts of morning sex—the third one being mostly her fault—she still managed to feel fresh. She'd once again tried to return the favor of the amazing oral sex he'd given her the night before, and he'd once again ended up inside of her, this time rolling her over on her back and rutting her so thoroughly, she finally understood the meaning of "caveman sex."

He'd actually been apologetic afterward. *Can't seem to keep my hands off of you long enough to let you finish the job, baby,* he'd said. Then he'd insisted that she "deserved a good soak after all that" and that they both needed to eat. But the croissants and coffee had gone cold, so he'd ignored her protests about the cost and ordered room service.

Now here they were in the prettiest-smelling bath she'd ever taken, her back nestled against his chest, while he fed both himself and her strawberries off the plate he'd had sent up. She then reminded herself that this was only a vacation with a very finite end. She should in no way get used to it.

Determined to make this scene a little less romantic, she reached toward the plate and grabbed a square of chocolate only to have it gently slapped out of her hand. "What you doing?" he asked behind her.

"I was just going to unwrap one of those squares of chocolate," she answered. "I can feed myself."

"See, that's why you'd be better off letting me do the heavy lifting when it comes to this breakfast business," he said while deftly unwrapping the chocolate himself.

He then tore off a third of one of the croissants and buttered it. "Here's how you do it. Take your buttered bread. Open it up and put the bit of chocolate in between like so, and voilà, you got the best breakfast this side of the Atlantic."

She bit into the piece of croissant he put up to her lips, and her taste buds reeled; the butter and chocolate melting together in her mouth tasted so good. "Oh, my gosh, I can't believe we don't eat them that way in America."

"Lots of things are hard to believe about America. You don't like our kind of football over there either. How's that?"

"Well," she said, pretending to give his question serious consideration. "American football is interesting and exciting with really funny commercials in between. While your kind of football is let me see…insanely boring. Even the cute guys aren't worth watching go back and forth on a field, barely ever scoring."

She felt him go still behind her.

"You really hate football that much?"

"No, not really," she answered. "I guess when it comes down to it, I don't feel any kind of way toward it. Just, you know, meh."

She expected him to return her disinterest with some extreme comment of his own. She'd heard Europeans were as caught up in soccer as Americans were in their kind of football. But instead he asked, "So if a big footballer came along, someone with real flash and enough money to stay at this place without somebody else having to put up the dosh—the kind of footballer them paps outside would be gagging to get a picture of—if one of 'em had also put it to you on that plane, you're saying you'd be like, 'Thanks for the offer, mate, but I'd rather with this one. Toodle-loo.'"

She squinted because she wasn't sure she completely understood the question. "Are you asking me if I'd rather get with a famous soccer player than with you?"

"Yeah."

"No," she said, her answer immediate. "First of all, I don't ever want to get with any kind of player ever again, especially one in the limelight. Football, baseball, soccer. I don't care. I did it once and I'll never set myself up like that again. As far as I can tell, even the ones who seem nice are liars and cheats."

The warm water sloshed against her as she turned around to face him. "And second of all, I don't want to sound too forward, but I like you. And it's not just about the sex. I think you're kind and smart and funny…" Her cheeks heated with self-consciousness, but she pressed on. "I mean, you're a really great and down-to-earth guy, and I'd rather watch you fix a downed electric power line than watch any kind of sports star play whatever he plays any day of the week."

He abruptly set her away from him before climbing out of the bath.

"Mick?" she said.

He didn't answer. Instead she watched as he dried off his large body with a towel. The beginning of the erection that she'd felt earlier in the bath was long gone.

"Mick?" she called again.

He left the bathroom without a word of explanation, leaving Kayla alone in the bath to feel not only awkward, but also really, really embarrassed.

She took her time draining the bath and thoroughly drying off. But she needn't have stalled. When she stepped into the bedroom, she found Mick had also vacated that room. Why had she said that? She hadn't known the man even twenty-four hours and she'd already gone completely moony-eyed over him. All because he was great in bed, made her laugh and had held her while she cried over her ex-boyfriend the night before.

This is why you can't have nice things, she told herself as she gathered up her clothes from different places in the room and yanked them back on.

She came out of the bedroom like a prisoner emerging from jail, shame-faced and remorseful over what she'd said. She felt even more so when she found Mick in the main living area, fully dressed in nice pants and a button-up shirt.

"I'm sorry," she said, wishing she could make it even a few hours without saying or doing anything mind-bogglingly embarrassing that required an apology. "I didn't mean to creep you out."

For moments on end he just stared at her. Then he asked, "Where's your suitcase?"

Wow, he must really be ready to have her out of here. "Um, I took it to my hotel earlier when I went out to get croissants and coffee."

"Why'd you do that?"

"Because that's technically where I'm staying," she answered carefully, not sure why he wasn't happy she'd moved her things out.

He rubbed a hand over his short hair. "All right, I have to go somewhere now. Somewhere having to do with the prize package. They've got a car waiting for me in the garage, but I can't take you with me."

She shifted on her feet, just wanting this over. "I understand."

"While I'm gone, I want you to go back to your hotel—"

She launched herself toward the door then. "Okay, I get it."

But quick as a jaguar, he got in front of her. "I'm not finished."

"I'm a big girl. You don't have to spell it out."

She canted to the side and tried to get around him, but with that unusually athletic swiftness of his, he got in front of her again. "Kayla, let me finish."

Kayla shook her head, her body now clammy with humiliation. She couldn't allow him to finish letting her down easily—no way. She had to get out of there. But when she tried to get around him again, he grabbed her around the back of her neck with both hands, his thumbs on her jaw as he lowered his head until it was level with hers.

"Kayla, listen to me. I ain't trying to get rid of you. I'm telling you to go back to your hotel, get your bag and bring it back here."

She stopped struggling. "Why?"

"'Cos you never should've taken it out of here in the first place," he answered.

Then he pulled her to him and gave her a kiss so hot, so laced with obvious desire, she felt it all the way in her toes. Her heart slowly began to come back to life as his lips moved over hers. "I thought you were mad at me for going too fast."

"No, I was mad 'cos..." He stopped kissing her and let his forehead rest against hers. "...'cos I really like you, too. I'm not used to that, liking a girl the way I like you, and I want you to keep on liking me the way you do."

She looked into his eyes then, and she believed him. She saw fear there and a hungry desperation that made her want to reassure him that she'd never stop liking him even though they'd only known each other for this short time. "Are you sure I can't come with you?" she asked.

"No, it's a one-person thing. A peek-in on the Paris L'élite football club's afternoon practice, hosted by the president of the club himself. Made the reservation for me only a few weeks ago. And soccer's 'insanely boring,' innit what you said?"

She had said that, and she chided herself for being disappointed about not being able to go with him.

"I'll be gone for at least five hours, so do whatever you want today. But when I get back, I want you here with your bag. You understand?"

She nodded, happier than she had any right to be to follow his command.

"All right, then." He kissed her again. And again, then one more time before raising his hands and backing away from her like she was a sinkhole and he was afraid of falling in. "Enough of that. Stop tempting me, woman! If I let m'self kiss you one more time, you'll be on your back, and I'll be later than I already am."

She giggled.

"Why are you laughing *again?*" he asked her with amused exasperation. "I still have yet to make a joke."

Chapter Eight

Kayla was still laughing when Mick made it to the other side of the door. He knew because he could still hear her giggles.

But the easy and light feeling that he'd left the room with disappeared as soon as she was out of sight. Christ, what had he done?

It had seemed like a game at first, misleading her about who he was. But what she'd said in the bath about liking who he was pretending to be more than she could ever like a big-star soccer player like he was in real life left him unexpectedly hit by two extreme emotions.

On one hand, his heart swelled to enormous proportions hearing that she'd choose him—the real him—not the big-name soccer player most women from his side of the pond saw when they looked at him.

On the other hand, he'd had to get out of the tub because he liked this girl. He really liked her. He didn't want to lie to her anymore, but then he also didn't want to let her go. Not yet anyway. However, he also didn't think he could keep her if she knew the truth about who he really was.

But he had never been a coward. He'd told some of the biggest soccer players in the world exactly what was on his mind before knocking them in their teeth. He could handle the girl he'd met on a plane. He'd decided then and there to tell her everything, and if she slapped him across the face, so be it.

After he'd left the tub and pulled on some clothes, he occupied himself with checking his many voice mail and text messages from Gerald while he waited for her to finish in the bath. "Where are you? Why aren't you answering your phone?" the first messages screamed. Then came the text messages, these all in caps, "WHY DID YOU TELL THE FRONT DESK NOT TO LET ANY CALLS THROUGH??? THERE'S A CAR WAITING FOR YOU DOWNSTAIRS. HAS BEEN FOR HOURS NOW."

Just as he'd been typing back for Gerald to get his knickers unbunched, she'd come out of the bedroom, once again dressed in the shorts and Suns tank she'd been wearing when she'd entered his bedroom that morning. That very morning when she'd come back after he'd thought he'd lost her.

An image of her pulling the yellow-and-orange tank over her head hit him like a lorry. Followed immediately by one of her smiling up at him in her bra and knickers as she took him in his mouth. His erection sprang up anew then, straining against his pants, demanding to be let out, demanding to get inside her for a fourth time. Because *he* just couldn't get enough of her.

That was when he realized he'd been lying to himself. He was a coward, a coward for misleading her in the first place and a coward for what he was about to do, which was continue to lie to her. At that moment he couldn't risk losing her. Not yet.

It had felt like the right thing to do while he was doing it. She really liked him. He really liked her. Lies needed to be told to maintain that equilibrium. But after he left her, the guilt dogged him all the way to the French team's practice facilities. He could barely pay attention while the club's new Qatari president showed him around the recently renovated grounds and then out to a full-course lunch at a swanky restaurant. Then to watch the Paris team's afternoon practice. Then the starting lineup decided to take him to a strip club.

"You are here with us, but maybe your mind is somewhere else, yes?" asked Bruno Monceaux, the French team's star midfielder.

The club wasn't like the ones they had in Britain. The women on stage were on par with professional dancers and performed well-choreographed, raunchy numbers designed to both impress and titillate the mostly male crowd.

However, Mick could barely work up the enthusiasm to clap, much less hoot and whistle like the rest of French team members sitting in the club's special VIP area.

"Maybe you do not like the girls?" Bruno, who had been yelling the loudest of all, suggested. He pulled his phone out. "This is fine. We have those kinds of clubs in Paris, too. I will message my sister. She has many gay friends who will know where to send us."

"Appreciate that, mate, but I'm all right with the girls," Mick told him. "Just not these girls."

Bruno put his phone away. "I see. This girl, I am assuming she is the one who made you miss our practice,

the one you brought to France with you. You are thinking of her now?"

"It's a long story."

"I like long stories," Bruno answered. "I read Victor
Hugo's *Les Miserables* when I was twelve. Two times.
Tell me."

So Mick did. He didn't know why. He'd been playing on a team since his single-digit years, but he'd never
been much of a team player. Always kept to himself, had
never enjoyed the close friendships that seemed so easy for
other players on his team. He was even half-afraid Bruno
would tease him for being this twisted up over a girl he'd
only just met.

Instead, Bruno nodded when Mick finished with his
story. "I knew this kind of romance once. An American I
met while doing charity work in Cameroon. We were both
there with an international aid organization and we grew
very close even though our time together was very short.
She knew I played football, but she did not comprehend
what that meant. I very much liked her not understanding
this part of my life."

"And how did that end, mate?"

Bruno answered with a Gallic shrug. "Not well. There
was a misunderstanding between us and we never saw
each other again." His face darkened with the memory of
whatever had happened between him and his girl, but then
his face lit up with an idea.

"We are planning to take you to Kentucky after this."

Mick looked at him. "Kentucky the state?"

Bruno waved off his confusion. "In America it is a state.
Here in Paris it is *un club*. Very discreet—no paparazzi allowed. And if anyone is caught taking a picture of someone
famous, they are put out and banned for life. You should

invite your woman. We will be in the VIP area, so there
will only be you, her and us footballers. You can tell her
it is part of your—what did you call it—*prize package*."

"So you don't think I should just tell her? Come clean
about who I really am?"

Bruno shook his head with a wave of his hand. "No!
No! No! It is certain she will leave you if you tell her the
truth now. Show her the very best of times for the next two
days, and make it so she likes you very much. So much she
does not care who you are and that you lied to her. Then
you may tell her. This is a good plan, no?"

The question must have been rhetorical because Bruno
didn't wait for a reply before standing up and yelling something in French to the rest of the team. They all listened
intently and then let out a big cheer.

"What you'd say to them?" Mick asked.

"I told them that we are moving on to Kentucky. That
you are inviting a girl who must not know who you are.
That we must pretend you have won a night with our football club in the VIP area so that you can continue to sleep
with her."

Mick shook his head. "And they're cheering?"

Bruno placed a hand on his shoulder and said, "Mick,
mon ami, you must understand. The French do well in three
areas above all others." He ticked them off on his fingers,
"Le sexe. L'art dramatique. La déception."

Even with his severely limited French, Mick understood what Bruno had just said. The French excelled at
sex, drama and deceit.

Chapter Nine

Mick didn't know about the sex bit, but Bruno was right about the drama and deceit parts. The French starting lineup not only played their parts to a T, but they also made a big show of asking Mick over and over again how he was enjoying France, as if they hadn't met him many times before on the opposing sides at stadiums all over the world.

Magically all women were turned away at the VIP lounge's velvet rope unless they were married to or dating a member of the team. The girlfriends and wives who did get through were quickly cornered by Bruno and obviously given the drill because when they came over to Mick and Kayla, sitting together on one of the cushioned settee benches, they introduced themselves and acted as if they had no idea who he was. The team also managed a feat he'd never seen performed by a group of soccer players in his life, which was not talking shop. Or at least not talking shop to him. But for all he knew that was all they were talking to each other about in French and various other languages. After a while, Bruno sat down on the other side of Kayla and peppered her with questions about her trip and prize.

"Mine isn't nearly as nice as Mick's," she shouted over the loud electronic music blasting from all the speakers. "I mean, they flew me first-class from California, but my hotel is basically a small box compared to his, and no extras, just the hotel and flight. That's it. Nothing like this."

"Oui, Mick's package is very generous," Bruno agreed. "We will be taking him to breakfast tomorrow morning and then he will sit in on one of our morning practices. But after I believe there is—how do you say—a shopping spree, at Je T'aime Tourdin, a very nice boutique in the Golden Triangle. My female friends all love it, and of course, Mick will take you."

Kayla quickly shook her head. "Oh, no, I couldn't possibly—"

"'Course you could," Mick said, slinging an arm around her shoulder. "I'm not one for the fancy stuff meself. You want me to just leave all those shopping spree euros unclaimed?"

He could see Kayla's practical mind weighing his argument.

"I guess not. And I was planning on getting a few new outfits for work when I got back home…"

"Oui! Oui!" Bruno said approvingly. "Dress for success as they say."

"Okay," Kayla said, smiling at Mick shyly. "As long as it's part of the package and not costing you any money."

Mick smiled back, not caring a bit how much money this shop Bruno had suggested would cost him.

"I've got to go the bathroom," she said.

"Yeah, sure." He stood up with her and watched her go, appreciating the view from behind as she left.

Almost as soon as she left, Bruno and the rest of the French team gathered around Mick, congratulating themselves on their acting and wondering if they shouldn't have their own reality show. Mick laughed along with them, relieved that they'd been able to pull it off as promised. He was taken aback by the easy camaraderie he felt with them.

Bristol United actually had movies made about their particularly violent fan base, and the team tended to court young hotheads like himself—real aggro players who could barely stand to be in a room with themselves, much less with each other. But the Paris L'élite footballers were a great time. They were easy to talk to, warm and able to have fun without busting heads.

Which was why it took him so long to realize Kayla had yet to return from the toilet. About twenty minutes after she'd left, he went looking for her. There was a line outside the one-stall women's toilet, and the overly made-up brunette who emerged definitely wasn't Kayla. She had shown up to the club in a button-up yellow baby doll dress, which she apologized for, and a pair of orange Teva sandals, which she'd apologized for even more profusely.

"They were the only things close I could find in my suitcase," she'd said, eyeing the other women in VIP, most of whom were wearing designer gear. "I didn't have your number, and I didn't want to keep the car waiting, so I figured I better…"

"You look great, baby," he had told her. "Truth is, I'm just happy to see you outside a Suns jersey."

Now he asked the line of women dressed mostly in

fashionable black if they'd seen a black woman in a yellow dress.

One of the women pointed to the door at the end of the hallway. Then she asked him something in French that ended with "Mick Attwater." He didn't understand what she said, but it was easy to figure out from the way the other women in line turned and stared.

"Sorry, I don't speak French," he mumbled and made his way to the door at the end of the hallway before anyone could follow up in English.

The door let him out into an alley at the back of the club. And, sure enough, he found Kayla there, leaned up against the wall, head bent over her phone. From the intent way she was looking down, it was obvious that whatever she was reading had her full attention.

He thought of the ex-boyfriend who'd cheated on her. The wanker who'd let her get away. He'd himself had never pursued a girl again after breaking up with her, but there was one bloke on his team who'd begged his wife to take him back seven times after getting caught with various other women. He didn't know who was more stupid, his teammate for cheating or the wife for continuing to take him back.

He approached Kayla angrily. Had he misjudged her? Was she like his mother, always willing to stay on, no matter what kind of abuse his dad ladled on her?

"Kayla," he called out to her.

She looked up at him with such a guilty expression, he knew what he'd suspected was true. Jealousy reared up like a monster inside his chest, and his next words fell out of his mouth like sharp knives. "You came here to be with me, but you're on the phone with somebody else. Who is it?" Then he guessed, "Marcus?" He hated how much he sounded like his father.

His parents had barely been able to go out to the local without coming home in a screaming argument about some bloke his father insisted his mother had been flirting with. But Mick couldn't help himself. He had to know. "He's been texting you this whole time? And you're texting him back while I've been all over the club searching for you like some trained dog?"

Now her expression went from guilty to appalled. "Are you kidding me? Do you know how much international phone plans cost? Even if Marcus was texting me, they wouldn't get through and I definitely wouldn't be able to text him back without severe charges."

Her words took most of the wind out of his sails. "Then why'd you look like you'd been caught just now?" he demanded, still feeling defensive but also foolish.

"Because I was kind of with somebody else," she answered. She turned the phone toward him, and he saw what looked like an ebook pulled up on it. "Joseph and Mira. He's a one-hundred-year-old werewolf. And she's a human that needs math tutoring—they're both in college together because he likes to get a new degree every couple decades or so. He doesn't like humans, hates them for killing his kind, but he can't resist her. However, he has no idea that her dad is a werewolf slayer, and he'll stop at nothing to keep them apart." She stopped with a self-conscious roll of her eyes. "So yeah, anyway, I was over here reading a new adult novel when I was supposed to be hanging out with you in VIP. I'm sorry."

He shook his head and leaned his shoulder against the wall, the jealous monster letting him go. "If you were bored, why didn't you tell me? We got a car waiting for us outside. Could have said goodbye, no worries."

"Clubbing isn't exactly my thing and I can only hang out in the VIP section for so long, yelling at the top of my lungs to be heard, before I need a break. But you looked like you were having a good time with those guys, so I came out here to get a breather."

"I'd rather spend time with you."

She nodded. "Because we only have one more night together?"

He shook his head and cupped her face. "No, because I'd rather spend time with you. No matter what."

She decisively put her phone back in her purse. "I'd rather spend time with you, too," she told him.

He took her hand and walked them through the alley toward the side of the club where he was told their driver would be parked.

"Hey!" she said as they emerged from the alley. "There's the other Arc de Triomphe!" She pointed to the iconic stone landmark, sitting at the west end of the Champs-Élysées and illuminated from all sides by the lights of Paris. "I saw the other one when I went to the Louvre this afternoon, but it was smaller and it had statues on top of it. Three angels and four horses. Pretty neat, especially when you consider it was built back in the early-nineteenth century to commemorate the Napoleonic war victories. You'd never find anything like that in Los Angeles. If something was built in the thirties, we consider that really old. You'd have to go to the East Coast to see any big structures from the 1800s, and even then, most of isn't nearly as majestic as either of Arcs."

They arrived at the car, and he waved the driver off before opening the door to the limo for Kayla himself.

He could see the Seine in the distance as he got in on the other side of the car, and he wished he could walk her home along it. The hotel was only a couple of miles away and he knew she would enjoy seeing the river all lit up at night, just as he knew he would enjoy watching her take in the romantic sight.

He also knew that he'd never be able to do something like that—not without putting on a disguise first. At home he kept a collection of hats and sunglasses in the back of his car, just in case he wanted to go some place without being recognized. But half the time even disguises didn't work—probably because he drove a vintage Alfa Romeo, a 33 Stradale that would net at least a million pounds at auction now that he'd fixed it up. Either way, he really hadn't expected to do much more than visit the Paris L'élite football club and hang out in his hotel room, so he didn't have what he'd need to attempt such an impromptu act.

He closed the door on the view of the Seine and turned to Kayla. "Tell me more about your day. How'd you like the Louvre?"

She wrinkled her nose. "Seriously, you want to hear about my trip to the Louvre? I mean, you've been to France before so you've probably already been there, right?"

"Nope. Never been," he answered. He didn't add that being an easily recognized football player made going to places with tons of tourists impossible if he didn't want to get mobbed. The only landmarks he had seen anywhere outside of England had been visited at odd hours in the morning and had come with advert and/or photo-op obligations attached.

"Well, the lines to view certain exhibits are super long, especially for the Mona Lisa. But seeing all the paintings is worth it. I don't know much about art myself, but I mean, while looking at the Mona Lisa, it feels so alive…like it's a living, breathing thing. it made me realize how much power these paintings carry inside of them. Those artists are fortunate because when they die they've left piece a of themselves behind. Their hearts and souls are displayed all over the Louvre."

He nodded, loving the sound of her voice. Loving how she made going to the Louvre sound like more than just another tourist experience. Loving that she'd rather have a quiet conversation with him than enjoy one of the best VIP sections in France, loving…

He didn't let himself think it. But in the back of his secret heart, there came a whisper. *Loving her.*

Chapter Ten

Mick really did seem interested in what she had to say about her day, which Kayla had thought was pretty boring in comparison to his own. But in the back of the limo with his arm draped around her shoulders, he'd listened to her talk intently to the point that something occurred to her. "Maybe we could go to the Eiffel Tower after the shopping spree tomorrow."

His arm stiffened and he shifted in his seat before saying, "Don't think so."

"Oh," she said, feeling crestfallen. She'd liked the idea of going somewhere romantic with him, but romantic tourist attractions probably weren't his thing. "You don't want to go."

"No, I'd love to go there with you, but…" He shook his head, and he seemed like he was making a hard decision before he said, "Yeah, actually that's it. Eiffel Tower's not my bag. Plus I've already been, y'know."

"Sure," she said. "I understand." Though, she didn't completely. Refusing to go to the Eiffel Tower seemed more of a Marcus move than the man she'd come to know over the past two days.

"Now you think I'm a wanker like your ex," he said, as if reading her mind.

"No, I just…" She shook her head.

"Tell me," he said. "Tell me what you're thinking right now."

"It's stupid. I mean we only have one more night together after this. Why ruin it with real relationship expectations?"

"All right, then, if we were in one of those real relationships, if we were all about the communicating aspect of things, what would you be saying to me now?"

"I don't know." She shrugged, but her words came out with more passion than she realized she had on this particular subject. "Relationships are give and take. It can't be one person doing all the taking and the other person doing all the giving. If you want me to come out and do the things you want to do, you should be willing to do the things I want to do, too."

"Was that how it was between you and Marcus the Wanker, then? He'd have you come meet him at some club, and you'd be bored to death, reading 'bout your new adult vampires and whatnot on your phone, while he arsed about with his American football mates and all that."

"Werewolves," she corrected. But other than that he pretty much had it right.

"Hey," he said, squeezing her to his side. "I ain't him, all right."

"I know," she said, laying her head against his shoulder.

"I know that. And it's unfair of me to bring baggage from my old relationship into this…whatever it is. I'm sorry."

"Nope, you were right—I was being a right wanker. Thanks for calling me out on it. I appreciate you coming out tonight, especially considering that you were at a good part in your book and all that."

She laughed.

"I'm going to make it up to you."

"You don't have to."

"Ain't a question of have to. I want to. Understand?"

She nodded against his shoulder. "I understand and I'm grateful because you seriously don't have to. I'm over it."

"Hey, I'm over it, too. Another argument, and it's sorted like that. No yelling or beer bottles thrown. Knew there was a reason I liked you."

She suppressed her laughter. "I like you, too," she said.

Then his mouth was on her lobe warm and wet as he whispered in her ear, "Really, really like you." His hand moved down to underneath her skirt, then slipped under and caressed her sensitive inner thigh.

Her breath caught. "I really, really like you, too," she said. "But we can't. Not with the driver right there."

His hand got even closer to her womanhood, so close she could feel the outside of his index finger against the seat of her panties. "Right there behind a tinted partition. If we're quiet, he never has to know," he said, his voice low in her ear. "Let me see if I can make you come before we get back to the hotel."

Her heartbeat quickened at the thought of getting caught doing something as hedonistic as having sex with some-one in the back of a limo. She should have pushed his hand away and told him to stop.

But she didn't.

Instead she melted into him as she turned toward his seeking mouth. She loved the feel of his arm wrapped tight around the back of her neck, keeping her there, wanting her there, as his tongue delved in and out of her mouth.

She felt his hand move her panties aside, and his fingers began to do the same.

He pulled his lips away from hers to say, "If we're going to get this done before the hotel, I'm going to need you to get nice and wet. Can you do that for me?"

The stakes he presented excited her as much as the hooked fingers he was slowly pushing and pulling in and out of her. She could feel herself becoming wetter in answer to his question. She could also feel his erection, now hard and unforgiving against the side of her thigh.

"That's right, baby," he whispered in her ear. "Get hot for me. Make this next part one-two-three-four."

She was too turned on to ask what he meant by one-two-three-four. But she soon found out.

He removed his fingers from her, somehow unzipped his pants with one hand and took himself out. The hood of hard length was red and already dripping with pre-cum. "One," he said.

He easily lifted her onto his lap. "Two."

And just as easily slipped inside of her slick folds from behind, all the way to the hilt. "Three."

He then slapped his right hand over her mouth when she cried out with the pleasure of being entered so thoroughly. "Four."

He was so big inside of her but, oh, so right. She found herself whimpering against his hand as he started moving in and out of her in his seated position.

"Shh, baby," he said in her ear. "I know it feels good, but if you're too loud, we'll get caught."

She didn't want to get caught. She bit back on her whimpers, concentrating instead on her breathing and how it felt to have his thick length sliding in and out of her. He laid her back against him now and she felt like a doll, barely doing any work but receiving so much pleasure.

But her pleasure alone seemed to be enough to rev him up even further. He uncovered her mouth and used both of his hands to yank open the top of her bodice. Buttons went flying as he deftly opened the front clasp of her purple bra.

"Sorry, baby," he whispered in her ear, palming her left breast in his rough, calloused hand and circling his thumb around its taut nipple. "Can't get enough of these."

He then started to pump into her from behind, working inside of her with blazing speed, his hand cupping her breast so tightly, she couldn't have moved away even if she wanted to. And she definitely didn't want to.

"I love you like this," he said in a fierce whisper against her ear. "Totally exposed. Your knockers hanging out your dress, so wet I can tool in and out of ya, easy as you please." His lower-class accent seemed to get thicker the more excited he got. "Whaddya think 'ould 'appen if the driver opened the door now? 'Ould you let me keep going 'til you got what you was after?"

The question sent an almost painful lightning bolt of fresh lust through her body, and she very nearly cried out.

"Shh, baby! Remember to keep it quiet back here. Just nod or shake your head to answer me."

She nodded her head, not caring how it made her seem. It was true. At that moment, nothing would have made her stop receiving his sex inside of her. At the moment the whole city of Paris could be watching them and she wouldn't have made him stop.

"Look down," he said. "Look down at yourself."

She did, and he brought his free hand to rub at the button between her legs.

This time she did cry out. Loud enough for the driver and probably anybody else on the street to hear. It was one thing to get drilled in such a vulnerable and exposed position. But the sight of his hand, pale and heavily veined with muscle moving on top of her dark womanhood? What could she do but cry out and then scream when her release came just a few seconds later, sharp and alive and completely mind-splitting.

She could hear his dark, triumphant chuckle in her ear even as he continued to pound into her. However, all laughter stopped when he surged inside of her. He held her to him even tighter as he came with a long shout along with a set of curses.

Not until she felt him spilling the last of himself inside of her did she realize... "Oh, God, we forgot a condom."

She immediately scrambled off of him and they stared at each other, both breathing hard.

He sat up slowly and put himself back inside his underwear before zipping his pants. "Don't got anything to worry about from me. Got tested just a few months back and I'm clean."

"You haven't had sex since you got tested?" she asked him.

He shrugged. "Been busy."

"I—I'm on birth control," she told him. "And my last ob-gyn appointment was two months ago. They test for everything and it all came back clean. And I...um...haven't had sex since I was tested either."

Now he raised his eyebrows. "You and the wanker went two months without having sex? I can't keep my hands off you for two hours."

"No, we hadn't," she admitted, her face so hot it felt like it was burning. "Actually for over three months. Not since my birthday. He said he was too busy. That's why I went to the doctor. I thought something might be wrong down there because he didn't seem interested. But now that I'm looking back on it, I'm realizing that was right after the new cheerleader joined the Suns squad. Oh, my God, how could I have been so epically stupid?"

She let her head collapse into her hands but only for a moment because that was when she realized they were no longer in motion. The car was totally still, with the engine off, obviously parked somewhere. She looked at Mick. "Why aren't we moving?"

He had the good grace to look chagrined. "Well, you see, Kayla, we got to the hotel about ten minutes ago. But you were too busy to notice."

"And you kept going?" Then realizing that they no longer had the benefit of the car engine to mask their voices she lowered hers and repeated. "And you kept going?"

He raised his hand. "In me defense, baby, I'd have to argue that as close as you were, it would have been unfair of me to stop. I'm not sure you would have let me stop. And that's the *Law & Order* truth, both the U.K. and the U.S. versions."

"I can't believe…" She reclosed her bra with the speed of a teenage girl caught making out by the police. "Now the driver knows." She looked out the tinted window to see Jacques standing near the door that led into the hotel lobby. His hands were folded at the front, obviously waiting for them to get out of the car. "And Jacques!"

Mick just laughed. "Baby, it's fine. They're French. They know what's what. Plus, I think your screaming probably gave us away more than anything."

She held her hand out to him. "Give me your jacket and the room key. Now! Now! Now!"

He handed them both to her, clearly very amused as she jammed her arms through the blazer's sleeves and clutched the front together with a fisted hand to cover up her ruined dress.

"Bit big on you," he observed.

Kayla just put her hand on the door handle and raised her chin high. She refused to do the walk of shame.

Instead, she did the run of shame. Swiftly opening the car door and racing through the entrance Jacques hastily pulled open for her when he saw her barreling toward it. She was gone and headed back up to the penthouse before anyone could say as much as a *bonjour*.

Chapter Eleven

Kayla should have been exhausted. After the three bouts of morning sex, and the Louvre, and Kentucky—the night club, not the state—and the car sex, then the apologetic round of "I'm sorry we got caught" sex, she should have fallen asleep as soon as Mick rolled off of her.

But something he had said earlier had her brain turning and wouldn't let her go to sleep even after he pulled her nice and cozy to his side. "Hey, Mick?" she asked.

"Hmm," he answered.

"You keep saying that you don't joke."

"'Cos I don't," he answered.

"Earlier when you congratulated us on getting through that Eiffel Tower argument, you said we got it sorted without any yelling or cracked beer bottles. If you never joke, why would you say that?"

He went still, so still that she could tell she had stepped on some kind of emotional land mine and she wondered if he would even answer what she now understood to be an intrusive question.

Then he said, "Your parents, what're they like? Nice house, two jobs, three squares a day, church at least every other Sunday sort, right?"

"You forgot Suns season ticket holders, but other than that, you're right. They still live in the same house I grew up in. They're both lifelong members of the postal service. My dad's a mailman and my mom works the counter at our local post office. What are your parents like?"

Again he was silent for a long while, but he eventually answered. "Me dad's worked for the power company all his life, and me mom's been a hairdresser long as I can remember, but they're not like your parents. They're the sort who've got to keep moving from flat to flat because they get pissed and trash the place. Landlord finds out and they're on to the next. We moved three times the last year I lived with them. Ain't a clue where they're at now 'cos we don't keep in touch. If I got married or anything like that, I'd have to hire a private detective to find 'em. But then I'd never do that, would I? 'Cos they're the kind of parents you don't invite to posh events. They'd do things like sneak in beer to your youth league football games, get blind drunk, then break off 'em beer bottles like they're on one of 'em telly dramas and threaten to off each other with all your teammates looking on."

Kayla didn't need to be told this description wasn't hypothetical or even hyperbolic. Mick had lived these stories, had lived with these terrible people and was still living with them, even if they hadn't been in contact in years. Her heart broke for him.

But she kept her voice casual. "You're right. My parents aren't like yours. Especially my father. He was, still is, a great dad. Always supportive, always there for me. He played high school American football, and he's a big guy, really macho-looking. A lot of people are scared of him when they first meet. But he's a huge teddy bear. He gave my brother and me all the hugs we could ask for growing up, and he never picked us up late. Not once."

She entwined her fingers with Mick's. "He also never took us to meet his parents. We didn't even know they were alive until they died in a car accident. Drunk driving. They ran into a pole. We were pretty much the only people that came to their funeral. I couldn't believe those people raised my kind and loving dad. I told him that after the funeral as we were driving home. I was sitting in the backseat, and I'll never forget what he said to me. He said, 'It's easy for me to be a good dad. With every decision that comes up in regard to you two, all I gotta do is think, What would my parents do? Then I do the opposite.'"

She felt Mick's breath hitch in his chest underneath their intertwined hands. She suspected he was fighting back tears, but she'd learned enough about him by now to know that he wouldn't appreciate her drawing attention to it. She could envision him as a little boy, his eyes fierce and wide as he refused to cry, even when his parents humiliated him. So she continued with her story.

"When the stuff went down with Marcus, I turned off my phone. The plan was to spend the time I was supposed to be with Marcus here in Paris nursing my wounds at home in my condo. But my dad showed up at my door. And you know, he's my dad, so I had to let him in. I thought he'd be disappointed because the Suns were his favorite team. But he was mad at Marcus. Even madder than I was. He told me I was better than Marcus, that I should go on the trip anyway, even if I had to go alone. He would have gone with me, but he works for the government, and they don't let you take a week off with only a day's notice. He went into my room, packed a bag for me—that's why I've been wearing so much Suns apparel on this vacation—and drove me to the airport himself. Dad's not big on traveling himself, but he really didn't want me to let what Marcus did ruin my trip. So I came to Paris alone. And that's why I'm here with you now."

"And your mom, tell me about her."

"Well, she's a great mom. We're really close now, but when I was a teenager, we got into a lot of arguments. Now that I'm grown, I think it was because—"

"You were too much alike," he guessed. "She's soft-spoken, likes to read, doesn't like a lot of drama, thinks your dad's a softy even though everybody else is like, 'Hey, look at that bully.'"

She laughed. "Yeah, exactly. How did you know?"

He didn't answer, just pushed their intertwined hands above her head as he rolled on top of her. His lips found hers and soon he was pushing into her, his strokes rolling and unhurried. Like he had no destination in mind for them other than making their joining last as long as physically possible. It was heaven. She kissed him back, wanting the same thing and wondering what would happen when they had to part the day after tomorrow.

Chapter Twelve

Shopping sprees, as it turned out, took way longer than their name suggested. Especially at Je T'aime Tourdin, a boutique located in the heart of Paris's affluent Golden Triangle. An attendant, a tall and thin woman who wore her pencil skirt and pretty silk blouse like a uniform, was waiting for them when the car pulled up to the curb. She escorted them into a space with beautiful hardwood floors and pink-and-silver damask wallpaper.

It didn't look like any clothing store Kayla had ever been to. There was more open space than actual clothes, and with its sprinkling of settees throughout the front, the place looked more like a well-lit nightclub than a place to shop. Beautifully dressed mannequins seemed to be thrown into the boutique's large windows just because. A cash register wasn't even visible.

However, it must have been a store because a woman in a chic peplum dress welcomed them in a rapid, heavy accent. She then introduced herself as Giselle and informed them that she would be assisting with their shopping needs.

Giselle had two assistants, also dressed impeccably but in black dresses with much shorter hemlines than their middle-aged boss. They magically produced flutes of champagne, which they pushed into Mick's and her hands while Giselle asked Kayla if there was anything she wanted to see from their current collection.

Seeing as how Kayla had only just learned of the store's existence the night before, she had no idea about their current collection. Back in Los Angeles, where casual was king, she considered flipping through the latest Banana Republic catalog keeping up. "Um…" she said.

Mick quickly took over. "Right, fix her up with some work clothes 'cos she works in an office, yeah. We'll also take a couple of dresses, something properlike for a night out. And while you're at it, give us a look at your casual clothes."

She opened her mouth to protest that she already had enough casual clothes, but he stopped her with a raised hand. "Nothing against your dad, baby, but I'd appreciate seeing you in something other than American football gear."

Giselle and her two assistants tittered, and before Kayla could protest again, they were being escorted to a seating area with even plusher seats at the back of the store. A few minutes later, actual models came out and did a sort of runway show, walking along a raised L, pivoting in front of a stunned Kayla.

"What do you think?" Mick asked, taking another swig of his champagne. Kayla goggled at him. Even though he was a blue-collar worker, he seemed completely at home and not at all nonplussed by this experience. As if this was the way he shopped all the time.

"I wouldn't know," she whispered so she wouldn't hurt anyone's feelings. "All those models are like a size zero."

"Right, then," he said, putting his glass down on a side table.

He went over to Giselle, and they had a conversation that she couldn't hear from where she was seated. Giselle nodded, clapped her hands together twice and called out something to her assistants in French that had one of them rushing to the back of the store. Then Giselle indicated that Mick should follow her to a little room discreetly tucked away at the corner of the store.

"What's going on?" she asked as Mick passed by.

"Gotta give her my shopping spree coupon and all that," he answered without stopping. "Be right back."

Just then a little old lady appeared with a length of measuring tape around her neck and a pincushion strapped around her wrist. She had Kayla stand up and started taking her measurements.

"Wait—what's happening?" she asked the assistant who had come back with the tailor.

"Your…ah, friend said you were having trouble deciding, so he is choosing the clothes for you." She pulled out a notepad. "Also, we will need your address so that we may send you the clothes when they are ready."

Kayla's eyebrows nearly hit her hairline. "Wait a minute. You're tailoring whatever he picks out to fit my exact measurements?"

"*Oui,* of course," the assistant answered, as if they lived in a world where all clothes were made to order.

Kayla had no idea what to say. On one hand, it was weird to have a man pick out her clothes. On the other, it was Mick's shopping spree, so he should be allowed to spend the money however he chose. Mistaking her conflicted look for concern, the assistant hastily quickly added, "And do not worry about the dress. We will have it expedited and couriered to your hotel."

Kayla found out what the sales associate from Je T'aime Tourdin meant a few hours later when Jacques showed up at their door carrying a damask dress bag with the store's logo scrawled across it. She thanked him and took it back to the bedroom.

"What you got there?" Mick asked as he came out of the bathroom with a towel wrapped around his waist and another one he used to swipe his short hair dry.

The sight of him in nothing but a towel distracted her from the dress, which she'd been hanging up on the closet's outside door hook.

"What?" he asked when she openly stared.

"Has anyone ever told you have a really nice body?" she asked a little breathlessly. "I mean, none of the guys I see tending the power lines in my neighborhood look like you."

He grinned. "So that's why you're with me then? You're just using me for m' body?"

"No, I'm with you because you're easy to be with and because you're really great. I'm just saying the body doesn't hurt. You're more ripped than some of the players on the Suns."

"More—how did you call it—'ripped'—than Marcus the Wanker?" he asked.

"Yes, more ripped than him."

He seemed pleased by this piece of information, but he didn't dwell on it. "Go ahead and put on the dress. I'm starving, and we've got to be there in less than an hour."

She had no idea where *there* was. Some fancy restaurant he assured her was covered by the prize package but definitely wouldn't let her in wearing her flip-flops and a Suns T-shirt.

She unzipped the bag and almost let out an audible gasp.

"You shouldn't have. You really shouldn't have," she said, pulling out the shimmery strapless bandage tube dress. The detailed knitting on it was so fine, she could tell it must have been at least partially hand sewn. "I mean, how much did this cost? Was it really all covered by the shopping spree?"

"Put it on," he said. "I want to see it on you."

That's when she noticed the second hanger behind the first. It had a bustier made up of the finest white lace she'd ever seen and matching boy shorts made of the same material. "And you got the underwear, too?" She shook her head. "I really don't think I can accept this. Or at least let me pay the taxes on it. I mean, there's no prize package in the world that would cover the taxes, too…"

He came over to her and took the dress away from her. He put it on the closet hook, then turned back to face her. He then untied the hotel robe she'd put on after her own shower, exposing the full length of her naked body to his hooded eyes.

"This is why I took over at Tourdin," he said. He palmed her naked breasts with his large hands before slipping the robe off her shoulders. "You're the sort never buys anything for herself."

He took the boy shorts off their hanger. "And I'm the sort that won't let that stand."

He held out the lace underwear at her thigh line. "Step in."

She stepped in, putting a hand on his shoulder to maintain her balance as she did. "Seriously, I don't need you to help me get dressed. I was just saying…"

He let his hand skim over the V shape between her legs, an errant finger dipping into her tunnel. "I know what you were 'just saying,'" he said, sliding his finger in and out of her on each word.

He then took his hand away and pulled the delicate boy shorts up and over her butt before turning her around toward the room's mirror so that he could put on the matching bustier.

As he connected the hooks, she could feel his erection through his towel and heavy against her back. But after he was finished, he merely turned away from her and took the dress off its hanger and unzipped it.

"Step in," he said again.

She did as she was told, but she was disappointed when he simply pulled the cocktail dress up her body without any further intimate touches.

"Close your eyes," he said.

She did, and she heard him walk away and open a nearby drawer. He quickly came back and clasped something around her neck.

"Open your eyes," he said.

This time her gasp was audible. The necklace swimming in multicolored jewels fell all the way to her cleavage. It was less a necklace and more of a statement piece. Colored glass meant to dazzle. There was no way the green jewels could be emeralds, the blue jewels sapphires and so on. But even as a well-designed piece of costume jewelry, the necklace was no less stunning than it would have been if it had been the real thing. She could only gape at her image in the mirror.

Her speechless reaction seemed to please him, and he

wrapped his arms around her from behind. "Got it from the shop downstairs. Don't ask me how much it cost. This is our last night together. Let me give this to you."

Maybe it was because she had never in her life seen a necklace so beautiful, or because he was right, it was their last night together and she didn't want to spend it arguing his questionable spending habits. For whatever reason, she put her accounting brain aside and said a simple, "Thank you."

He turned her around in his arms, but before he could kiss her, she stiffened.

"What?" he asked.

She grimaced. "There's no way I'm going to get away with wearing Tevas with this dress."

It seemed that everything was easily acquired in Paris. A pair of black Louboutins in her size arrived in the room just a few minutes later. He gave her a warning look when she saw the label, and she didn't argue. She just put them on and swore to herself that she'd look up how much they cost, then go downstairs early tomorrow morning and discreetly pay for the shoes, the necklace and anything else he had tacked on to the room bill. It was the least she could do considering how generous he'd been about sharing his prize winnings with her. And who knew how much he had paid in taxes on the dress and whatever he'd had sent to her condo back in California.

Still, she had to wonder after he got dressed in a tuxedo that fit him to a T—she could only hope he'd rented it—just where he was taking her.

"This restaurant you made reservations at, it's so fancy you have to wear a tuxedo?" she asked him in the elevator as they made their way down to the car.

"Yep, that's what the prize package said."

"What's the restaurant called again? Maybe I ran across it in my guide book."

"The Third Level."

"Hmm, never heard of it."

He shrugged. "Well, I guess we'll see if it's worth all the fuss when we get there, right?"

Fewer than fifteen minutes later, Kayla's chin nearly hit the floor. They were standing in front of the Eiffel Tower.

"I told you I'd make it up to you," he said with a grin.

After a ride in two brightly colored hydraulic elevators with exposed wheelworks, she found out "The Third Level" was actually the third observation platform at the top of the tower. People came from all over the world to see Paris from the tower's highest observation deck, but tonight it had been closed off to the public. A table set for two awaited them, with the most stunning view of Paris in the background.

And that was when the last doubt left Kayla's mind. European prize packages beat American ones every day of the week.

Chapter Thirteen

The look on Kayla's face when he sat down across from her at the private observation deck table was worth everything he'd had to do over the past twenty-four hours to make this happen on such short notice. Including the one he knew his agent, Gerald, would be none-to-happy about.

A Bristol United player could not get a private table set up on the Eiffel Tower's most popular observation deck. But as a future member of the Paris L'élite, the city was his to do with as he pleased.

"Are you serious?" Kayla said as soon as the maître d' who had seated them disappeared behind the observation deck's wood-and-glass doors. "You can't be serious."

"I told you I don't kid," he answered.

"I know but this is…" She suddenly reached across the table and grabbed his hand. There were tears in her eyes. "Thank you."

"Don't cry, baby," he said, reversing the hold and enclosing her hand in both of his. "You deserve it."

"After I got on you about not coming to the Eiffel Tower with me, and all along you were planning this? I feel horrible."

So did Mick. He'd been throwing money at her all day in one way or another, yet it was doing nothing to assuage his guilt over continuing to lie to her. In fact, the more money he spent, the worse it became.

He pasted on a neutral smile and pretended like he was enjoying himself as much as she was as they made their way through several courses. And by the time they were finishing up the dessert course and sipping their *café au laits,* he had almost started to buy his own act. That they were two middle-classers who both won first-class trips to the same city and happened to meet on the way there.

"Just when I think this city can't get any more beautiful, we get to see it like this. I love it here." She looked away from the view, but he could still see the lights of Paris sparkling in her eyes when she said, "I love you."

His heart violently constricted in his chest upon hearing those words, then he completely flatlined.

The close-to-death feeling must have registered on his face because she gave him an apologetic grimace. "I know it's too soon. And I know we only just met each other. And I know that it's impractical to feel this way since you're leaving tomorrow and neither of us have the money in real life to be flying back and forth from London to L.A. all the time."

For a moment he couldn't talk because so many words were stuck in his throat.

But that seemed to make more words come spilling out of her mouth. "I'm sorry," she said. "Really, I shouldn't have said anything, just kept my feelings to myself. But this is the best time I've ever had in my whole life, and I couldn't let you go home without telling you that."

Finally he was able to speak. "Don't apologize to me ever again."

She blinked, obviously taken aback. "Okay," she said carefully.

"You're always with the 'I'm sorry' and you've never done anything to be sorry about. Not one thing."

Her eyes melted. "Okay," she said again.

"And I love you, too." The words he didn't think would ever cross his lips easily slipped out. "Have felt that way since you showed up at me hotel, I think," he added quietly, though he knew confessing this made him look like a romantic idiot.

Her smile was nothing short of beatific. But then, she gave him yet another apologetic look. "In that case I'm going to have to break your 'don't apologize' rule because now I'm sorry I didn't tell you sooner."

For Mick, the sex they had that night felt like a living manifestation of their recently confessed love. Every touch sizzled with it; every kiss labeled it by name. Mick loved each of her breasts, suckling each in his mouth for minutes on end.

He then moved down to the V shape between her legs, his mouth spelling out their love with every flick of his tongue until she came for him hard, pushing into his still-hungry mouth.

"Where does Marcus the Wanker get off making you think you ain't perfect?" he asked when he came back up to kiss her lips. "You know what you taste like, baby? Woman. Joy. Love. If my manhood wasn't such a selfish bastard, I'd stay down there all night. Don't laugh. You know I'm not joking."

Her laughter transformed into a soft gasp when he guided himself into her. She moaned, her hands finding his hips as he braced himself and established a rhythm.

"Open your legs wider, baby. I want to go deeper."

She did as he said, her hands moving to his bottom. He groaned when he sank deeper into her. As her breasts bounced every time he thrust inside her, he had to fight to maintain control. He curled his back to take one of her beautiful breasts in his mouth, and she went wild underneath him, bucking and squirming, until she managed to babble a few words, telling him how good it felt, how she had never experienced anything like this before.

The same was true for him, but he couldn't have put words to his feelings if he tried. He wished crazy stuff, like that she wasn't on birth control so that they could make a child together, a girl with her good nature and his athletic ability. He wished they could get married before she left, so that she'd have a reason to quit her job and come right back to France to be with him forever. He wished that they could defy the laws of physics, that he could sink deeper and deeper into her until they became one. He came then with a great yell, all of his wishes spilling out of his body and flooding into her. "I love you so much, baby," he said.

Somewhere in the distance he heard her say, "I love you, too," and that made him drive his release into her even harder. He didn't stop until he was totally spent.

It took them both a long time to come down from that. They clung to each other for what felt like hours, whispering "I love you" back and forth. And even when they both started to chill from the accumulated sweat on both of their bodies, he didn't let her go. He pulled the covers over them but kept her in his arms, tight against his chest, her legs trapped under his, so that she couldn't possibly have moved even if she wanted to.

"Mick?" she asked.

"Yeah, baby," he answered, hoping she didn't ask him to let up on his hold. He didn't know if he could, especially considering that this would be the last chance he'd have to hold her like this. Because tomorrow when he left for London, he'd be forced to tell her the truth. Who he was and how he'd been lying to her this entire time. This fantasy they had created together would all come crashing down around him.

But then she said, "I know it's hard to get unscheduled time off, but do you think you could stay? Just for a few more days? Until my trip is over?"

Chapter Fourteen

Mick woke up feeling like someone who'd been granted a stay of execution by the governor—even though Britain didn't have political governors…or the death penalty. Her request for him to stay through her trip had effectively given him three more days. Three more days to figure out how to tell her who he really was. He'd have to figure out a way to make her agree to continuing their stay at the Paris Grand, where he wouldn't be in constant threat of being mobbed by autograph seekers. And he'd have to figure out a good excuse for why he couldn't go to any major landmarks. He had faith that Bruno and the president of the Paris L'élite club could continue to weave their magic, especially now that he would be an official member of the club starting in August. None of those obstacles mattered.

But when Mick woke up in the bed that would be theirs for three more days, one thing was missing. Kayla. Her side of the bed was empty except for a note on the pillow beside him with 6:00 a.m. written in the corner. "Went down to the restaurant to grab some breakfast. Will probably be back before you get this."

He shook his head, guessing that she'd opted to make the trip herself rather than tack another room service charge on their bill. But then he frowned when he saw the time. 6:45. Why wasn't she back yet?

Mick could hear the shouting even before he reached the open entrance of the Paris Grand's main restaurant. His heart dropped all the way into his stomach when he spotted Kayla arguing with Jacques.

"Tell me!" she shouted. "Tell me the truth right now!"

"Madame, please calm down," Jacques said. "If you will just follow me, we can call Monsieur Attwater, and perhaps he can…"

"Perhaps he can do what? Lie to me some more?"

They argued underneath a flat-screen television, which was broadcasting a sports program. Mick quickly recognized the show as the same type of football highlights they showed in England. Except in the French version, the announcers were talking excitedly while a cartoon graphic of Mick wearing the Paris L'élite jersey and a mean scowl stood with arms folded at the bottom-right side of the screen. On the top-right side of the screen, video of him and Kayla ran on a loop. Him getting in the car outside of Kentucky, entering Je T'aime Tourdin. They even had a video of them giving each other a kiss as they left the Eiffel Tower.

What had happened was immediately obvious. Someone had leaked the news of his agreeing to join the Paris team. And now this French sports program was discussing not only the highlights of his career, but also the mystery woman he'd been running all over Paris with.

"Why would you help him do this to me? Did he pay you?" Kayla, who still hadn't seen Mick, shouted at Jacques.

Jacques looked poleaxed. "Madame, please. Do not make a scene. Come this way—"

"Mick," a voice called out from the cluster of tables in the middle of the restaurant. "Mick Attwater! Mick Attwater!"

Suddenly nearly everybody in the restaurant was cheering, with quite a few French men chanting his name. But he could barely hear them.

Everything had gotten quiet in his head as Kayla walked toward him, looking horrified and disoriented, like someone who had just witnessed a bombing.

"Why are these people chanting your name?" she asked when she reached him. "And why is there video of me and you all over the TV?"

"Kayla, let me explain. There's been a misunderstanding between us from the beginning."

She shook her head, her eyes completely devoid of the love that had shone so clearly in them last night at the Eiffel Tower. "So when you told me you were an electrician, that was a misunderstanding?"

"I said I came from a family of electricians. Never said I took that path meself."

"And when I told you explicitly that I would never want to date a sports star, that was a misunderstanding?"

"I thought that if you got to know me…"

"You thought that if I got to know you, I wouldn't mind you lying to me from the very beginning? Because that's what you did. There was never any prize package. You went out of your way to convince me you are someone you're not. And apparently you even got the entire French soccer team to help you do it. All so you could get in my pants."

"Wasn't the whole team, just the starting lineup," he said because that was the only point he could really refute. Christ, this was getting out of hand. Kayla was looking at him like he was a murderer of small children. As he looked around he could see several phones in the air, a few that were probably set to video record.

"But you lied to me," she said. "Do you admit to lying to me from the beginning?"

The utter disappointment in her eyes was so disheartening, he actually wanted to lie to her again. A thousand lies sprang to his mind, anything to keep her, to preserve what they had. He thought of how happy they had both been less than an hour ago, and desperation nearly overtook him.

But in the end, he loved her too much to continue with his charade. "Yeah, I lied to you. I've been lying to you this whole time," he admitted. He took her hand and brought it to his chest. He begged, "But, Kayla, I can explain. Come with me someplace private and I swear to you, I'll explain everything."

She slapped him so hard that his face turned sideways. "Don't touch me!" she whispered fiercely, yanking her hand out of his.

She stormed past him. "Wait—you can't leave," he called after her, following her into the hotel's main lobby. "What 'bout your suitcase? It's still in my room."

"Keep it," she said, swiping at her angry tears as she made her way to the lobby doors. "That's what I should have said four days ago."

She ran out of the hotel. Mick tried to follow her, but

he was nearly blinded by flashing bulbs as soon as he stepped a foot outside. The paparazzi let Kayla by, but they swarmed Mick, making it impossible for him to get through them. It left him with no choice but to stand there, helpless and trapped while Kayla hailed a cab and jumped in, speeding out of his life forever.

Chapter Fifteen

For once Kayla was grateful for the big end-of-the-quarter report. Reconciling all the payroll numbers and double-checking that no one had been overpaid or underpaid could be tedious, but at least she got to stay in the conference room all day. Just her and Suzie and nobody else. A sequestration from coworkers, for which she was immensely grateful.

It was true that Americans weren't big on soccer. It might be a huge sport everywhere else in the world, but it was barely even covered in the States. To the point where very few Americans would be able to pick Mick Attwater out on the street. Even if he was one of England's top players, known throughout Europe as the bad boy of soccer before he was ordered into anger management. A soccer player could literally kill someone and it still wouldn't make the American news cycle. It certainly wouldn't get picked up by the media if he got busted stringing along an American woman who had no idea who he really was until she came back home to California and found out his whole sordid backstory via Google.

But that same American woman had been publically cheated on by a Suns football player several days prior to her showing up all over the European news sites, slapping the face of "the bad boy of soccer" in front of a restaurant full of onlookers. In that case, Kayla had found out the hard way—the story would definitely get picked up. Over the past five days, the story and well-documented slap had been featured on several sports news programs and quite a few gossip blogs. Whatever humiliation she'd felt over Marcus—well, this was ten times worse.

Kayla could barely walk through the office when she reported back to work the following Monday under the weight of her coworkers' pitying stares.

The only one who didn't treat her like the most gullible woman on the planet was Suzie.

Girl, don't be embarrassed, she'd said after she flipped off the TV and scowled at the employees they'd found watching a recap of the story on a gossip show in the break room. *That man is around-the-way fine. And I personally would be happy to be misled into bed by him.*

Then she'd suggested that they get a head start on the end-of-the-quarter report to keep Kayla's mind off the situation.

But immersing herself in numbers wasn't making her feel any better.

She still hadn't been able to make herself stop missing Mick. Their relationship had been a complete lie, but she'd come to cherish it over their short time together. And now, as the news stories were finally dying down, she still found herself getting sliced up by bittersweet memories of how happy she'd been and how complete she had felt when they were together.

It also didn't help that on Saturday several wardrobe boxes had been brought to her door. The clothes Mick had brought her at Je T'aime Tourdin.

After signing for the deliveries, she'd grumpily ripped open the boxes, planning merely to catalog their contents so that she could decide which clothes should go to which charity. But what she'd found inside the box had been colorful and bright, like the underwear she always wore underneath her otherwise dull clothes. She'd known just by looking at the collection of tasteful pencil skirts and pretty blouses that she would look great in any of them. And that she'd feel like a million bucks—as opposed to the impostor she felt like when she used to dress to Marcus's tastes. She'd wondered how Mick had been able to do such a good job picking an entire wardrobe out for her when he'd only known her such a short time.

Now sorting through the end-of-the-quarter report with Suzie in the conference room, she thought of those wardrobe boxes, still taking up too much space in her living room. She hadn't had the heart to stuff any of the impeccably designed clothes into the trash bags she'd brought out for just that purpose.

"You know you've been staring at the same spreadsheet for over fifteen minutes, right?"

Kayla came out of the trance with a shake of her head. "I'm sorry," she said and then remembered Mick chastising her for apologizing too much. The memory was almost physically painful, and she cringed, thinking of how her heart had exploded with so much joy when he'd said, "I love you, too" soon after.

Across the table, Suzie gave her a sympathetic smile. "I

get it. I once let myself fall too far, too fast with the wrong person, too. That's how I got Daniel."

Daniel was Suzie's eleven-year-old son, smart as a whip and a true credit to Suzie's good parenting. But even though Suzie never complained, Kayla knew that being a single mother couldn't have been easy.

Suzie's eyes shadowed even further. "Speaking of wrong guys, Marcus had the nerve to call here last Friday. Said you didn't answer any of his calls or text messages, and that was unlike you, so he just wanted to make sure you were okay."

Kayla rolled her eyes. Of course, Marcus, who'd never thought she was interesting or pretty enough when they'd been together, was acting as if he just had to have her back now that she was famous in the sports world. Perhaps remembering a different relationship than she did, he'd left her several long messages about how they needed to be together, how they couldn't let stupid people keep them apart. As if it had been outside forces that had split them up and not his blatant cheating caught on camera for the whole world to see.

"As soon as we're done with this I'll send him a text message telling him never to call here again," she told Suzie.

Then she started going down the list of numbers, but Suzie stopped her with a gentle, "C'mon, Kay, you're not really here. Why don't you take the rest of the day off? I can finish up."

Kayla shook her head. "No, I don't want to stick you with all of this."

"I swear, it's no big deal," Suzie said, taking the spreadsheet out of her hands. "Remember how you and your mom brought me ice cream when Latrell Jordan stood me up for junior prom? This is more like you cashing in a long overdue IOU—"

"'Scuse me, 'scuse me. This thing on?" said a voice over the interoffice PA system.

Kayla froze. The accent was unmistakably English. But just in case she thought some other guy with a growly London accent had gotten hold of the office intercom system, the man said, "This is Mick. Mick Attwater, doing something I shoulda done two weeks ago when I met the best woman I've ever known—that would be your own Kayla Edwards." He heaved a sad sigh. "I'm going to be honest with her."

"Oh. My. God," Kayla said.

"You see, Kayla thinks I misled her for kicks and giggles. And she's right. I did do that at first. Planned to get in her underpants and then get right out. The plan worked, and it was supposed to be like, 'Well done, mate, let's move on.' But here's where a simple story gets complicated—I couldn't. I couldn't move on because she was wonderful and she really seemed to get me and she's soddin' gorgeous. When you meet somebody whose wonderful, who gets you—even the bad parts—and is…soddin' gorgeous but who has gone off professional athletes because of her wanker ex, what are you going to do? Tell Miss Wonderful, that's all right, then, maybe next lifetime? So I misled her, and here's the really bad part—the more I fell in love with her, the more I misled her. It wasn't my best moment, mates, but what you don't understand, what I don't think she understood, is that the guy I was pretending to be so I could remain in her knicker territory—that guy is who I really am, who I always wanted to be. More than anything I wanted to be somebody who could make a woman like Kayla look at him like he was worthy of her, like he deserved a role in her universe. So yeah, I lied and all that. But not about the important stuff, not about how totally, completely, impractically in love I was with her from day one."

Kayla exchanged a stunned look with Suzie.

"So why am I telling you lot this? Quite frankly, because I haven't really slept in five days. That's another thing about Kayla. When I was with her, I'll tell you this, mate, I slept like a baby. Now that she's gone…no sleep for Mick. And the next thing I know I'm on a plane to Los Angeles, taking a taxi from the airport all the way here because all I really know about Kayla's life here is that she has great parents, she has a best friend who's also her boss and she works in payroll for the Suns. So here I am at her place of business to say, please, Kayla. Please believe me when I say I really do love you. Also, I want you to quit your job without notice and come back to Paris with me right now because I got a burning need to marry you and have a family. Preferably two girls because if I learned anything from this experience, it's that boys are stupid. Please, Kayla, do it for your coworkers, who probably want me off the loudspeaker, though quite a few of them seem to be video recording this. Cheers, mates—hope you get a lot of money for the footage. Also, Kayla. *Listen to me closely, Kayla.* I've got your suitcase here with me, and I'm completely willing to return it to you…provided you agree to marry me and come back to France."

Kayla could barely breathe her heart was beating so fast. She looked at Suzie, who said, "Girl, I will write your letter of resignation my damn self. You better go to that man."

Kayla ripped open the door and ran into the main office, where she found Mick leaned over the microphone at reception, his neck craning around. "Kayla? Kayla? I'm beginning to suspect she's not here and none of you got round to telling me that before I made a fool of myself. If so, let me tell you, that's completely out of bounds."

He stopped when he saw her, standing outside the conference room door, and his whole face lit up. "Oh, there you are, love."

Kayla rushed past the cubicles into his arms. He caught her easily and kissed her like a man long deprived of oxygen, holding on to her like he would never let her go. And at that moment, she knew three things: they would both sleep like babies tonight, he was definitely not joking about how much he loved her and...

Their *three* wild and sexy nights had just been extended to a lifetime.

* * * * *

A sizzling new miniseries set in the wide-open spaces of Montana!

THE BROWARDS OF MONTANA
Passionate love in the West

JACQUELIN THOMAS	DARA GIRARD	HARMONY EVANS

WRANGLING WES	ENGAGING BROOKE	LOVING LANEY
Available April 2014	*Available May 2014*	*Available June 2014*

www.Harlequin.com

KPBOMC14

REQUEST YOUR FREE BOOKS!

2 FREE NOVELS
PLUS 2 FREE GIFTS!

KIMANI™
ROMANCE

Love's ultimate destination!

KROMI13R

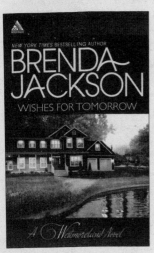

The mesmerizing Westmoreland family stars in these
two full-length stories in one great volume...

From *New York Times* bestselling author

BRENDA JACKSON

After biding his time, the perfect
opportunity has finally arrived
for Callum Austell to pursue the
ultimate object of his affections.
But Gemma Westmoreland is no
pushover, and if Callum is to get
what he wants, he may just have
to utter those three little words...in
What a Westmoreland Wants.

After a passionate night together,
Derringer Westmoreland wants
and needs to see Lucia Conyers
again. But for the first time in his
charmed life, the rancher has
some persuading to do...in
A Wife for a Westmoreland.

"Sexy and sizzling."
—*Library Journal* on *Intimate Seduction*

Available May 2014 wherever books are sold!